THE KALEIDOSCOPIC WORLDS OF POE BLACK

THE DARK ENERGY

THE
KALEIDOSCOPIC
WORLDS
OF
POE BLACK

The Dark Energy

MARK ROLAND LANGDALE

ILLUSTRATIONS BY ESTHER ROSE HARVEY

Matador
Unit E2 Airfield Business Park,
Harrison Road, Market Harborough,
Leicestershire. LE16 7UL
Tel: 0116 2792299
Email: books@troubador.co.uk
Web: www.troubador.co.uk/matador
Twitter: @matadorbooks

ISBN 978 1805141 174

British Library Cataloguing in Publication Data.
A catalogue record for this book is available from the British Library.

Printed and bound in the UK by TJ Books Limited, Padstow, Cornwall
Typeset in 12pt Adobe Jenson Pro by Troubador Publishing Ltd, Leicester, UK

Matador is an imprint of Troubador Publishing Ltd

Dedications go to the following people: Esther Rose Harvey, my brilliant illustrator; my niece Briony; Anastasia, who I imagine popped out of a book entitled *Russian Fairy Tales*; and finally Yarra, a woman I never knew but imagined was a character out of a dark Nordic fairy tale, this one, for once upon a time, I passed a cottage named Yarra's House, which one day vanished into thin air. The opening line to a German folk or fairy tale is… Back in the old days when wishing was still effective, if wishing was still effective, and sometimes in the modern world, I wonder if it still is, then I would wish for Yarra's House to reappear upon the road it stood upon, for in truth I miss the old house.

The truth is, Yarra's House was knocked down and replaced with a new build, and I never got to meet Yarra or tell her that the name of her house inspired in part my character Yarra, aka Sorrow.

This book was written in the times of "The Lockdown", a dark time when coronavirus swept the globe. The tale is set in Finland where my brother Vern and his wife Selvie live, which I have visited several times, travelling to the edge of Finland and the Russian border in my travels.

I also dedicate this to anyone who is struggling with their mental health, as I myself was diagnosed with bipolar twelve years ago. There is a light at the end of the dark tunnel, and help is never far away.

One must first look through a microscope then through a kaleidoscope if one is to see the world in its true light, for the truth lays somewhere in between these two most magical instruments

Mark Roland Langdale

Life is but a dream inside a dream

Edgar Allan Poe

Poe Black lives in many different worlds, worlds he has created in his mind, world building on a grand and imaginative scale. Each tale is set in a different parallel world, some slightly different, some very different, as in the many worlds theory of the maverick genius Hugh Everett III.

Prologue

In the darkling hour when wishing was no longer as effective as it had been once upon a time, there lived a boy named Poe Black, and this is his dark fairy life story. This Nordic tale is set in three entirely different worlds: the real world (so-called real world), a parallel world and the spirit world, three being the magic number, dark magic in this extraordinary case.

A very brief history of the timeline of one Poe Black, in effect, Poe's backstory: Poe's mother had died in childbirth. Poe had never known his father, as he left his mother a few months before Poe was born. Poe was looked after by his grandparents until they both died and he was left alone, an orphan. That is when Poe came upon the abandoned ramshackle wood shack close to a forest, and where he had lived ever since, as he was beginning to believe he was simply a character in a dark fairy tale, one written by the Brothers Grimm.

1

The House of Poe

A pale, willowy young man with large black, pearl-shaped eyes was sitting on the top of the world watching it pass by, a young man with a most unusual-sounding name: Poe Black.

Poe was one of life's great bystanders, happy to be an observer and not a participant. The truth over the fairy tale was that Poe was sitting on the roof of an old wooden shack in Finland, within spitting distance of a most magical silver birch forest, which is how Poe had always thought of the forest. The young man appeared to be waiting for something to happen, Poe having recently swapped wishful thinking and dreaming for daydreaming, or so it may have appeared from a distance. However, appearances can be deceiving, for Poe was happy that nothing was happening. For in that nothingness, the old steady state theory cosmologists used to believe in was where he found his happiness.

Poe had swapped his normal haunt, the darkly magical space of the attic, for the magical space of nature, which as night turned to day was flooded with light, the light of the Earth Star. In truth, Poe wouldn't have minded swapping that light for another magical light, that of an aurora, but you can't have the world, just a small piece of it. From space, you were able to see two giant green, purple and red magic circles spinning around the poles, the Aurora Borealis, the Northern Lights, Aurora Australis, the Southern Lights, also known as the Wind, and the Zodiacal Lights. Spinning fairy circles, Poe imagined, were made of snow and ice, fairy circles that were visibly shrinking with every passing year. It would not be long before those magic circles of snow and ice disappeared forever, unless global warming was reversed.

Poe imagined renting rooms out in his shack to runaways from other times, ones who were trying to escape their past. Princess Anastasia Romanov and Rasputin, known as "the mad monk", the Russian Prince Ivan IV, also from the Romanov dynasty, Anne Frank and King Ludwig II, the dream king. In effect, Poe's house would become a safe house, a sanctuary for time travellers. But when cold-blooded assassins came looking for them with ice picks and axes in hand, Poe would play the part of the heartless landlord, telling them in no uncertain terms that it was time to move on, to another time and space.

Poe sometimes imagined his wooden house had been built at the edge of the world, the edge of the world to his imaginative mind being a forest in Finland.

In reality (whatever that was), Poe had just entered that space between the ears known in Norway as *Lykkaland*. Translated into English, it means "state of happiness". In front of him lay a magical white carpet of snow and beyond that a magical forest full of silver birch trees.

Poe began to feel a surge of electrical particles pulsating around his entire body, the hairs standing up on end like iron filings, as if a magnet was pulling the hairs upwards. When he was a child, Poe would have said they were fairy sparks, static electricity, but the days of fairy tales for Poe Black had long since passed. The faerie had died and Fairyland was now little more than a barren landscape covered in cobwebs and broken fairy wings. These days, Poe preferred facts to fiction, swapping fairy tales for quantum wonder tales. In truth, most people did not think of these as facts; most folk thought quantum physics was nothing more than fairy tales or wonder tales, the sort dreamt up by Lewis Carroll.

There was a ghostly full moon in the sky, even though it was the middle of the day, concealed, almost invisible to the naked eye. So, perhaps it was the pull of the moon that was making the hairs on his head stand up on end. Poe half expected to be pulled off his feet, as if gravity no longer existed in this dark neck of the woods. Poe felt he was now in the middle of a dark energy field. This should not have unduly surprised him, given the fact that for half of the year it was dark during the day as well as the night, as if for half of the year the Nordic countries had uprooted and set up home on the dark side of the moon.

The air was so cold that Poe could easily imagine it turning to ice as the sky froze over, so it appeared as if he was looking into a giant mirror of ice. But when the sun came out from behind the clouds, the sky and the giant ice mirror cracked, causing a million tiny shards of ice to fall to earth, cutting Poe to ribbons. As snowflakes fell from the sky in winter, they glistened in the sun, a most magical effect and one Poe never tired of, as he imagined he was gazing through a kaleidoscope made of ice, ice crystals replacing the coloured glass.

Poe knew the spot he was sitting on was not officially the top of the world; not even with his kaleidoscopic mind could he twist the globe so that became possible. Having said that, Finland was not a million miles away from the giant magic circle that was the Arctic Circle. Sitting on the roof of the wooden house, Poe seemed transfixed by the fairy tale-like landscape. In his hand he had hold of an old brass spyglass, one normally associated with old sailing vessels and salty seadogs. Poe could well have been imagining he was standing in a crow's nest on a tall ship or an ice breaker on its way to the Arctic Circle.

Eventually, Poe blinked like the shutters of an old Victorian box camera, or perhaps a better description and one more poetical was a camera obscura. For a boy known for overthinking everything under the moon, stars and sun, he did not recall the fact to mind that Anne Frank received a book entitled *Camera Obscura* on her birthday. She wrote in her famous diary that she thought this a good book.

Whatever he was waiting for, Poe imagined it would come out of left field, but whatever he was waiting for, he would have to wait for it to come to him. Nature and the universe did not like it if you pushed it, for if you did, it was liable to push right back. You must be patient, like a Buddhist monk high up in the mountains, but waiting was the worst thing in the world. If this "happening" was to be a bad one, he wanted it to be over. When nature and the universe were good and ready, only then would they perform a giant sleight of hand trick, pulling the rug from underneath Poe, shifting the landscape around via an earth tremor, landslide or an avalanche; a dirty trick.

Poe was tired of tricks; he longed for a treat.

The treat was when spring came as the sun shone its magical rays through the trees and they hit the skin. The sun was the elixir of life, not a mythical stone that only existed in the world of the storybook. Spring was like a kind of magic as the landscape turned from barren to full of life. Both plants and animals and man benefitted from this magical transformation.

Then something hit Poe like a bolt from the blue. If this was a thunderbolt, it was a tiny one, as if Thor had shrunk like Ant- Man, a quantum bolt of lightning. The truth was, it wasn't a bolt of lightning that had struck him but the sun striking something shiny that had bounced off that object, honing in on the centre of his retina.

Poe looked more closely. He was amazed to see a creature. It was dark black. Surely there were no wildcats, panthers or jaguars in this neck of the woods. Such wildcats lived in the rainforest, not the forests of Finland. Poe rubbed his eyes, blinked several times and tried to refocus both his mind and the antique retractable brass spyglass, a prop from a movie theatre, which meant it wasn't meant for use in the real world as it blurred the image, thus it appeared to the user as if they were looking through mottled glass, like that in a fisherman's tavern. The world of the movies was about as far from reality as could be. It was almost as if you had slipped into a parallel world, the world of Hollywood.

It seemed all anybody did these days was escape the real world through one medium or another; computer games, television, radio, theatre, cinema, theme parks, arcades, sports arenas; so much so that one had to wonder if there was any need for the real world anymore. Some scientists and philosophers believed the universe was a projection, a holographic image, in which case the world was a hollow one. For Poe Black, the wonders of nature were the best way he knew to escape reality, even if that world was full of danger. As for the world of so-called technological wonders, the computer world, well, to Poe's mind that world really did feel hollow, as hollow as the hollow earth theory, one any self-respecting scientist would tell you was a fiction, like the horror film *Sleepy Hollow*, one of Poe's favourite movies.

Poe rubbed his eyes for a third time, three being the magic number; better that than pinching himself, the old Alice trick. The dark creature seemed to have gone through some kind of metamorphosis. Thankfully, it had not transformed into a giant cockroach as in the book *Metamorphosis* but into a woman, dressed in black, wearing oversized dark glasses with a red scarf wrapped around her neck, as if she were an old-time movie icon. Alternatively, she was the fairy-tale legend Little Red Riding Hood, as this tale was fast becoming a dark fairy tale of the Brothers Grimm variety. Poe imagined that the red scarf was dripping in blood from the last victim she had strangled, and whose heart she had then ripped out of their chest with her bare hands.

Although he did not know it, Poe was starved of the stimuli that made a person feel truly alive, the company of other like-minded souls. Poe sensed his self-imposed isolation was about to come to an end, but what sort of end? This thought alone made him want to run away as far as possible, to the dark side of the moon perhaps.

'*Priv-yet*, hello, I'm sorry to disturb. I'm lost. Could you point me towards nearest town? You can't get signal up here, it's like I've fallen off edge of world,' cried the young woman in broken English.

The girl had a Russian accent, a girl to Poe's mind who had seemingly appeared out of thin air, as he turned around to see a young girl tramping towards him in the snow. The first word the girl had spoken was Russian *priv-yet*, simply meaning hi, short for hello, or at least that was how it sounded, for the written word was more complex, the letters more like symbols or hieroglyphs seen through the eyes of those from other lands. Poe knew a few Russian words, the basics; hello, pronounced *zdrast-vuyt-ye*, and goodbye, *da svi-dan-ya*, a word everybody knew from the movies, mostly spy films or films starring deadly assassins. Russian men were often portrayed as the bad guys in such films, whereas Russian women were portrayed as attractive, dark, alluring, mysterious creatures, often as cold as ice.

The question he was asking himself was how on earth did the girl sneak up on him without him being aware of it? One moment she was a dot on the horizon, the next almost in his face, unless he had turned the spyglass the wrong way around? Perhaps she had wings. With a pinch of fairy dust, the girl may even be the frost fairy out of a Finnish fairy tale, with her long, icy reach which stretched from summer all the way into winter. Poe's heart was now lying in the snow after she had drained it of life. It beat one more time for old times' sake then stopped. A raven appeared out of nowhere and pecked at Poe's black heart then croaked, 'Never more,' a one-liner from the pen of Edgar Allen Poe and his epic poem *The Raven*.

Poe was now imagining this was a scene from the film *Doctor Zhivago*, which meant Poe was playing the part of Yuri (played by the actor Omar Sharif), and the girl was playing the part of Lara (played by the actress Julie Christie). Poe felt he was about to make a scene as his body let him down, his legs turning to jelly as his tongue tied itself into a fisherman's knot.

Poe loved old novels, especially the genre known as "scientific romancers", the forerunner of science-fiction novels. The trouble was, romance was not exactly scientific. There was no equation for romance or love; you could not put it under a microscope. Poe was putting this strange girl under the microscope, taking a sample of her blood, hoping it did not confirm his worst fears that she was a vampire. If she was, he'd toss her aside, like a work of art, one in your collection that you find out is a fake, a copy, as his fictional anti-hero Dorian Gray heartlessly tossed his lover aside in the novel *The Picture of Dorian Gray*. Poe Black and Dorian Gray, they were practically blood brothers, or at least half-brothers, separated in time and space, separated by the paper-thin yellowing pages of a novella, half-fact, half-fiction, science friction!

'Fallen off the edge of the world, yes, I'm not surprised. All the people in this part of the world have fallen off the edge of the world, so you should feel right at home in Forest Finland. It's a parallel world, one set in another time and dimension. Falling off the edge of the world is the new normal, and the new normal is the world of the paranormal,' Poe heard himself say, as if in a nightmare, quite possibly a waking nightmare if Poe fell for this female assassin.

'*Da-da*, I'll be right with you,' stammered Poe, half in Russian and half in English. It seemed at long last that Poe had finally found his real voice as he dropped the spyglass on the roof of the house then quickly kicked it out of the way. The last thing in the world, parallel or otherwise, he wanted the girl to think was that he was some kind of weirdo who liked spying on young girls. Frankly, the spyglass wasn't much good, for the image was blurred, or perhaps it was his mind that was blurring fantasy with reality, fact with far-fetched fictions.

'*Spa-si-bal-sho-ye.* Thank you very much,' the girl replied, firstly in Russian then in English.

In truth, the spyglass Poe had been looking through may just as well been a kaleidoscope, for Poe had seen several images of the girl, and each one appeared to be different. Every time he turned the scope to get a clear image, it changed like a kaleidoscope. There was a good reason a kaleidoscope was called a kaleidoscope... because it lied. Poe sometimes called it a "fairy- tale scope", for another word for fairy tale in the thesaurus was a lie. But lie was such an ugly word for such a beautiful instrument, a work of art, and one that should be displayed in a glass case, in an art gallery.

To Poe's mind, one had first to put life under a microscope, then under a kaleidoscope, for the truth lay somewhere in between.

Poe was shocked by seeing this strange creature that seemed to have appeared out of thin air, so much so that he almost fell off the edge of the roof, and off the edge of the world, at least in Poe's mind. The girl was now wearing an old fur coat and a large fur hat, so Poe imagined she had stepped out of a fairy tale or a copy of the book *Doctor Zhivago*, or perhaps she had stepped out of a bowed mirror, for she did not have the traditional features of a fairy-tale princess.

The lost girl Poe was re-imagining as Anastasia, the Russian fairy-tale princess who, having escaped from her assassins, had been chased through one fairy-tale forest after the other, both enchanted and disenchanted forests. No wonder the girl appeared a little dishevelled, or at least her fur coat did. The more likely modern fairy tale (lie) was that she probably picked it up at a charity shop, fake fur, and she was a fake princess impersonating Princess Anastasia from the doomed Romanov family. But the tale of the Romanov dynasty was another dark fairy tale from another dark time, and one that Poe did not have time for at this present moment, a magic moment perhaps?

Then Poe fell... fell hopelessly in love with the strange girl as he tripped over his tongue and then tripped over his two left feet, and with every action having an equal and opposite reaction, Poe slipped and fell off the ladder attached to the side of the house. Everything went as black as the dark side of the moon and as black as the Black Sea as Poe blacked out.

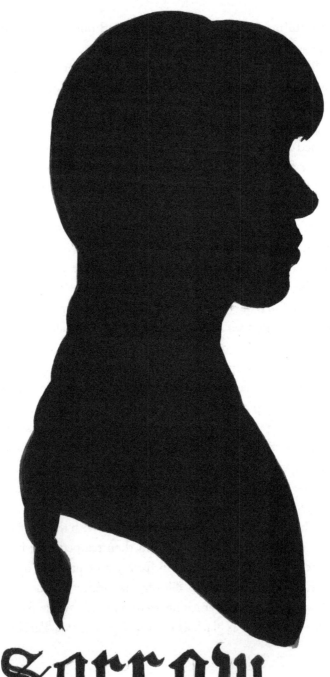

Sorrow

2

The House of Sorrows (Yarra's House)

'Where on earth am I?' grunted Poe, unable to maintain his equilibrium. Thankfully, he just about managed to grab hold of the ladder to stop him falling to his death, a macabre one at that, as if written by the ghostly pen of Edgar Allen Poe himself. An epitaph written by your hero; at least that made his parting from this world a little easier to take, as Poe imagined his soul departing this world for the spirit world.

Poe was doing his level best to right his small world, a world which was spinning wildly like a gyroscope or a compass in the Bermuda Triangle. For a second, Poe thought he was dead and this was heaven, as this figure was clearly an angel. But what if she were a dark angel, an angel of death? Even in death, Poe was looking on the dark side of the afterlife. Had this dark, mysterious creature been sucked into his world from another universe along with the dark energy, energy the physicists had predicted in their latest "way-out theory"? The girl was black poison. Like a black widow spider, she had obviously walked straight through his mind, body and soul, infecting him with her dark energy. And in doing so, had it changed his DNA forever, twisting the strand so that he, Poe Black, like the girl, was a changeling? Poe could not stop his mind twisting the dark tale this way and that, trying to get a clearer picture, but with a kaleidoscopic mind that was never going to happen.

'Pa-zhal-sta. Be careful. I don't want you to break your neck. I don't want our second meeting to be at a funeral, yours,' laughed the girl, trying her best to smile, as she reached out to stop Poe from falling off the bottom of the icy ladder. Smiling clearly did not come easily to the girl, for the smile did not sit easily upon her face. It looked slightly wonky, half-smile, half-grimace. But then again, as she was a teenage girl, she probably didn't want to break her air of cool. The ice maiden was indeed a cool look in or outside the Arctic Circle.

To Poe's mind, the laugh seemed somehow forced. Perhaps she really did want him to fall to his death for an assassin; that would make her life so much easier. Poe chastised himself for thinking the worst of this strange girl, for wasn't he, Poe Black, a stranger in most folk's eyes? Even through his own eyes, when Poe looked into a mirror, he felt like a stranger, a stranger to himself, as if he were possessing someone's else's body.

Poe then found himself imagining the girl as Snow White, as white as the driven snow, and so polite you would be happy to bring her home to meet your parents, even if your parents resided in the local cemetery. The first word the girl had spoken was in Russian, the word please. No self-respecting assassin would use the word please before they stuck an ice pick in your heart; it just wasn't what assassins did. Assassins were the strong, silent type. Actions spoke louder than words. If the girl was really a cold-hearted assassin, Poe would already be trying to pull the ice pick out of his chest, the worst thing you can do to a protruding object, for if you remove it, you will almost certainly bleed to death.

Poe was under the spell of the fairy tale, and possibly under a love spell as well.

Poe had always loved the sound of a Russian accent, or at least when it came from the lips of a Russian princess. Finland was within spitting distance of Russia and although the two countries were no longer at each other's throats, as they had been once upon a dark time, there was still bad blood between them. However, there was no reason why simply because she was of Russian descent she should give him the cold shoulder, the ice maiden treatment. The last thing Poe wanted to do was get into a war of words or, worse still, start a new cold war.

Then the ladder began to shudder as it started to slide sideways, causing Poe to lose his balance. Hopefully, the girl, being his guardian angel, would catch his fall.

Wishful thinking perhaps. The opening line to old fairy tales went as follows… Back in the old times when wishing was still effective. Poe found himself hoping the lost art of wishful thinking was a gift he possessed, for he was now wishing for all the world that this girl's appearance would not be a fleeting one, as fleeting as a Nordic summer.

Many people believed in doors that led from one time and dimension to another. Hugh Everett III, one of Poe's heroes, most certainly did with his "many worlds theory".

The movement of the ladder broke the spell Poe was under as time moved on. As the girl reached out to break Poe's fall, it seemed the art of wishful thinking wasn't dead after all. Poe noticed something else as he fell into her arms: she had a silver chain hanging around her neck, with a yin and yang symbol attached to it. However, that was only half the story, as the pendant was of the yin symbol, a large teardrop-shaped yin without the yang, as if the pendant had been cut in half using a metal work tool. Poe looked down at his chest, for under his t-shirt he had the same pendant, except he had the other half of the symbol, the yang.

Surely this was too much of a coincidence, the science of synchronicity in action, the psychologist Carl Jung's weird and wonderful theory of how the universe really worked. Poe had had the pendant made, for he had always felt a part of him was missing, known in psychology as "the shadow self". Except there was more to it than simple psychology, although psychology was anything but simple. A psychologist would probably tell him, as he lay on an uncomfortable couch (which felt like a bed of nails) that this really was wishful thinking, a feeling which gave a lonely young man some much-needed comfort. This could have been the reason the girl had had the yin pendant made, for she, like Poe, felt as if a part of her was missing.

'I see you couldn't get a signal either. I wonder how high you have to go to be able to get a signal. The stars, heaven perhaps, the dark side of the moon?' the girl said, trying to ease the awkwardness between them, as first meetings for young folk are anything but easy. The girl could see Poe did not know many Russian words so did her best to speak English, however broken it was.

'I can get a signal up here, or at least for the radio. I know this is going to sound strange but I like to listen to dead air, static, the background radiation from the Big Bang. I find it soothing. It feels a bit like listening to God whispering in my ear, or at least the creator,' Poe replied, fearing he was sounding like a geek or a dead philosopher; not the effect he was looking for. He was searching for the air of cool of a hero of the silver screen, or any dead cool vampire out of any number of vampire movies and TV series over the years. Perhaps he would be better choosing the young Tom Cruise in *Interview with the Vampire* to base his cool character upon.

'Isn't it funny how all vampires have cheekbones to die for,' Poe mumbled under his breath, trying out a line in his head, thinking this was not a bad line to break the ice with. And, after all, teenage girls loved vampires to death; it was a fact right up there with the fact that earth was not a sphere, it was an oblate spheroid. This meant the earth was slightly misshapen, not unlike Poe's small world.

Poe felt another charge of electricity surge through his body, for it felt to him as if he had finally been given the gift of sound and vision, as in the David Bowie song of the same name. Poe had always loved this, the opening upbeat bars of music which seemed somehow at odds with the downbeat lyrics, sweet, bittersweet like first love.

'M-my name's Poe, by the way. Poe Black,' stuttered Poe, looking down at his shoes as if they needed a good polishing. Where was a shoeshine boy when you needed one?

'A most unusual name. And you, Poe Black, I imagine, are a most unusual boy. And my name's,' the girl hesitated for a moment then said shyly, 'my name's Sorrow.'

The name Sorrow repeated three times inside Poe's mind as if her voice had been recorded on a record and the needle on the record had got stuck.

'Born on Sunday like Solomon Grundy, Sunday is favourite day of week. I know most people hate it, it being slow gloomy-grey, and too close to Monday, has most working people wishing Sunday, Monday separated by giant iron curtain,' said the girl in her broken English. With her Russian accent, Poe was smitten, finding her charming and adorable, so much so that he wanted to call her Babushka.

Poe did not for he did not want to scare the girl off. She might think he was one of those clingy, drippy types who apologise for being alive. Poe apologised, not for being alive but for not being dead, as he apologised to Edgar Allen Poe's ghost every time he saw him enter his attic.

It is another well-known fact that young Russian girls hug and kiss one another like long-lost friends every time they meet. If this was indeed a fact and not a fiction, Poe considered if somewhere in his attic there was a dressing-up box. A quick change and he was sure he could pass for a teenage girl as he had the soft features of those of a female of the species, a pretty boy; at least he had as a child. Nowadays, there wasn't an ounce of fat on him. He had cheekbones to die for, which meant he was definitely vampire material. Yes, Poe could suck the girls in with his girlfriend act then suck the blood from them. Trouble was, Poe hated the sight of blood, so the vampire-walking-dead act was a complete non-starter.

Teenage girls also loved horoscopes and astrology. Poe had learnt that fact from school, the one he rarely attended, so perhaps he could ask Sorrow what her star sign was. After which he could ask her if she thought their meeting was written in the stars, serendipity. To Poe's mind, the word horoscope was far too close to the word horror for his liking. Today, you will meet a tall, dark, handsome stranger with cheekbones to die for in a dark alley. Don't be afraid, he isn't the big bad werewolf, as according to the stargazers there isn't a full moon out tonight!

'Poetry, your name, it's poetry,' said Poe, as if he were the living embodiment of a dead poet like Percy Bysshe Shelley. Poe hoped the girl did not think he meant that she looked like a sorrowful soul, one who brought sorrow to all those she met. No sooner had the words come out of Poe's mouth than he immediately wished they hadn't, but you couldn't put the wish back into the wishing well once you had fished it out. 'I-I mean, it's a nice name, Sorrow, yes, most unusual it is. It has a kind of bittersweet poetry to it,' Poe added, wondering where the poetry came from and whether he had just joined the Dead Poets Society. In truth, he knew exactly where the poetry had come from: his mother and his grandmother, who both loved writing and reading poetry. Poe wondered if in part that was how he got his name, along with the fact that his mother must have loved reading the gothic tales of Edgar Allen Poe.

'My real name is Yarra Eloise Pandora, Romanarov not Romanov. Unfortunately, I am not distant relation of Romanov family. I got nickname of Sorrow given to me because I do not smile much,' Sorrow added, shrugging her shoulders theatrically, struggling with her English but determined to press on, for Yarra knew that English broke down barriers, whereas her mother tongue only made her more misunderstood. The Russian language had a poetry about it. No sooner had Poe heard the name Romanov than he imagined he had conjured up the girl from his own mind, for Poe had always been fascinated by the Romanov dynasty, some may say even obsessed by the deaths of the Romanov family assassinated in 1918 by the Bolsheviks, either that or the girl was a fantasist, not unlike Poe himself.

It appeared Poe did not hear the girl say she was not related to the Romanov family, but then at times we all hear what we want to hear. Then Sorrow went on to tell Poe how she got the name of Yarra, that it was on an old cottage in the woods which her mother passed by every day when she went to work. One day, the house was gone, vanished off the face of the earth. The truth was, the old cottage was crumbling away and was knocked down when the owner, presumably a woman named Yarra, died. The only thing left of the house was an old wooden sign which read *Yarra's House*. Sorrow's mother took the sign and put it on a playhouse she had built for her daughter with her own fair hands. Yarra's mother had a small plot of land where a small wood stood and where the playhouse stood. Yarra made up many stories while in the playhouse about the life and times of a woman and girl named Yarra, almost as many tales as there were made up about Anastasia – the lost girl and the Romanov family. Yarra's House may no longer exist but thanks to Yarra, aka Sorrow, the memory of the cottage and its owner lived on. Yarra said if wishing was still effective, as in the opening line to German folk and fairy tales, she would wish Yarra's House was still standing, as if it was a house from a giant child's Victorian pop-up book, and then she would be able to meet her namesake.

As Sorrow was telling this short but poignant tale Poe noticed the deadpan expression on the girl's sullen face as Poe began to imagine the girl named Sorrow, Yarra, Eloise Pandora, Romanarov; the girl with a hundred and one personalities. His first imagining turned the girl into a vampire, like Lucy Westenra from the novel *Dracula*, and as the girl looked deathly pale, this wasn't so hard to imagine. Perhaps the girl suffered from mental illness multiple personalities. In a certain light, Poe could imagine the girl to be an albino, so white was her skin, and in another light... silvery moonlight... her skin could be compared to that of a silver birch tree.

So, the girl was a tree witch now, was she? Poe needed to live in the real world and not the world of his imagination if he was ever to get to know this girl properly. Poe decided to call the girl a "changeling", that way, no matter how many times she changed, he would know he was still talking to the same person. Beauty was skin-deep. Poe was sure 'the changeling' was beautiful on the inside, and inside, her sweet disposition never changed.

'Yarra and Eloise are also very poetical names, and as for Pandora, well, I have always loved her backstory, Pandora's Jar,' said Poe, as his tongue untied itself and he loosened up a bit from the straitjacket he felt he was wearing. Young men never were that fashion conscious, but wearing a straitjacket, well, that was just crazy, and the sort of thing that was guaranteed to lead to the madhouse.

'Pretty unusual girl, yes, I am, if truth be told. I collect antique sweets. I have edible Easter egg made by Fabergé. Once upon a time, egg belonged to Princess Anastasia Romanov, oh, and believe it or not, I collect antique tears,' said the girl, drawing a long breath, which gave Poe a chance to take some of this information in. He found himself wondering if this was a blind date by the way the girl was telling him her hobbies. Poe felt this may well be the case and a curious case indeed. It soon became clear that Sorrow, aka Yarra, was trying to blind him with science, although this definitely came under the heading of weird science.

'Tears were a part of school science project on emotions. Science teacher also big on psychology. Every time I cry, I catch tears in a glass jar, tears of sorrow and tears of joy. I label the jars of tears with time, date and year I shed them. I watched tear-jerker movies, went to funerals, cried a lot when I didn't win the first prize at science fair. I thought that unfair, a waste of good tears, too late to do me any good. Still, I did get third prize and praise from teachers for my original mind. I expect you think that a little weird,' said Sorrow, coyly twisting her hair around her finger into a ringlet.

Once again, this was all in his vivid imagination, for outwardly at least the girl showed little emotion, which to Poe's mind, full of books on psychology by Freud, Jung and Nietzsche, meant that inside she was a volcano about to erupt. If this was the case then Poe wondered if he should run for the hills, or at least the forest set upon a hill.

'We live in a mad, mad world. You'd have to be mad not to think this was our reality,' Poe blurted out, then wished he hadn't. He was desperate not to say the wrong thing, but it was as if his head had been shaken up so that all the thoughts and words were mixed up.

'Poe Black, you have old head on young shoulders as old saying goes. I try to keep madness locked inside the Pandora's Box in my head,' Sorrow replied.

'Easier said than done, for madness often leaks from the Pandora's Box inside my head, like dark energy leaks into our world from another universe,' Poe added wistfully, sounding like a philosopher from another age, until he realised he was now speaking in broken English. The girl must think he was mimicking her, making fun of her, thought Poe, turning as red as the beauty spot on Jupiter.

'*Iz-vi-nit-yepa-zhal-sta.* Sorry, Poe Black, I have to go. Perhaps we will meet another time?' stuttered Sorrow as she turned away, as if being called by an angry father or a wicked stepmother as she hadn't finished her chores. The truth was, Sorrow's mobile phone had rung. It was a text from somebody dear to her heart, one she could not ignore: her poor mother on her deathbed.

'*Da, da,* yes, yes, of course. Take care. I'll be here when you get back, on my lonesome as usual. I don't go out much. In the meantime, I'll continue sticking pins in my eyes and building gothic castles out of matchsticks.' Poe sighed, heavy of heart, then under his breath added the Shakespeare lament, '"Parting is such sweet sorrow."' Poe was already kicking himself for a wasted opportunity, and the girl hadn't even gone yet. Poe had tried to tell the girl he didn't want her to go, but the words stuck in his throat as in a nightmare. Perhaps it was for the best; he didn't want to seem desperate or lose his air of cool. Cool was the word, as the temperature began to plummet to well below freezing, whereas before, thanks to the warmth of the girl's closeness, Poe had felt as warm as a forest fire from a distance. Perhaps this was Poe's last chance at love. Nobody knew what the future would bring. He may fall off the edge of the world as he turned over in his sleep tonight… the end of the Life and Times of Poe Black… end of dark fairy story! Who on earth in their right mind would sleep in a bed on the edge of the world? If that did not qualify as madness, nothing did!

The Boy Who Fell Off the Edge of the World: a tale Poe had written when he was younger and one he was beginning to wish would come true.

'Don't worry, Poe Black, you're never alone in this world, or any other. Remember, there are a thousand and one other Poe Blacks in a thousand and one other universes. If you get lonely, jump in wardrobe in attic and have mad tea party with other Poe Blacks and be back in time for mad tea party with Alice, the Hatter, the White Witch from Narnia and the Starman David Bowie, *da-svi-dan-ya,*' cried Sorrow, in floods of tears, enough to make Alice's pool of tears seem little more than a damp patch in an attic, or so Poe imagined, undoubtedly an imagining he'd got wrong. 'Meet another time.' Perhaps the girl meant in another world, a parallel world, for Poe felt sure he would not meet this strange creature again in this one.

Poe thought he heard a faint voice floating on the wind that said, *We'll meet again on the Bridge of Sighs in Venice,* or perhaps it was simply a voice inside his head putting words into the mouth of the mysterious girl named Sorrow.

Poe was more than a little woebegone, a favourite word from the lexicon of Victorian writers.

Poe often saw the beauty in death, as if watching the last breath of a butterfly and a moth in a jar before their wings were clipped forevermore, only being observed behind a wall of glass as Poe re-imagined the Life and Dark Times of Edgar Allen Poe.

'What had he just said?' sighed Poe, with an excess of horror upon his face, an Edgar Allen Poe line if ever there was one as he feverishly pored over the line that had just come out of his mouth. Poe knew he was sure to go over and over the line again, picking over the bones of the conversation, like a black vulture wishing he could rewrite it so it came out better. 'I'll be waiting, waiting for a cold day in hell!'

It seemed for Poe Black that *Lykkeland*, "the state of happiness", was a shambles from all sides, which made it an omnishambles.

Poe craved a metamorphosis from ugly moth via chrysalis status to beautiful butterfly, in keeping with his butterfly mind. For right now his beautiful mind seemed to be twisting itself into psychosis rather than metamorphosis, "Strange days indeed, most peculiar, mamma." And the strains of John Lennon's song *Strange Days* echoed in his head, as if being played in a gothic cathedral. This song was followed by the Stranglers' song *Strange Little Girl*, the lyric being "Strange little girl where are you going?" Where indeed? Poe wondered. This song was followed on the black jukebox in Poe's head by a downbeat Doors song, *Strange Days*, to end this strange day. Poe pulled the plug from the cracked jukebox in his head, the one covered in cobwebs, for he was sure the next 45 disc on the jukebox would be *Sorrow* by David Bowie. Then Poe's mind started to shut down.

Poe wondered why the Doors' downbeat-upbeat song *People are Strange* had not popped up in the jukebox in his head. With all the strangeness going on in the kaleidoscopic worlds of Poe Black, you would have imagined it would. Boy, were some people strange, and as Poe looked into the mirror of the mind, he knew he was one of those strange folk, a stranger to everyone he met and most of the time a stranger to himself. Will the real Poe Black please stand up, as a thousand and one Poe Blacks stood up in one parallel world or another.

There was only so much strangeness a boy could take in one lifetime. Poe was sure all the other Poe Blacks in parallel worlds would agree with him right now if they were in his shiny black pointy leather snowshoes.

3

The Metamorphosis of Poe Black

Poe did not see the changeling girl again, aka Sorrow or Yarra, Eloise or Pandora, although of course they were one and the same. Poe had only known the girl a few minutes, but those few minutes were magical ones, and ones that seemed to go on forever, or at least they did in his mind. Every time he shut his eyes, Poe could see the girl's face, as pale as a ghost, as if her skin was made of quicksilver. Poe was acting as if he was suffering from a bad case of lovesickness, pining over a long-lost lover. But what was time? It was an illusion; Einstein said as much, and Max Plank the physicist agreed. Max Plank time, in theory at least, made time vanish, splitting time like the atom. So many times it disappeared into thin air, just like the mysterious girl with the string of poetical names engraved upon a charm bracelet had done.

Yarra was Sorrow's first given name, and having given herself the name of Sorrow was now in the guise of her alter ego Pandora, a vampire who slept in a giant ebony box that looked awfully like an Egyptian sarcophagus as in the 1924 horror movie *The Cabinet of Dr. Caligari*. Pandora then transformed into a Russian doll which shrank before his very eyes, one blink at a time in an old black and white stop-go motion animated film. With each blink, the Russian doll named Pandora jumped out of one wooden doll, unscrewed the one inside it and then jumped in and screwed the head back on. It had all the hallmarks of a nightmare inside a nightmare, the opposite to Edgar Allen Poe's quote of, "Life is like a dream inside a dream." Life was hardly a bowl of cherries, unless they were black cherries.

Poe wondered if Yarra had been nicknamed Sorrow for a good reason, in that she brought her friends nothing but sorrow, so in the end they had no choice but to turn away from her, either that or have to suffer the sorrows she had to endure. Perhaps this was a punishment for crimes in another lifetime, reincarnation. Poe often wondered if his mother had been reincarnated as a flower, a black rose, for according to his grandmother she dressed in black from head to toe, as if a widow in mourning, like Queen Victoria.

It had been a blind date, one in which Poe imagined he was Charles Babbage and Sorrow was Ada Lovelace, a meeting of minds; one brilliant, one beautiful. Poe stretched this meeting out so it lasted a lifetime. Poe cut the meeting up into sequence as if he was a producer editing a movie, all played out on what he imaginatively referred to as the Doorstep Theatre. This was a one-man one-woman play as he dressed himself and Sorrow up in elaborate costumes from a fancy-dress box that Poe imagined once upon a time belonged to Pandora in the Greek tale. Poe played Prince Albert to Sorrow's Princess Victoria,

Tsar Nicholas II to Sorrow's Tsarina Alexander, the Duke of Essex to Sorrow's Queen Elizabeth I.

In the blinking of an eye, a year passed by and nothing happened, well, nothing out of the ordinary, unlike the extraordinary meeting Poe had had with this strange and mysterious creature that he was now beginning to imagine was conjured up either by the frost fairy or the silver birch goddess. That was until Poe Black and the world found themselves trapped inside a giant nightmare, inside a glass Pandora's box, as a pandemic swept the globe; coronavirus, COVID-19. In the strange days that followed, the abnormal became the new normal. Then a giant witches' broom appeared out of the darkness and swept the virus clean away, but it did not sweep the girl under the carpet, for the carpet of a forest was like a giant magic carpet.

Poe then awoke from a dream, although as he walked around in a dream most of the time, it may have been a daydream, one in which he was talking to a strange creature, all dressed in black. It is said we control daydreams, while at night dreams control us, except in Poe Black's upside-down world where it appeared to be the other way around.

Poe knew he had fallen in love with Sorrow's beautiful mind, a girl who clearly loved figures as much as he did. And it was not just Sorrow's beautiful mind that attracted Poe to her, as she had a figure to die for. A body to die for, he hoped not!

Since Sorrow had disappeared off the face of the planet, or fallen off the edge of the world, Poe had turned his back on the world, shutting himself away, disappearing back into a world of his own making. 'My soul is unwell. It is lucky that I am leaving this cruel world far behind me,' Poe sighed, sounding like Hans Christian Andersen as he left his European tour and headed for home in Denmark. The truth was, Poe had turned his back on the world a long time ago, way before his sorrows were down to a girl named Sorrow.

Poe's world was a small world, the attic. It was in this dark world, this dark space, that Poe, surprisingly, was at his happiest.

The old shack house had five rooms as well as the attic. Two of the rooms were bedrooms, yet he chose this poky little dark room to spend most of his time. It was almost as if he was quarantining himself off from the rest of the family of ghosts in the attic, as if he had the virus COVID-19, an unseen virus. Poe had likened this virus to dark energy, the sort quantum physicists were trying to track down. Poe was happy in his unhappiness, listening to dark music, reading dark material, thinking dark thoughts. For most, it would have been like being shut in a prison cell, devoid of light, but for Poe Black it was a cathartic experience. Poe embraced the darkness or "the dark energy" as he poetically referred to it.

Then, one dark night, Poe heard scratching. A giant rat had scrambled up onto his bed, or at least it had in the nightmare. Eventually, after trying to fight the rat off, Poe awoke in a cold sweat. 'A nightmare, nothing to write home about. Just add it to all the others in my nightmare journal.'

Poe soon realised the scratching was real and coming from behind the wall, so reluctantly he got out of bed, more curious than scared, wondering if a bird had got trapped behind the wall. Poe pressed his ear against the wall. He was sure he could hear a voice saying, 'Your time has come.' He must be imagining it. He pressed his ear even tighter to the wall in the hope of hearing more clearly. It was probably the fluttering of a bird's wings. It must have got in under the roof and was now trapped in a panic.

Poe was a soft-hearted boy, with skin as thin as a butterfly's wing or the skin of an old man, and as most people said, he was old before his time. That was about right. Poe hated to see anything suffer. He'd rather suffer himself. If he didn't rescue the poor thing, he would beat himself up for months afterwards. The bird would turn from a pigeon to a nightjar, to a raven, visiting him regularly in his nightmares. The thing was, Poe had always had a soft spot for the raven, a bird that in most people's eyes was a harbinger of doom, which always appeared in Medieval Tales. Perhaps the reason for this love of the raven was because of Edgar Allen Poe's epic poem *The Raven*.

'Don't be scared, boy. It was written this way,' whispered the voice behind the wall, but this time in a louder tone, a tone that sent chills right through Poe's whole body. He felt so cold that he imagined he had been turned into an ice sculpture, although he did not imagine for one moment he had been turned into the ice sculpture of the artist Tove Jansson who wrote the *Moomintroll* books, her statue being in an underground car park in Helsinki.

Trolls belonged in dark fairy tales, entangled in the dark web like flies trapped in a spider's web waiting to be devoured by a giant spider, an ending they deserved and one they had brought upon themselves. Poe did not have an internet connection. In fact, he didn't even have a computer, of which he was glad. Poe would leave his avatar self, or one of his many parallel selves, to do battle with imaginary black dragons, vampires and werewolves in the cyberworld. And if one or more of his parallel Poe Blacks ever darkened his doorstep from the multiverse, hoping Poe would join forces with them, he would send them packing. And he would do this by setting a pack of wolves upon them, ones he kept in the attic as his guard dogs. Poe had thousands of parallel selves, perhaps hundreds of thousands, so he wouldn't miss one or two, and, after all, one had to keep the wolf from the door somehow, the werewolf!

For a few seconds, Poe wondered if he was still trapped in the nightmare as he stepped on something sharp. It was a loose tack from the ragged-looking moth-eaten carpet, and he soon realised that was not the case as he howled out in pain just like a werewolf in the process of changing. This was not a metamorphosis Poe much cared for; it was bad enough going through the changes, physical and mental, that all teenagers went through, without making it any worse.

The wall was covered in old, fading wallpaper that looked like tangled ivy, poison ivy, which often came alive, wrapping itself around him like a boa constrictor squeezing the life out of him, or at least in his nightmare. Poe tore at the paper as if his life depended upon it until, much to his astonishment, behind the wallpaper he saw a black wooden door. The door did not seem to fit the attic; it looked out of place. A garden would have suited the door down to the ground. It was not because Poe imagined the gate to have a soul, like some religions believed inanimate objects had, or the Nordic people believed trees had souls, but because it looked for all the world to be a garden gate. Poe was now imagining this unassuming-looking gate as a gate to another world. Poe saw a picture of the forester in his mind's eye. His instincts and sixth sense told him that he should lay the blame for this nightmare at his door. The forester was the man who had built the house, one that was fast turning into a house of horrors. Poe had found this bit of information out after discovering a small black tin under the floorboards. Inside the tin were the blueprints for the house and the deeds, along with several fading black and white photographs of the man, suitably dressed with an axe in his hand, an axe Poe had always imagined dripping in blood.

Poe tugged at the door, expecting it to be stuck fast after years of not being used, but once again, much to his surprise, the door opened easily as if it was brand new.

Poe peered into the gloom. He could have done with a torch, or at least a candle, but all he had on his bedside cabinet was a green laser pen. Poe had had this pen for years. Most of the time it barely worked, the batteries worn down by all the times he had used it to fight off imaginary dragons, black dragons, shadow dragons. Such dragons possessed a dark energy so powerful that one flame from their dark mouth, one beat of their giant wing could destroy a whole world! Even Poe had to admit teenagers could be a little melodramatic at times, as if they imagined they were starring in a Victorian melodrama on stage.

The beam of the laser pen created three-dimensional patterns like those a Spiro-giro graph created. If one shined the pen on a wall far away, it was as if it created a parallel world, a 4D one that you could climb into and disappear. Sometimes, Poe would go up onto the roof of the house at night and shine the beam onto the snow. It created amazing patterns, almost as amazing as the pattern of a snowflake.

Poe shined the beam of the light into the room, but the beam was so weak that he could hardly see anything at all, other than cobwebs. He had no other choice than to climb into the room and hope the bird, bat, hopefully not a vampire bat, the vampire or whatever it was, didn't in its panic take his eye out like in his nightmare. If this happened, it would be as if the bird had flown out of his nightmare into the real world.

Poe stepped into the room, shielding his eyes, fully expecting to hear the creak of the floorboards underfoot, or perhaps to hear the floorboards crack as the floor gave way and he fell to his death. One last nightmare for old times' sake before he met the grim reaper. It was grim, all right, as grim as a Brothers Grimm folk tale.

Poe felt as if he was walking on a carpet, and low and behold, as he looked down, he was amazed to see a thick green carpet beneath his bare feet. Not a traditional carpet but a magic carpet made of leaves, lichens and moss. 'It's like I'm walking through a forest. I can't be. It must be a loft space. The wind must have brought the leaves in, and the moss has grown because the loft is damp,' said Poe, trying to figure things out logically, but if this was a dream then maybe it would be better if he tried to figure things out illogically.

But this wasn't a dream. Poe was now even more sure than ever of that; perhaps this was a door to a parallel world, a time portal.

Then the door slammed shut, as if a great wind had sprung up in the loft space, causing leaves, dust and old webs to swirl all about him, the webs covering his face. In his panic, Poe clawed at his face, scratching it, drawing blood. If there were vampires living in the attic space, he would soon know it. Poe spun on his heels as if he were a whirling dervish, no mean feat in this small space, and, in doing so, almost fell flat on his face. The door was now in front of him and if the nightmare ran to form, the door would slam in his face and he would be locked in, locked into the nightmare when he wanted to be locked out of the nightmare.

In a cold sweat, Poe grabbed at the door handle, pulling at it, shaking it violently, but it would not budge. It was as if the door hadn't been opened for years.

Poe wanted to reverse the dream, or time, or dream time, but if this was a nightmare, he felt reversing the dream would not be possible. Anything and everything was possible in the quantum world, the impossible dream made possible. It was in all the adverts in his *New Scientist* magazine. Poe was trying not to imagine shrinking down to the size of Hans Christian Andersen's fairy-tale character Thumbelina, or miniature Alice, in which case this was a Nightmare in Wonderland.

4

The Twisted Forest

A ghostly face appeared out of the gloom, except it wasn't a ghost but the face of a large white wolf. So, this was how this nightmare ended, thought Poe, with him admiring the lining of a wolf's stomach. The tale of White Fang, the old Victorian horror story written by Jack London, sprang to mind and he wished it had not. Poe wondered if it was the old man Wolf Witcher, the down-and- out who once upon a time was an actor. Poe had put the old man up for a while in one of his spare rooms. One day, he disappeared without leaving a note to say goodbye, which Poe had thought was odd. If Wolf Witcher was a werewolf and one who, like Poe, had entered this alternate reality, then it all made a strange kind of sense. That's if this was an alternate reality and not a delusion of the tired and diseased mind, brought about from spending too much time on one's own. Another strange thought occurred. Could this be the spirit of his mother who was now watching over him? Highly unlikely; a human need to put human spirits in the form of other creatures to give them comfort.

Of course, it could be the spirit of his father, who left his mother a few months before Poe was born. Poe was not sure he wanted to meet his father. After all, he was hardly the sort of man a son looks up to. He hoped he had more of his mother's DNA than his father's, the black sheep of the family.

'Welcome to your dream, Poe Black. On this journey, you will find yourself, your true self and your true nature. You cannot turn back. The only way to get out of the forest is to keep going until you reach the end of the forest. When you reach the end, your dream will be revealed to you like a clever conjuring trick. Good luck, my boy, you will need it.' The white wolf spoke then spoke no more as it disappeared back into the gloom.

Poe imagined the wolf had been reincarnated from a Buddhist monk, so Zen-like was his speech and manner. He then recalled the writing on the back of his dream journal, which read –

This dream journal is here to guide you on a path of reflection, self-evaluation and being more mindful. Blah, blah, blah, cut to the chase... By the time you have filled this journal, you will be on a solid path to mindfulness and have a better understanding of your true self.

Poe felt he was off to a rocky start on this journey through the self and through the dream world, as to his dark mind the dream already appeared to be heading towards a nightmare faster than the speed of light. What next? Would he be surrounded by his worst nightmare, a pack of wolves ready to rip him limb from limb, drink his blood, thus turning them all into giant wolfmen? Poe imagined the shadow wolves from his nightmares had leapt across time and space into the present.

Poe didn't mind putting the dream or himself under the microscope, but he had reservations when it came to putting the nightmare under the microscope, for a nightmare was like a bad virus, like the Black Death, not to mention the fact it was highly infectious. As was the nightmare catcher, who most certainly was not too slow to catch a cold and was more than happy to pass it on to anyone who was at death's door.

At this exact moment of time, Poe felt as if he was in a trance or under a spell as he found himself wondering if the wolf had got the line muddled up, like an old actor fluffing his line, and what he meant to say was, 'Welcome to your worst nightmare!' If this was the case, Poe had a good mind to tell the wolf he was welcome to the nightmare, as he was back off to the land of dreams, where he hoped to meet his dream date.

Then another wolf appeared, except this wolf was in his head. It had been in his head as long as he could remember, an old nightmare coming back to haunt him. It was a red wolf, the sort one sees in the Bayou swamp land in America, but no, Poe had got it horribly wrong, for this wasn't a red wolf as Poe had first thought, as it now became clear to Poe that the wolf was covered in blood, but whose blood, its own or its victims?

Poe's blood ran cold, for he imagined this blood could well be his own! Poe had never been the sort of boy to cry wolf, like in the children's fairy tale; however, this may be the time to start!

Poe walked on further, the twigs and dry leaves underfoot sounding as if he was walking on rusty metal. Poe felt compelled to put one foot in front of the other when all his instincts told him he should be walking backwards towards the door of the attic. Then he saw a light, so, naturally, he walked towards it, and as he did so, he was amazed to see shining through the canopy of the forest a bright silvery moon. Poe could no longer see the wooden walls of the house; he could only see the wooden trunks of the trees. 'I can't see the woods for the trees!' mumbled Poe, as if he was in a trance, or sleepwalking, in the state of REM, the period in sleep when one dreams their most vivid Technicolor dreams, whereas nightmares are always filmed in sepia or black and white.

The magical rays of the moon had transformed the forest from a forest of shadows into a forest of silver. Even Poe's shadow was made out of silver. If the wolf appeared again, Poe hoped his silver shadow could move like quicksilver. Poe wondered if Yarra, or as she preferred to be known, Sorrow, was hiding behind one of these trees. After all, Sorrow was always in his dreams, unless like in a previous dream she had transformed into a silver birch tree right before his very startled eyes. For a moment, Poe was frozen to the spot in fear and imagined he had been turned into a petrified tree made of stone. Thankfully, this was not the case. His foot was caught in a trap, yet he felt no pain. This must be a dream, he thought, until he realised the trap was rusty and old and with a little jiggling of his foot soon fell apart and his foot was free.

Just how old was this forest? Charles Darwin would had turned in his grave, or the ghost of Darwin would have told Poe he had sawdust for brains, for all he had to do was cut down one of the older trees in the forest and count the rings. Charles Darwin, you should be ashamed of yourself, Poe would have retorted, for nothing but nothing would make him cut down one of his beloved silver birch trees, not even on the advice of one of his heroes, Charles Darwin. Thinning out the forest helped restore it to its former glory; it was the tried and trusted method for a forester, but still Poe grimaced when he saw this happening. It was as if he was sharing the forest's pain.

Then something caught the corner of his eye. Poe's first reaction was to shout out, 'Who goes there?' although he wasn't sure if this was the wisest course of action. Besides, who goes there was the sort of line one heard in old movies. What if the shadow was a mad axeman, or, even worse, a tiger, for perhaps he had wandered so far from home that he had entered the Tiger Forest. Believe it or not, this forest was a fact, not a fiction, for there was such a place in Finland as the Tiger Forest, although thanks to the decline of tigers in the world, tigers were rarely seen in this poetically named forest. 'Hey, you, stop. I need help. I'm lost!' Poe cried, as the shadow stopped dead in its tracks.

Poe fumbled about in his pocket like an aged magician well past his prime, before eventually producing an old fob watch that once upon a time belonged to his grandfather. The hands of the watch were spinning wildly like a compass in the Bermuda Triangle. As the moon had disappeared behind the clouds, it felt to Poe as if he was on the dark side of the moon. The forest became illuminated as the cloud passed over the moon, but the shadow was nowhere to be seen.

The more Poe walked on through the forest, the more he felt a sense of *déjà vu*, and not just *déjà vu* but the sense he was walking through the nightmare. Several of his nightmares by the thickness of the undergrowth he was clawing his way through; thick virgin forest covered in snake-like vines. Poe wished he had a map or a compass to guide him as in the sport orienteering; but maps and compasses in a forest were for greenhorns, and that included forests of the mind. It was as if Poe was trapped in the Nightmare of the Twisted Forest in his Victorian perambulator, surrounded by baying wolves. One minute the forest seemed twisted and the next it untwisted itself as if by dark magic. The trees all looked as if a giant woodsman had ripped every single tree out of the earth and twisted their trunks then replanted them.

At times, all Poe could see were trees, then he could see the walls of the attic, as if the forest was a kaleidoscope or he was looking through a kaleidoscope. Of course, Poe knew this instrument could distort things, lie, hence the name kaleidoscope, although the word lie was itself twisted.

Many people twisted your words for their own ends. Poe hoped this nightmare had an end and one he found palatable. His fondest wish was that the nightmare had a fairy-tale end but not a dark or grim one as in a Brothers Grimm, Hans Christian Andersen. Poe imagined the white wolf had lied, told him a fairy tale, sucking him into the nightmare. It felt at times to Poe as if he really did have a kaleidoscope in his head. This was no bad thing if you wanted to be an original film maker or a director, like one of his directing heroes, F.W. Murnau, who directed the classic 1920s horror film – *Nosferatu, A Symphony of Horror.*

Poe walked on a little further, his throat as dry as a desert. If he had still been in bed, half awake and half asleep, he would have automatically reached out and drank from a glass of water he kept by his bedside. It was best to be prepared for the nightmare if you knew you were prone to them. Poe already had a clove of garlic and a cross on his bedside table and a gun with six silver bullets in its chambers, just in case he ran into a vampire or a werewolf in his nightmares, waking nightmares.

Poe was half expecting an old deserted run-down lunatic asylum to spring up like a Victorian pop-up book, but, touch wood, one hand on his head, one on the trunk of a tree, so far this had not happened. Everybody was world building these days, even vampires and werewolves. Poe preferred his worlds to be deconstructed rather than constructed; art houses, museums, movie houses, houses of fun in funfairs. And all these small worlds would be run-down, covered in cobwebs, overgrown, surrounded by trees.

As a child, Poe never talked much. This caused his grandparents to worry that he may be autistic, so they sent him to a child psychologist. The psychologist, who Poe thought looked like a cross between Sigmund Freud, Carl Jung and Friedrich Nietzsche, asked him to complete a few simple tests, putting square pegs in round holes, something which later made him smile, for he felt he was a round peg in a square hole, and for his interpretation of ink stains, butterflies, dead moths. The child psychologist later informed Poe's grandparents that he was living behind a wall of glass, metaphorically speaking, that people couldn't reach him and he couldn't reach them. Alternatively, people could see his lips move but could not hear his voice, and the same went for Poe. It really felt as if he was looking at the reflection of the world in a giant black bowed mirror.

Then Poe saw a silver-haired man with a scythe in his hand. At first, Poe imagined the man to be a forester or a ghost, a spirit of a forester that like him had entered the forest and being unable to escape died here. The grim reaper, or the ghost of one of the Brothers Grimm, was Poe's next wild imagining. There was a full moon out, so perhaps the man was simply suffering from the mental condition known as "lunacy", brought on by a full moon. Another fiction, as there was no scientific evidence to back up this weird and not-so-wonderful mental malady. The man was scything down the twisted silver birch trees. Perhaps he imagined them to be infected by a disease.

Although the forest was dark when the moonlight went behind the cloud, it still looked as if it was dusk or twilight, due to the silver birch trees, Poe presumed. That was the magical power the silver birch tree had to illuminate, which is why if ever Poe got a bad case of the blues, he often found himself in the Forest of Lumen (the Forest of Light), as Poe referred to the forest. When this happened, Poe couldn't even recall how he got there. It was as if he had been sleepwalking.

The silver birch trees always rejuvenated him. Forest Bathing had become all the rage nowadays. You could even get it on prescription. But this was normally only for city folk as, for the most part, the only forest they ever saw was the concrete forest or jungle.

Poe could see a man in the forest sleeping rough, a man who was clearly having a nightmare like himself, for he was tossing and turning this way and that, as if wrestling with a nightmare. The man looked familiar to Poe. Was this the tramp who he found sleeping rough in the wooden house? This had been the tramp Wolf Witcher, an old actor and manager of a theatre company who had helped him to purchase the house. At the time, Poe, being only fourteen, was too young to buy it himself. The tramp played the part of a long-lost relative Atticus Eugenius Black III, who signed the papers that allowed Poe to buy the house. Poe paid the tramp a princely sum and let him stay in one of the rooms. Eventually, the tramp moved on. Or perhaps once again Poe was being led astray by his wild imagination. After all, one tramp pretty much looked like another tramp.

Tramps all wore the same uniform, one with as many creases in it as the face of an old witch, and carried around their worldly belongings in an old moth-eaten carpet bag. Poe imagined in the cold winter months that the tramps climbed into the carpet bag and used it as a sleeping bag, and if they had the old flying dream, well, after all, it was a magic carpet bag! Of course, the moth-eaten old carpet bag may well be well past its sell-by date, and if the magic ran out, well, then the old falling dream came into play as the dream was replaced by a nightmare!

The shadow figure bent down over the man and then did something quite extraordinary. He drew out a pair of bellows from the inside pockets of his large black frockcoat. A few seconds later, he drew out a pair of long silver tongs and several glass jars from the inside pockets of the frockcoat. To Poe's mind, he imagined the Edwardian-style frockcoat once upon a time belonged to a magician, probably Merlin the Magician. The shadowy figure then proceeded to push the bellows into the tramp's ears. The man then feverishly pumped the bellows as if pumping up the tyre of a bicycle while humming to himself what to Poe's ears sounded like a lullaby. The shadowy figure appeared to have sucked something dark and misshapen out of the tramp's ears. Still with the bellows in his hand, he pumped the object, now slithering like an eel, into one of the glass jars. The object circled the jar, thrashing around like a fish in a net, causing the jar to turn as black as night, as if the glass had turned from opaque to smoke glass.

A black rabbit appeared nearby and as it ran past, as quickly as the flash Victorian villain Spring-Heeled Jack, he grabbed it roughly by the neck. The man then picked up the ghastly-looking misshapen object out of the glass jar with the pair of long silver tongs and held it up to the light. For a second, Poe thought the man was about to swallow the object but instead he inserted it into one of the rabbit's large ears. The rabbit struggled, trying to free itself from the man's vice-like grip but could not and was almost strangulated as it attempted to break the man's stranglehold. The man in black then bent down and gently placed the black rabbit back down onto the ground and watched as it shook violently. Then the rabbit died, possibly from shock, although here Poe was guessing, for he had no medical training or degree in animal husbandry. The man then took out a sharp silver paper knife and gutted the rabbit, wiping the blood from his hands on the rabbit's thick fur.

Poe turned away. He was squeamish at the best of times, watching horror movies through his hands or from behind the settee. Poe forced himself to watch. He was mesmerised by the man in black as he pulled the writhing, slithering object out of the body of the rabbit and put it back into the jar. The jar shook so violently that it toppled over. Poe imagined that if this continued much longer, the object would smash the glass jar and escape. Poe backed off, fearing the worst, the very worst, when he knew this was the worst thing he could do, as if bringing the worst upon himself.

The tramp had stopped thrashing about like a fish on a hook on a line no sooner had the man in the black frockcoat removed the object from his ear, the nightmare, as Poe imagined the object to be. The tramp rolled over and went back to what looked like a dreamless sleep, as he seemed content, now sleeping like a baby.

'Like the grim reaper, the nightmare catcher's work is never done. We'd make a fine team, the reaper and I, a fine team, perhaps not a dream team, more a team to deliver the perfect nightmare, two nightmares for the price of three. It's amazing how popular my nightmares are, inserted in the ear of any enemy while they sleep, and a few moments later, the nightmare gets to work, and by the morning they would have gone raving mad. Guaranteed or your money back,' the nightmare catcher sniggered in a low voice as if, like Rumpelstiltskin, he did not want anyone to know his name.

'Wolf, is that you, is that you?' Poe cried out, but the tramp did not answer. Perhaps he had turned into a wolf and had run off into the forest, fearing he too would be gutted by the man in black.

Poe woke up with a start and looked all about him, as if half in a dream, half in a daydream, although this had all the hallmarks of a nightmare rather than a dream. Poe had always found it hard to distinguish the world of reality from the world of dreams, but now he was finding it nigh on impossible to tell one from the other. He could not be sure what was real and what was not. Poe walked around in a daze until he came to a wishing well. He leant over the side of the well then felt a large hand in the small of his back. 'If you want a better look, may I suggest I give you a helping hand,' laughed a shadowy figure in manic fashion as Poe fell to his death, then added, 'The question was, did the boy fall or was he pushed? If pushed on the matter, I'd say the boy was pushed.'

Poe woke up with a start, quickly realising he'd had a recurring nightmare, the oldest nightmare in the book, the one in which you fell to your death. Thankfully, this time, the nightmare was not a waking nightmare, just a bad dream. Poe decided not to go back to sleep for fear of the nightmare waiting for him there, so he walked on through the forest, with only the moon to guide his way.

Then Poe came to a large wooden building and outside in the garden – half garden, half woods – a group of people were gathered round. Poe did not want to disturb them. Also, he wasn't sure if, being a stranger, he would be welcome in this neck of the dark woods. So, he sneaked slowly up, hid in the bushes like a spy and listened in on the rather strange conversations that were going on.

'Hans Christian, your session with the psychiatrist Mr F Nietzsche is in ten minutes after the brothers Wilhelm and Jacob Grimm have had their joint session. Oh, and Rumpelstiltskin, it's no good spinning some tale that you're well enough to leave. I think we all know that's never going to happen. You're as mad as the Hatter. Besides, since you've been at the asylum, you've become quite a skilled milliner. Your mad hats are selling like hot cakes,' laughed the man, who was clearly one of the orderlies working in the madhouse. In truth, to Poe, he sounded as if he was well on the way to the madhouse himself. 'Yes, probably shouldn't have mentioned hot cakes, not with the witch who liked to bake children in the oven close by. Don't want to set her recovery back a hundred years, not to mention Snow White, what with her evil twin cosying up to the wicked prince.'

'Snow Black, Snow White's evil twin sister, and the wicked prince are getting on too well for my liking,' a big burly man snapped, giving these characters the evil eye.

'I thought that's why they were here, because they were unwell. At least their souls were unwell,' replied a man poring over some notes.

'There's getting on well and there is getting on too well. I wonder if the lunatics will soon be taking over the asylum, as in a dark fairy tale when the staff become the patients, and I'm not sure how patient Rumpelstiltskin and the wicked prince are going to be,' the big burly man grimaced.

Upon hearing this comment, Poe thought that the lunatics, the power-mad leaders of the world, had taken over the asylum a long, long time ago.

'I don't think you're mad, just a little crazy. Well, we all get a little crazy at times,' a little girl with a box of matches in her hand said, setting light to a tree just to watch it burn.

'You're clearly spinning me and yourself a nice little fairy tale, Little Match Girl. Take a look in the glass admirer if you don't believe me,' a large man with not a stitch on replied, handing the girl a hand mirror.

The girl immediately dropped the mirror when she saw that the flames from the tree had set her clothes on fire as

she looked all about her, wildly, her eyes as large as saucers, screaming, 'Who set my clothes on fire, who!'

'Emperor, please, could you put some clothes on. Otherwise, you'll catch your death of cold. It's snowing. That's down to the Snow Queen,' an orderly exclaimed, passing the man a large black kimono with a red and gold dragon on the back of it.

'I'm wearing my best suit. You're clearly mad if you cannot see that it cost me a small fortune at the Forest Bazaar,' cried the man known as the Emperor.

'You mean the Forest Bizarre. If I were you, I'd ask the Big Bad Wolf if you could borrow his fur coat. It's real fur!' the orderly sniggered then, out of the corner of his eye.

The Snow Queen had a large ice pick in her hand and was just about to use it to pierce the wicked prince's black heart. You see, the Snow Queen was convinced that the wicked prince had been cheating on her behind her back with Snow White.

Poe rubbed his eyes and his ears, for he could not believe any of his senses, fearing he was going mad. Poe thought it best he quickly move on; otherwise, he too may end up in this madhouse for fairy-tale characters. But Poe Black wasn't a one-dimensional character out of a fairy tale; he was three-dimensional, made of flesh and blood, perhaps even four-dimensional. After all, this was a parallel world.

Poe looked nervously over his shoulder, fearing a great big crook might appear out of the dark and hook him away by the neck, and that would be the end of that. Alternatively, another dark fairy-tale character, the nightmare catcher, still to make his name in any neck of the wood, was standing in the shadows with his giant net covered in cobwebs, just waiting for Poe to pass by.

But this happening seemed all too real to Poe's mind. It was a nightmare, all right. There was no mistaking a nightmare. It had all the right ingredients. It was dark, fractured, and Poe couldn't move a muscle. It felt a little like he was wearing a straitjacket!

Poe did not want to judge these characters too harshly, for he felt sorry for them, for they were little more than puppets on a string, as was he. Some of these strange, deranged minds were little more than shadow puppets, shadows of their former selves, especially the character the Shadow. In truth, the fact that these dark, twisted characters were shadows of their former selves was probably no bad thing. It was little wonder these fairy-tale characters had lost their minds, given the terrible things they had been subjected to in their dark fairy life stories.

This is how Poe imagined the psychologists Freud and Young and the philosopher Nietzsche would have diagnosed their mental state. As most of these characters were figments of a storyteller's dark imagination, it was rather the storytellers they would have liked to have had on their couches, oh, and Poe Black too, as this dark fairy story could well be playing out inside the Attic Theatre inside his head. Hans Christian Andersen wrote four biographies, the last one entitled *My Fairy Life Story*. Hans Christian Andersen suffered badly with neurosis, enough to keep Sigmund Freud interested in his extraordinary case for the rest of his life.

As Poe walked away, he saw his own shadow waving the characters goodbye, wondering if everybody in this madhouse was mad. By this, Poe meant that he imagined everybody in the asylum took on the mantle of a fairy-tale character, writer or famous psychiatrist.

Mental health was no laughing matter. At times, it was as if you were sticking the knife into your own brain and twisting it, unable to help yourself from digging the knife in deeper and deeper. People did not see the real you; they only saw your shadow, which is why the sufferer was always painted black, bone- black. These were the dark thoughts from the *Dream Journal of Master Poe Black Esq.*, written in mirror writing in invisible ink.

That dark night, Poe imagined all the dark characters from fairy tales chasing him with pick axes, bones saws, ice picks and clubs in their hands. If they caught him, Poe was sure his head would be served on a silver platter at the Mad Fairy-Tale Tea Party.

5

Strange Days Indeed

Now deep within the forest, Poe could see that the trees in the forest were as twisted as if a giant had twisted them with his bare hands. The giant had squeezed all the life and all the blood out of them, at least dark red sap, which had congealed upon the trunks of the trees, trapping insects as if in amber. In fact, it seemed as if all the trees in the forest were made out of nothing more than shadows, as if he was in Plato's world, not the real world but the shadow or mirror world of which Plato talked about in his theories on forms. Then the moon came out of the clouds and shined its quicksilver beams upon the forest, and Poe could see the forest was, in part at least, full of magical silver birch trees, his favourite tree along with the weeping willow tree. Poe thought of Yarra, or Sorrow as she preferred to be called. He imagined her favourite tree was the weeping willow. He wished she was here now.

Then a giant ghostly apparition appeared before him. He pulled back only to see it was a giant cloud that had shaped itself into a giant figure. It seemed the old saying was correct; every cloud did have a silver lining.

Then Poe saw a soldier, a Prussian soldier. He knew this because he recognised the style of the uniform; the soldier had a tiger on a lead, a white tiger. In truth, the tiger could be a ghost tiger if the Prussian soldier was a ghost, a spirit from the world beyond.

Poe wasn't sure if he should call out to the man. After all, he may run him through with his sword. Poe hid behind a tree as the soldier turned towards him. Had he seen him or had he simply changed his mind as to what direction he was going in? Here, Poe recalled the fact to mind about turning a corner to the one you were going to take, which then changes your whole life, a quantum equation that he believed in, although to most it sounded like a fairy tale or a wonder tale.

Perhaps the Prussian soldier was not leading the tiger; perhaps the tiger was leading the soldier. The soldier had a bandage around his head and a patch over one eye. Poe wondered if the soldier had been blinded in the war.

'Hey you, boy, behind the tree, please don't be scared. All I want to know is, is the war over?' cried the soldier, his pace and the pace of the white tiger quickening as Poe's heart quickened to the point where he thought it would burst.

'What war would that be?' Poe replied, not sure what else he could say. After all, he had no idea what time frame he was in, that's if he was in any time frame at all. For all he knew, time may have got all muddled up in this world. Hundreds of parallel worlds, times and dimensions may have become entangled with one another, creating a microcosm, a hybrid world. Or this could simply be a dream, although a nightmare was the more likely story.

'What war? The War to End all Wars, of course!' spat the soldier, reaching for his sword then drawing it out as if he meant to use it.

Poe found he was frozen to the spot; he could not move. The Prussian soldier stepped forward. Poe tried to close his eyes but he could not. The pen was mightier than the sword. If Poe had his ink fountain pen on him then he would find out if this thought experiment was correct or another fairy tale, a lie. In his head, he pictured a poster by a Russian artist of a man with a giant pen stabbing another man to death, not the sort of imaginings he wanted in his head at any time, least of all now. Crossing swords with a Prussian soldier with their fearsome reputation, armed with nothing more than an ink pen, he didn't fancy his chances, although he could squirt him in the eye with the ink. What had he done with his laser pen? He quickly rifled through his pockets and found it then shone it into the eyes of the solider. The battery was dead and soon so would he be.

The soldier wielded his sword and cried, 'Welcome to the Forest of Blood!' cutting through Poe like a knife through butter. Poe was expecting to hear the hiss of the blade cutting through the air, but he heard no sound but the big bass drum that was his own heartbeat. Poe felt no pain. It was a quick death, but he wasn't dead. The sword and the soldier had passed right through his body. The soldier was clearly a ghost, a spirit. The soldier disappeared but the tiger did not. Poe reached out to stroke the animal, imagining his hand would go straight through the creature, only to find it did not. The white tiger, or snow tiger as Poe was now thinking of the beast, was real, and to prove it the tiger swiped at Poe with his paw. Poe pulled back in horror as blood seeped down his arm. Thankfully, it was only a scratch then Poe realised the tiger was as blind as a bat as he waved his hands in front of the animal's face but got no reaction.

'There, there, boy, I mean you no harm. No, you can be my eyes in this forest,' Poe said, not sure why he had said that, for it made little sense. There was something about the animal; it was as if it had a sixth sense. All animals sensed when danger was not far off their sense of smell. If a person lost one sense, their other senses were heightened. Poe felt that if he could gain the animal's trust, he may well end up saving his life. The tiger probably knew the lay of the land far better than he did, and anybody who meant him harm would shudder at the thought of taking him on with a wildcat by his side.

The animal did not give the impression it was blind and as already shown, it could defend itself. Animals could often tell if something or somebody meant them harm. The white tiger soon realised Poe was a friend and not a foe. Poe untied the lead that was attached to the tiger so the animal could go free if it so desired to. The Prussian soldier, or the spirit of the soldier, clearly thought it had the beast at its beck and call. The animal obviously sensed the soldier was trying to find the light so he could go over to the other side, the spirit world, and would not leave his side until he did so.

'You have your freedom if you want it, although I could do with a guide,' said Poe, talking to the animal as if it understood his every word and went to take the collar and the lead from around the tiger's neck. The tiger lifted its paw and Poe stepped back, fearing the worst. The tiger then sat down. Poe took this as a sign that the tiger did not want to go on alone. So Poe sat down by the animal's side, removed the collar and lead and slowly began to stroke its soft fur in a reassuring manner. The tiger purred, and so did Poe. As he stroked the animal, he felt as if his grandmother was stroking his hair. It was a sensation that he could only describe as Zen-like. Poe then fell asleep, resting his head against the tiger, and soon the animal fell asleep too, their heads touching. If one was looking upon this curious scene, they may have wondered if the two creatures were having the same dream for both were smiling serenely.

Time moved on, although as there were no clocks in a forest, not even a sun or a moon dial, it was hard to know what time it was.

Unless, of course, the forest was in an attic where a grandfather clock stood. If the attic would only reveal itself to Poe, like in a cleverly staged illusion, then perhaps he would get a glimpse of the clock. As there was a calendar on the wall of the attic, Poe would also be able to find out the date; more wishful thinking from the mind of Poe Black.

Then, as Poe began to feel lost, a voice cried out that he thought he recognised.

'Poe, Poe Black, it's me!' cried a shadowy figure from behind a tree, so it looked as if the tree was crying out. If this tree was a weeping willow then that may be a little more understandable.

'Who or what are you!' Poe cried, waking up with a start to find his head inside the mouth of a tiger, or so he imagined wrongly, for the tiger was yawning. Poe fell back as the tiger moved forward and started licking him. 'Okay, boy, okay, I had a bath last week!'

Poe got to his feet and the white tiger stood in front of him, as if to protect him.

The shadow appeared from behind the tree and then stood beside the tree, now bathed in moonlight shadow. At first, Poe could not distinguish between the tree and the willowy figure, as if they were Siamese twins.

Poe wished these shadowy figures would not keep jumping

out from behind trees. One of these not-so-fine days, one of them was going to scare him to death. Still, there was no need to fear, not now he had his guardian earth angel by his side, the tiger, or so he imagined. Poe could not trust his senses or the forest. He had a sense that this may be a trick, a trap, for he was sure the forest was reading his mind. The forest must know how much he wanted to see this strange girl, the one he'd briefly met in another world. It felt like a lifetime ago when they had met. If this was a dream, it was hard to know how much time had passed, for dream time was as illusive and illusionary as quicksilver.

Poe kept feeling his face to see if he had any age lines. As there were no mirrors in the forest, it made it hard to know for sure. If he came to a stream, a river or a pond, he would use that as a mirror. Poe just hoped these mirrors did not deceive as the forest seemed able to do. The forest was playing mind games with him, twisting his own thoughts first one way then the other, until he wasn't sure what was real and what wasn't.

The tiger sensed that this shadow meant them no harm and pawed at Poe, as if trying to communicate this to him.

'It's me, Sorrow. Don't you remember me, the lost girl with strange accent from Siberia?' pleaded the girl, sounding like the Little Match Girl from the fairy tale. Sorrow was clearly crestfallen that the boy of her dreams could forget her so easily. Perhaps he was not the boy of her dreams, more the boy of her nightmares?

'Sorrow, is it really you?' cried Poe, real tears in his eyes as he stepped forward to embrace the girl, then realised he was being rather forward. After all, they had only met for a brief time and then she had disappeared into thin air.

'If it's not me then I don't know who it is,' Sorrow laughed, although the laughter quickly died, for she knew what she had said in jest rang true. Sorrow, Yarra, Eloise, Pandora…

whatever she was calling herself in this world was going through a metamorphosis of her own. For all young people, this was a painful process, a journey of self-discovery and one at times that was dark, beset with self-doubt and sometimes self-loathing.

Then Poe recalled their first meeting when he'd finally made up his mind, after much self-doubt, that the strange-looking girl was in fact a changeling. This meant whether she was in the form of an insect; butterfly, moth, dragonfly; bird, animal or mammal, or a hybrid of the three, she was still the same old Sorrow, the one he had known for… five minutes! Yes, that was true. He had not known the changeling very long, but as we all know, five minutes, both in the real world, the dream world and in the world of parallel worlds, which feature many different times and dimensions, can feel like a lifetime.

The lifespan of certain tiny insects is little more than five minutes, so one second in the life of an insect equals a month in a human's life, and one minute equals a decade. Having said that, Sorrow, in whatever form she appeared to Poe, had not gone through a metamorphosis, turning into a moth or a moth girl, or at least not at this exact moment in time, or in the life story of Poe Black. The short time Sorrow had been in the forest, she had to ask herself who she was, wondering if she too was locked in an insane asylum, having being diagnosed with multiple personality syndrome.

'Who is your friend? I take it, it is a friend and not a foe?' Sorrow asked nervously, looking at Poe and the white tiger at the same time so that it appeared she was cross eyed.

'Oh, he's a friend, a long-lost friend, or so I imagine. He's my guide through this twisted forest,' Poe replied, deciding wisely not to fill Sorrow in on the whole story, that a stranger, a Prussian soldier, at least the ghost, the spirit of a Prussian soldier, had lent him the creature out of the kindness of his heart. Technically speaking, the soldier did not have a heart, not having a body.

Sorrow tried to smile but only ended up grimacing, making Poe feel uncomfortable, as if she sensed the beast was somehow to be the death of him, perhaps of both of them.

Poe and Sorrow walked hand in hand towards the nightmare, when every fibre of their beings told them they should be walking away from it towards the dream. The problem was, the dream was impossible, and with no dream in sight they were trapped between a bad dream and a bad case of the night terrors. Fight or flight, neither being Peter Pan, Tinker Bell or the Snow Man, Poe and Sorrow decided to enter fight mode.

The shadows of the forest beasts, monsters and dragons, both real and imaginary, twisted and contorted themselves first one way then the other, coiling their bodies around the trees. First appearing then disappearing, as if conjured out of thin air as Poe and Sorrow walked deeper and deeper into the forest and deeper and deeper into the nightmare. They could not be sure which beasts, monsters and dragons were real and which were imaginary, conjured from the mind. Trees in woods and forests from a distance often took on the appearance of a witch, monster or dragon, their twisted trunks covered in knots and what appeared to be armour plating. Twisted branches covered in moss and ivy made one take a step backward, especially when night fell, as the trees appeared to be alive.

As such, Poe and Sorrow felt they had no other choice than to treat both the real and the imaginary with the exact same caution.

'Where's the tiger gone? I can't see it,' Poe exclaimed, as the tiger ran off into the forest.

'It's probably gone hunting. I'm sure it will return. It's

probably watching over us as we speak,' Sorrow replied, as if she imagined the animal was an angel, a spirit of the forest.

'I get the feeling we are being hunted and being watched,' Poe said nervously.

After a lot of soul-searching, Poe and Sorrow felt they were ready for whatever life or the forest with its twisted mind threw at them. Perhaps these two lost souls were doing just that, searching for their souls, which naturally made them… VAMPIRES! This, however, was not the case; there were enough vampires running around out there without digging up any more!

'Ready?' Poe said, turning to Sorrow.

'I'd like to say I was born ready but I was not. However, as there appears to be no turning back, it looks as if we must go on,' Sorrow said nervously, glancing over her shoulder as if she imagined the trees in the twisted forest had already begun to close in to block their escape route.

'To end this dark fairy tale, we must play out the rest of this nightmare in the hope this nightmare will end,' Poe replied, drawing in a deep breath, for he and Sorrow were of the same mind. What if this nightmare had no end, like Nietzsche's theory of a never-ending circle of life where we repeat the same mistakes we made in the last life?

Sorrow and Poe clasped hands so tightly that their knuckles turned white, as together they stepped into the unknown with their eyes closed, for this was not one of those times when you went into a situation with your eyes wide open. Poe and Sorrow disappeared through a giant curtain of weeping willow trees, as if they were nothing more than ghosts, spirits in the spirit realm.

6

The Wicker Maker

Poe and Sorrow found themselves in a clearing, although it was far from clear where they actually were. Were they trapped in a dream, a nightmare, an alternate reality, or the mind of a malevolent entity, a dark energy? The possibilities were as endless as the universe itself, for the universe itself could well be an entity of some kind, both benevolent and malevolent. God the creator; both a light and a dark energy.

'Hello, welcome, welcome to my humble abode,' cried a man, popping out of thin air, or so Poe imagined. Forest magic, the forest up to its old tricks again as once again the forest went through another change, a metamorphosis of a kind. Poe had already wondered if the forest itself was alive with the ability of a changeling, unlikely as it may seem. The longer Poe spent in the forest, the more he felt this unlikely story could well be true. Nordic folk tales were full of tales of trees having souls and spirits. Modern-day scientists were now saying all living things had consciousness.

'Welcome, strangers, it's good to see another human being. I haven't seen another living soul for years. Let me introduce myself. The name's Octavius, Otto, Oddly-Strange.' The man laughed, his face cracking like a piece of old manuscript papyrus. Poe was not sure if the old coot was laughing at his name or himself or because he wasn't all there, one penny short of a shilling.

'He seems a harmless sort, a friendly old man, even if he has an odd name,' hissed Poe out of the corner of his mouth, as if a poor man's ventriloquist, as Poe did not wish to alarm Sorrow, whose face was a picture, that picture being of the painting *The Scream* by the Norwegian artist Edvard Munch.

'Let's hope he isn't an odd bod, one estranged from reality!' Sorrow replied, mirroring Poe in her actions if not in the words, as she edged away from the stranger, fearing he wasn't as simple a soul as he first appeared to be. Sorrow was beginning to wonder if he wasn't one of those wolves dressed in sheep's clothing.

'I'm sure he isn't any more estranged from reality than we are,' Poe replied, crossing his fingers behind his back, hoping the old man was not deranged, just a little strange. And, after all, people were strange, as were the doors of perception, doors that led from one reality to another. The question was, what reality was the old man living in? In truth, living alone in a forest for years with no human company was bound to make you a little odd, uncomfortable around strangers while still seeking the company of others. Poe imagined the man welcoming them in with open arms to the Strangers' Society, a society who welcomed all strangers in, however strange, with open arms. No doubt Dr Strange was the president and founder member of this strange order. In truth, with a surname like Oddly-Strange, he may well have been a member of the now defunct Odd Fellow Society in America.

Poe did not see Sorrow as his sad ventriloquist's dummy, one he kept in the dark in an old suitcase or a moth-eaten carpet bag in an attic. A carpet bag that was magical, as was the ventriloquist's dummy, who was anything but a dummy, with a mind as sharp as a tack and with fingernails sharper than shards of broken glass. Poe had already had a macabre nightmare about a ventriloquist's dummy clawing its way out of a coffin buried in the earth. After which the dummy then clawed its way across the floorboards in his room, scratching his eyes out. Poe had actually found a ventriloquist's dummy in a box in the attic, one with a fixed grin and big wild staring eyes, a ventriloquist's dummy right out of a horror film.

There was also a Jack-in-the-Box in the darkly magical attic space, one Poe had imagined springing out of the box then dancing manically around his bed, crying, 'You can't catch me, you can't catch me. I'm free. I've broken out of my dark prison and now I'm about to flee!' It was funny, Poe thought at the time of this nightmare, how the man named Jack looked remarkably like the Victorian character Spring-Heeled Jack, as the Jack out of the box showed a clean pair of heels as he jumped out of the attic window and into the snow, leaving small footprints behind him. If he ran into Bigfoot, it would be an interesting turn of events, a twist in the fairy tale.

'What are you making?' Sorrow enquired of the old man as she attempted to break the ice, while trying not to imagine the forest floor being made of ice or salt liquorice, as if the man was the husband of the witch in the Hansel and Gretel story. She further tried not to imagine that the man was hiding an ice pick behind his back, with which he would stab her and Poe to death, as if he was possessed by the character in the horror movie *Psycho*. The old coot may well be a psycho, but by the looks of his dishevelled appearance, he was a retired psycho, so they should both be safe, unless his darker side, his shadow, was about to grow to the size of a giant!

'A wicker chair. I've made wicker baskets, wicker animals. I can make anything you like,' the old man replied, his bloodshot eyes flickering like the flame of a tinderbox before lighting up like two miniature bonfires. The Wicker Maker, the name Poe had already conjured out of his imagination for the man, was clearly a magician who weaved magic wicker carpets entwined with ivy and vines. And by the way the Wicker Maker's old feeble-looking hands nimbly threaded the wicker, one could easily have imagined that to be the case. Poe was trying hard not to imagine this character as Rumpelstiltskin; he really must not try and see this dark fairy-tale character wherever he looked, even seeing his face staring back at him from the trunks of the trees. It wasn't hard to imagine some of the trees as fairy-tale characters by their stooped, mangled witch-like appearance.

If the forest was really a living entity, a changeling, and one with a dark mind, one that appeared to want to twist everything into a thousand knots, trying not to imagine the worst might be the best course of action.

As the old man spun them a fairy tale, for that was what Poe was thinking, he carried on weaving the wicker basket. He could have been blind, for all they knew. The old man probably wove baskets in his sleep. Poe watched the man's fingers as they weaved their magic. He was spellbound, almost in a trace as he watched. As he watched the Wicker Maker, Poe wondered if the forest was taking his and Sorrow's thoughts and entwining them then twisting them into new thoughts.

'Come on in, I've got the pot cooking,' Octavius cried, glancing over to a pot boiling over a fire, his hands still in the process of completing the basket. The old man finished the wicker basket in what seemed to be no time at all, but then again perhaps time did not exist in this strange place. 'The objects I create are not perfect, but you tell me, who wants perfect! Folk want something unique, something handcrafted, crafted with love and life, life experience. I'm not working in a sweat factory, thank God!'

'The Wicker Man!' Poe gasped, as he gulped down hard, unable to stop his mind turning to the old British horror film from the 1960s shot in black and white. The Wicker Maker then transformed into the Wicker Man, a giant of a man made of wicker, before Poe's startled eyes, or at least in his mind's eye. Poe was imagining this man was made of wicker and was possessed by an evil spirit, perhaps that of the forester, the man who built the house that Poe now lived in: the House of Poe. In truth, it was beginning to feel like a house of horrors to Poe Black. The forester was a changeling, a man for every season, and every nightmare. For the life of him, Poe could not recall who wrote or directed *The Wicker Man*, which for anybody else would not have been a surprise. However, Poe had a photographic memory, and he was obsessed by the men and women who worked in movies, men and women who for a large part stayed in the shadows; the writers, producers, editors and in some cases directors.

These names were imprinted on his brain, tattooed there, so why couldn't he bring them to mind? Was he losing his mind and his memory, Poe wondered, as another worry line creased his face.

'The Wicker Maker, thanks, boy. I think I'll call myself that from now on. Been so long in this forest, can't remember my own name at times.' The old man laughed as if once again poking fun at his unusual name, although no more unusual than Poe or Sorrow.

'It's a film. You must have heard of it?' Poe said, looking puzzled, wondering if he should tell the man he had already given him his name, and giving him two names was confusing. The last thing Poe wanted was more confusion, as for a large part of the time Poe found himself in two minds, sometimes even more, as if he had a split personality.

'No, I have never…' the man said, pausing, as if Poe had freeze framed the man in his head, like in the still photograph of a movie, fully expecting him to say, *I've never heard of the film*, when instead he said, 'I have never heard of a film. What is a film?'

For a second, Poe was too stunned to speak. He wasn't sure if the old man was pulling his leg or not. Surely the old man hadn't been lost in the forest so long that the movie industry had passed him by. Poe decided the man must be joking so let it slide. Poe had been going to ask the man where he had come from and what era he was born in. However, as the man seemed more than a little confused, Poe did not want to confuse him any further. If someone was suffering from dementia, too much information just confused the issue. Surprisingly, the thought that the Wicker Maker could have been a previous owner of the house, the one Poe was now living in, did not occur to him at this moment in time. Perhaps that was because his house was now a forest, or time had speeded up and a forest had sprung up in the house, as trees often did in old houses, growing through the floorboards.

Things were happening so fast that it was hard for the mind to keep up. It was as if the film kept jumping ahead, a trick the director employed to confuse the audience. Either that or jumping back or jumbling time up, it was most disconcerting. Once upon a dark fairy time, his house may have been a lunatic asylum, or perhaps it had been built on the land where an old asylum stood.

'Rumpelstiltskin,' Sorrow muttered under her breath. 'Rumpelstiltskin. Not sure that name suits me. Besides, it's far too long. I'd never remember it in a million years, that and I'm illiterate. Can't write. Forgotten the language, being on my own so long. I talk to myself, don't get much sense there, and to the animals and the trees. They talk a lot of sense, especially the trees. They can teach you a lot if you only listen. Man's not big on listening, prefers to jib jabber like the monkeys. Folk like the sound of their own voices. That is why I love the forest. Silence is not something to be scared of. I guess some folk don't like their own thoughts, I can understand that. I guess too many voices, ghosts, of the past bleeding into the present, so much so that some need a necromancer to help them understand what the voices are trying to tell them.'

Now the old man had started talking he didn't seem to know how to stop, as if he was a clockwork toy that had been overwound. Or perhaps now he had finally found his voice, he had a lot to say, a lot to get off his chest. Octavius then stopped talking to stoke the fire and stir the pot as he smiled and waved Sorrow and Poe over to the fire. The three lost souls ate a hearty meal. The man was a good cook, or maybe it was because Sorrow and Poe were so hungry they ate every last bit. Neither Poe nor Sorrow thought of the films *The Hunger Games* and *The Huntsman,* or the Hansel and Gretel story, and Poe did not imagine for one moment that this was his last meal.

Sorrow and Poe soon fell asleep, as did the old man, but it wasn't long before Poe's restless mind started to turn, unable to suppress the dark thoughts in his head. Poe had wrestled his dark thoughts and wild imaginings all day long, trying not to let them escape, turning thought into reality, in some kind of twisted Neitzcher-Jekyll and Hyde-like thought experiment. Time seemed to have no meaning in the forest, although that was the same in a real forest, both worlds mirroring the other, or was this Poe's mirror mind twisting things? Regardless of whether Poe was awake or asleep or daydreaming, the steam wheels of his mind kept turning. It was Poe's subconscious mind that was now dreaming up another nightmare for him. Poe could even quote Shelley in his dreams: "Here like some weird Archimage sit I, plotting dark spells and devilish enginery, the self-impelling steam wheels of the mind..."

The forest was full of twisted shadows and twisted trees, as Poe imagined animals, birds and people twisted beyond all recognition. He pondered upon a twisted man or woman and whether their body mirrored their mind or vice versa. There must be an effect on the mind if the body is twisted; society did not like to see twisted bodies. In the times of the Victorians, there were freak shows. Nowadays, the freak shows had gone viral on the dark web, virtual freak shows, a giant freak show. Perfect was the form we all desired; the imperfect was shunned.

Poe recalled the phrase, holding a mirror up to society and twisting it into holding a cracked mirror up to society, then twisting it further, holding a bowed mirror up to society, and then twisting it one more time with his kaleidoscopic mind, so the phrase became "holding a computer screen up to society". To Poe Black's mind, that phrase seemed to fit the dark times we were living through admirably.

It seemed to Poe's mind there were too many people online and in society that rarely, if ever, looked in the proverbial mirror. The trolls who hide in the shadows on the Dark Net should take a long, hard look in that computer screen before they got out their poison pens. Killer lines were all well and good, but not if those reading them were mentally unwell, for then the killer lines really could kill. Karma was something both Poe and Sorrow believed in; what goes around comes around.

Too many young people appeared overly fond of gazing into the screen of their computer longingly when it was switched off, admiring their own reflection, like Narcissus. Poe re-imagined the black mirror of the computer screen as an iPad or a Victorian glass admirer, in other words, a hand mirror. The phrase by Sigmund Freud, "the Narcissus of little difference", sprang to Poe's mind whenever the character trait narcissistic was mentioned on TV, radio, literature or online. It meant that we as human beings wanted people to be like us but not so like us that they were carbon copies of us mirror images. Yet to Poe it appeared there were millions of people mirroring one another's behaviour, but not in a good way.

Of course, Poe could not be sure which dark times he was now living through, for whichever time and dimension he was in, it seemed dark. If there was a darker shade of dark, Poe Black was just the man to find that darker dark.

Poe woke in a cold sweat, and as he did so, Sorrow woke also, and it was not because Poe had disturbed her. It appeared that Sorrow and Poe really were, as Carl Jung had once written in one of his journals, "psychic dreamers". But Poe and Sorrow had not been dreaming, as they were both having a nightmare. The dream may have been hard to recall; however, the nightmare remained embedded in the mind, like a rusty nail in a coffin, and as such was not so easily removed from the mind. Even if the nightmare was surgically removed from the mind by a mind doctor, it often reappeared as if by dark magic or the magic of the movies.

'I heard a noise, something moving, something calling from the woodshed,' Sorrow whispered, looking at Poe, trying not to wake up the old man.

'Yes, something trapped,' Poe replied, leading the way, as if he had a map in his head, a map of the nightmare. As Poe and Sorrow made their way towards the woodshed, they passed several large shadows, fearing they were wild animals, until they realised they were simply animals made out of wicker.

'I was sure that wicker animal moved,' Poe hissed, looking nervously about him, wondering if the old man had made the trees out of wicker.

'Just your imagination.' Sorrow grimaced then the wicker deer fell over onto the ground, but instead of remaining still, it continued to move, twitching like an animal that had been shot.

'That's some imagination. Perhaps I do have a career in the movies after all.' Poe smiled, imagining Sorrow was mirroring his smile, smiling on the inside.

'It… it's bleeding, the wicker deer, it's come to life. We really are trapped in the house of horrors!' Sorrow grunted as the wicker deer yelped, as if in pain, and blood dripped out of the wicker animal. The trees in this part of the forest were bone- black. Sorrow wondered if the trees were not black but simply shadows, not shadows of the trees, for there were no trees, just the shadows of the trees, Plato's world, the form and the formless.

'Better that than the House of Wax or the House of Usher that are on fire,' replied Poe, a wild look in his eyes, as if they were on fire as in his mind's eye he pictured a movie house ablaze and one that soon became an inferno. 'The eyes of the deer, they're moving. I-I think there's a real deer inside that wicker basket!' stuttered Poe, as he found himself wondering if he had woken up the forest. The old man, on the other hand, still seemed fast asleep, away with the faeries, dark faerie folk who no doubt drank the blood of elves and wood nymphs. 'I think I've just woken the dead. There's blood pouring out of the animal encaged inside the wicker basket!'

'As long as you haven't woken the waking dead,' replied Sorrow, trying to reassure Poe and moreover herself. Sorrow was also trying not to imagine blood seeping out of the trees, as they too wept like weeping willows, flooding the forest with a river of blood. It would be this blood they would eventually drown in, as it rose higher and higher until it reached the ceiling, not of the forest but of the attic in which they were trapped. Sorrow tried not to imagine the Bloody Countess Bathoray, who bathed in her victim's blood. A bloodbath was not one that Sorrow imagined would cleanse mind, body and soul.

Then the deer stopped twitching. 'I think the poor thing's dead, scared to death.' Sorrow sighed, kneeling down and stroking the wicker deer as if trying to comfort it.

'I see things in colour for the first time and find myself wishing I didn't. Blood looks so much worse in Technicolor!' Poe said, without thinking, for by this he meant his nightmares, which, unlike his dreams which were always in colour, were always in monochrome.

'Just be grateful the blood isn't your own,' Sorrow said, counting her blessings.

'Come on, we must go,' grunted Poe, roughly pulling Sorrow away from the wicker deer and towards the image in his mind of a woodshed, somewhere even deeper into the forest. Or, alternatively, deeper into the subconscious mind, if this was a nightmare the two were sharing, as in Carl Jung's weird and wonderful theory of psychic dreamers.

They trekked through virgin forest, suffering many cuts and bruises from the bracken, vines and broken branches, which appeared to be guarding the woodshed as if the trees were alive. This was a twist from the old horror movie *The Hills Have Eyes*, another dark twist from the Twisted Forest.

'Thou shall not pass!' Poe heard a voice, hoping it was one his imagination had conjured up and was not real.

'The door's open!' Sorrow hissed, creeping quietly towards

the door, trying not to make a sound, as she was sure there was a nasty surprise waiting for her in the woodshed.

Now it was Sorrow's turn to hear voices, or at least one voice. 'If you go down to the woodshed today, you're sure to be in for a nasty surprise. If you go down to the woodshed today, be careful you do not die!'

'Shut up, shut up!' snapped Sorrow irritably.

'I didn't say anything!' Poe hissed, giving Sorrow a black look Dracula would have been proud of.

'Not you, the voice in my head. It won't shut up. I wouldn't mind, but when the voice tries to sing, it's like fingernails being scraped down a blackboard!' Sorrow replied, wanting to tell the voice in her head that the rhyme did not scan, but she feared that if she did, her mind would turn to the horror film *Scanners*. The poster for the movie was of the horrific face of a crazed character with a thousand pins sticking out of his face. It was enough to give you a thousand nightmares. Acupuncture could cure many things, but Sorrow was not sure that it could cure maladies of the mind. She must control her mind and push the voices back into her subconscious where they belonged, out of sight, out of mind.

'The voice inside my head is hardly likely to join a choir of angels either. Be careful, it may be a trap,' exclaimed Poe, not trusting anything he heard or saw either inside or outside of his mind. Poe was sure his own senses were being manipulated. He had to concentrate; he did not want to lose control of his own mind for therein lay madness.

Poe was trying not to let his mind dig out a copy of the old American comic *Creepy Tales*, one he had seen in a box in the attic. Perhaps Poe should have let his mind pull up this image, for then the attic would appear and the forest start to fade, as it had done before.

Perhaps, perhaps, perhaps not! Wishful thinking may

not help them in this case as the saying "Be careful what you wish for" sprang to Poe's feverish mind, for thinking about the stories inside the magazine might make things even worse. There was a tale in the magazine Poe had speed-read as he looked through the junk in the attic where a man finds himself alone in an overgrown city. The comic was first published in 1970; the pages were yellowing and fading. Poe felt as if the writer of the story had been able to predict the future, as it was not a million miles away from the present day due to the coronavirus with its deserted cities. Or alternatively a future where cities were nothing but deserted concrete Jungles, petrified forests.

For a few seconds, the forest seemed to ripple as if it were made of quicksilver, an illusion created by the quicksilver moonlight, reflecting on and off the leaves of the silver birch trees that were gently swaying in the breeze. Poe blinked, shutting his eyes like an old camera, wondering if when he next opened his eyes, he would be standing in a petrified forest.

7

A World Turned Upside Down

Poe eventually opened his eyes and immediately wished he had not, as his eyes were met with a most horrific sight, one he imagined would be imprinted upon his mind forever, like the negative of a film.

'Look, hundreds of wicker models of animals, and over here, even models of men and women, wicker men and woman!' Poe exclaimed, opening his eyes as he forced his mind to concentrate on one world at a time. The trouble was that Poe had both a kaleidoscopic mind that lied to him, skewing his perspective on everything around him. The further trouble was that the deeper Poe and Sorrow got into the Twisted Forest, the deeper the trouble that they found themselves in.

Poe was beginning to feel it was the nightmare that was getting deeper and deeper and thicker and thicker, mirroring the forest. Deep Time, as if they were going deeper and deeper into the past, digging themselves deeper and deeper into a hole, a black hole. This meant they were getting further and further away from the present, and further and further away from reality. If Poe and Sorrow were not careful, they would be digging their own graves. Poe saw a flash like the bulb of an old press man's camera, a vision of the future, the Wicker Maker standing over them as he made them dig their own graves. Then he made them climb into a wicker coffin before burying them alive, forcing them to recreate Houdini's buried alive illusion.

'That… that wicker man moved, and I know this time it isn't my imagination!' Sorrow cried, wishing she could shrink back into the shadows. Sorrow was desperately trying to be strong, trying not to cry or cry out like a hysterical character out of an old movie in which the woman was always depicted as helpless and weak.

'They're coffins, wicker coffins, in which case either there is a man or a woman still alive in there or-or they've come back to life,' stuttered Poe, trying to catch his breath. 'You know, I just realised you're speaking perfect English,' Poe said, turning to look at Sorrow, who looked at Poe as if he had lost his mind.

'We are in the middle of a nightmare and you choose this time to point out the fact my English has improved, not that I'm complaining, as I don't get many compliments in any neck of the woods.'

'Well, don't you think it a mite odd that your English has got better while my memory has got worse. It's almost as if you borrowed some of my memory. In fact, it's almost as if our two minds are becoming as one.' Poe grimaced, scratching his head, not quite sure what in fact he meant as his head continued spinning like a spiral galaxy. 'I think I'm going to be violently sick. Look, a wicker version of an Iron Maiden,

the Medieval Torture device. There's blood seeping out of the holes, and look, there are thin wooden spikes sticking out of the sides,' heaved Poe, turning his head away.

Sorrow appeared to be getting ahead of herself, for she was now imagining that these figures were all part of a mad magician's act, apart from the fact that this act had a twist, the wicker casket replacing the tall black wooden box containing the magician's beautiful assistant and the spikes replacing the swords.

Sorrow caught something out of the corner of her eye and spun on her heels like a whirling dervish, raw and bloody from trekking through the wild forest. Sorrow was sure she saw a shadowy figure running away from the scene of the crime. Or perhaps it was her own shadow. After all, people often said that as a child she was scared of her own shadow. Maybe it was a good thing her shadow was making a run for it. At least her shadow might get out of this nightmare alive! Hans Christian Andersen, the father of the fairy tale, wrote a macabre fairy tale entitled *The Shadow*, where a man's own shadow turned upon him. Hans Christian, as he preferred to be called, sure had a twisted mind, and a twisted sense of humour, and one which both Sorrow and Poe loved as much as they loved the gothic writer Edgar Allen Poe.

'Get me out, please, get me out!' pleaded a voice from inside the wicker casket.

'They're still alive!' Sorrow cried, unable to help herself and backing away in horror as the wicker casket toppled over and crashed to the floor, causing leaves upon the forest floor to fly upwards towards the canopy on the forest floor, or the ceiling of the attic in the wooden shack where Poe lived.

'Quick, quick, help me get them out.' Poe grimaced in panic as he wrestled to get the casket open.

'Thank you, you saved my life. The old man's stark raving mad, completely deranged, a lunatic,' a young pale-looking man whimpered. The gaunt-looking young man was dressed in rags soaked in blood.'I thought I was either going to suffocate, starve or bleed to death. Every time I fell asleep, I had a nightmare. They were the worst nightmares I have ever experienced in my life, only to wake to realise I was still trapped in the wicker coffin, trapped in the nightmare, a waking nightmare that only death could release me from. I was ready to welcome death in with open arms, hoping the grim reaper would lead me into the Valley of Death where I would fear no evil.' The young man sobbed, at the end of his tether.

Time was running out for Poe Black; things could not have looked much blacker unless they were bone-black. Poe could not see himself making old bones, but he could see the old man making a work of forest art out of his young bones, hanging his bones or his skeleton from a tree to scare away the crows.

'Come on, we have to get out of here,' yelled Poe. 'Sorrow, help me carry the boy. He can barely stand.'

And with that the three young souls made their getaway, or at least they tried to, for as they did so, a voice stopped them dead in their tracks. The voice was the voice of the old, crippled man who no longer sounded like an old man. In fact, his voice was strong and firm, even commanding. Poe felt he was a puppet on a string and the old man the puppet master, and as such he felt compelled to stop and turn around. When he did so, Poe's horrified eyes were met with the man standing as tall as a giant, whereas before his shoulders had been hunched up and his chest caved. Sorrow turned her head, compelled by the voice, as did the poor half dead young man, who in truth was already dead on his feet, his face as pale as a ghost from loss of blood.

'Bang!' The sound of a gun went off as Poe, Sorrow and the young man were sure their time was up, but there was no sound of a firearm being discharged; it was all in their minds. Fear had triggered the sound of a gun. The old man was holding a movie prop, and sticking out of the barrel on a long stick was a flag with the word *BANG*, followed by a large exclamation mark. Poe wanted to hold up a sign which read *NIGHTMARE* and on the other side of the sign it read *DREAM*, which he would quickly turn around and then hold up. Poe breathed again. He had seen this prop before in the attic, and as his mind recalled the fact, the walls and ceiling of the attic appeared to him, as if in a clever conjuring trick, the illusion of the forest shattered. If, thought Poe, sighing heavily, his heart was so heavy that it felt as if it was a hot water bottle blown up by a strong man in a travelling freak show and one about to explode. On Poe Black's Death Certificate, it would read – *Frightened to Death*, or so Poe found himself imagining, wild and tangled thoughts as the nightmare gathered pace. Poe might well need a pacemaker if he ever got out of this nightmare alive. At this rate, Poe might have to re-imagine that Death Certificate, which might read – *Poe Black Laughed Himself to Death* or *Died Laughing*.

'Run, run for your life!' spat Poe. However, he soon found this was easier said than done, for his legs felt as if they had turned to lead, or as if he was now running in black treacle in a nightmare. Running over this ankle-twisting terrain was never going to be a walk in the park. Poe found himself frozen in the pose of a runner on the starting blocks, unable to move a muscle. Poe wondered if the old man had spiked their food, using magic mushrooms, which were said to make a person hallucinate wildly. It was from this thought that another thought followed: that magic mushrooms in some quarters were used to treat depression. Hallucinations followed this unusual treatment, which was why a psychiatric nurse had to be by their side until the hallucinations came to an end.

Poe rubbed his sore eyes and slapped his cheeks in an attempt to wake himself from his torpor. Sorrow seemed more fleet of foot as she helped the young man by putting her arms around his shoulder. Another bang went off. Once again, there was no bullet fired, for this gun was a starting pistol inside the agitated mind of Poe Black. Poe's legs began to twitch like a frog with electrodes attached to its legs, as in the experiment on electrical currents by the Italian scientist Luigi Galvani. Then Poe sprang to life; however, Poe's run for freedom was a short one as he, Sorrow and the young man ran straight into a trap, two unseen nets lying on the forest floor covered in leaves. The next moment, Poe and Sorrow found themselves swept up by the nets and hanging upside down from the trees like bats in a cave. 'The nightmare catcher has finally caught up with us,' sighed Poe, feeling more than a little woebegone.

'What happened to the young man?' Sorrow asked, turning to Poe, looking down as the blood rushed to her head.

'Don't look!' Poe grimaced through gritted teeth, for he had seen exactly what had happened to the poor unfortunate young man, who had stepped out of one nightmare only to find he had fallen straight into another one. But at least his nightmare had reached the end.

'Oh my God, no,' Sorrow cried, for she saw the full horror of the young man's fate; a trapdoor in the forest floor had opened and he had fallen into a bear trap. The trap contained hundreds of sharp wooden spikes, one of which the young man had been impaled upon.

'You should be thanking me. He was a vampire. The best and kindest course of action was to stick a spike in his black heart. Vampires need tough love. It's the only thing they understand.' The old man was laughing so hard that Poe hoped the man might laugh himself to death. The trouble with that scenario was they would still be trapped in the nets, vulnerable to birds and wolves picking over their bones.

'Well, having woken me early, I feel hungry so if you don't mind, I'll get myself something to eat then sit down and enjoy the show.' Octavius chuckled, moving his wicker chair directly in between where Sorrow and Poe were hanging at opposite sides of the forest. Sorrow and Poe began to fear the worst, that the old man might be a cannibal and roast the young man's heart on a spit over a roaring fire. Worse still, Poe and Sorrow feared that after he had eaten the young man, they would be next on the forest menu, as it seemed this old man had a monstrous appetite. The old man had a healthy appetite for life, but it seemed he had an even bigger appetite for death!

'Let us out, let us go. I swear on my life that we won't tell anybody, for there is nobody around here to tell, and we certainly won't come back, cross my heart and hope to...' Poe whimpered, his spirit broken, along with his body, as the last word die got stuck in his throat, exactly like in a nightmare. As this was clearly a nightmare, for all the signs and warning bells were telling Poe and Sorrow this was the case, it followed that the only way out of this trap, this nightmare, was to wake up. The problem was that their hands were tied, so they were unable to attempt the old Alice trick of pinching either themselves or each other.

'Nice try, boy. Perhaps you should get your sweetheart to plead your case, sweet talk me, that's if she has a heart, probably won't have one much longer. The old hunger pains are coming back. I do hate pain of any kind, although, funnily enough, I do appear to like inflicting it upon others. Now if this doesn't light your fire, boy, get you all fired up, then my name's not Beelzebub,' spat Octavius, as he lit a fire directly underneath where Sorrow was hanging, helpless to do anything but accept her grizzly fate. Joan of Arc, who had been burnt at the stake, had always been a heroine to Sorrow. However, she never dreamt she would suffer a similar fate.

'You... you old devil, you'll burn in hell for this,' Poe spat, getting so fired up that he did not know what he was saying. Sorrow was worried he may suffer the Victorian malady of human spontaneous combustion.

Eventually, the old man fell asleep and the fire began to die. This gave Poe a chance to cut himself out of the net with a multipurpose penknife his grandfather had given him, a one-man survival kit, as his grandfather had always told him. Now all Poe had to do was get his hands free then they both had a chance of getting free from this evil old man, easy really and, surprisingly enough, for Poe it was. You see, Poe's grandfather had been a magician and escapologist in another life. His grandfather had taught Poe how to escape from both handcuffs and ropes that were tied tightly around the wrists. Thankfully, the old man had been careless and had not tied the ropes around Poe's wrists as tightly as he had tied the ones around Sorrow's wrists. Poe twisted his hands and wrists this way and that until the ropes loosened, to the point they were free.

Now free, Poe decided it might be better to cut the rope he was hanging from like a bat, a vampire bat, and so he did. Eventually, he cut through the rope and it snapped and he fell, landing with a thud onto the sodden ground. He wanted to cry out in pain but he did not want to wake the old man, so he bit his tongue. This produced blood. He hoped he did not get to like the taste of blood. After all, he had just spent the last few hours hanging upside down like a vampire bat! Poe was on the ground, still trapped within the net. Although his grampa had taught him all he knew, he was still no Harry

Houdini. Poe pictured the great escape artist freeing himself from a straitjacket in an old black and white newsreel, or rising from the dead in his trick of being buried alive. Harry Houdini starred in movies where he was the hero. In truth, he was a real-life Hero and one Poe had always admired, for he was a spy in the First World War.

Poe had wondered if Houdini had faked his own death, given the fact he died on Halloween Night. How theatrical! Houdini's wife, Bess, held a séance on the roof of a building every year on Halloween in the hope of contacting him. She never did contact Houdini, and the reason for that, Poe imagined, was because Harry Houdini's real name, Erich Weiss, was still alive and well. It seemed Harry Houdini had perfected the Lazarus Trick and then like others had disappeared into history, or, like Poe, had found a portal to another time and place.

Octavius stirred as if about to wake up, rocking back and forth in the wicker rocking chair, which looked most macabre, as if a scene out of the film *Psycho* or any number of films on the supernatural. Poe and Sorrow both held their breath. Thankfully, the old man did not wake. He was clearly having a dream by the big smile upon his face, or perhaps it was a nightmare, for the man clearly enjoyed a good nightmare. And here he was, the Wicker Maker, creating a bespoke nightmare for Poe and Sorrow. They should be grateful, dead grateful, instead of moaning about life and their slow, painful, agonising deaths. That's the trouble with some folk. They're never happy; they don't know when they've got it good.

Poe rolled himself across the floor of the forest and down a small incline littered with sinks of dead leaves, and within seconds he found himself at the bottom of a hollow. Looking up, he could not see the top of the hollow. How this could be? Poe had no idea, for it had taken no more than a split second to roll from the top to the bottom. Poe was hoping he had not fallen into another world, separating him from Sorrow, even though it may be a dream world and one without any danger. The more likely story was that he was just about to re-enact a scene from the film *Sleepy Hollow*, starring Johnny Depp, in which case he might well lose his head in more ways than one.

Poe's head was now spinning faster than the sails of a windmill in a storm. Poe hadn't immediately realised but he had almost been swallowed up by a large hole caused by a giant tree, the roots of which had been pulled out of the earth, presumably by one of the many forest giants.

Poe's head may have been spinning but it hadn't stopped his mind spinning dark fairy tales. A group of inquisitive squirrels poked around him in a playful manner then scampered away to be replaced with some hungry rodents, rats the size of stray cats. 'Go away, go away!' Poe hissed, but it was no use. They kept on going, gnawing at his clothes, close to breaking the skin. But every dark cloud has a silver lining, for the rats, in trying to get to their meal, were also gnawing through the net. Poe was free in no time at all; bruised, scratched, bitten and bleeding, but free to play the hero of the hour, and for Sorrow, time was running out.

Actions speak louder than words, so the words for the moment could stay inside his head, as in the blinking of an eye Poe jumped into action, scaling the tree like a monkey, cutting Sorrow down and then freeing her from the net.

'You're my hero,' Sorrow sobbed, flinging herself around Poe then quickly withdrawing, as if embarrassed, feeling it was uncool to show such emotions, or perhaps Yarra, aka Sorrow, did not want to play the part of the helpless damsel in distress.

'What's going on?' carped Octavius, struggling like a pike in a fisherman's net, his eyes bulging as they came into focus, as now it was his turn for his small world to be turned upside down. Poe was imagining the man with the head of a pike. He was a slippery customer, so he'd better be careful the old coot didn't trick him into letting him go with some sob story about not knowing what he was doing, as if the devil had gotten into him for one mad moment. Poe couldn't afford to let this catch off the hook, fearing he would end up hung up like a fish on a hook in a fish market if he did.

'What's going on? Being a Trickster, you should know all about tricks, and this is the oldest, dirtiest trick in the movie book, turning the tables. I expect you do have a wicker table somewhere in your wicker collection.' Poe smiled then added, with a sense of irony, 'But of course you've never heard of the movies.'

'Let me down, please. I promise I won't do anything bad ever again,' the old man pleaded, the blood rushing to his head.

'It's funny but the villain always says that line in the movies, and nobody ever believes him. The best I can do for you is leave you hanging. In the movies, this is called "the cliffhanger moment". Obviously, you're not dangling over a cliff, so you're already ahead of the game. Now to show you I'm not a monster like you, I'll give you the old heads-up, let you into what might become of you. The worst-case scenario is you're starved to death, no, sorry, best-case scenario is you starve to death. Worst- case scenario is the ravens and crows in this forest will peck your eyes out, the tree won't support your weight and you'll come crashing down, breaking most of your brittle bones. After that, my guess is that the wolves in the forest, who no doubt will be dying for a good feed, will rip you limb from limb, or something along those general lines. I'm afraid I don't have much of an imagination. I'm mind blind. It's a sad, sorry tale of the boy with no imagination. In truth, I imagine it's got nightmare written all over it. That should give you a few nightmares to be getting on with, old man, after which you can send me a cheque in the post. Better backdate it.' Poe grinned as he and Sorrow walked off into the sunset, or so they imagined.

The more likely story was that they were simply walking from one nightmare into the next nightmare. 'When this waking nightmare has died down and we are back in the land of the living, and no longer in the land of the living dead, we can sit down and watch the film *The Wicker Man* and laugh about it,' said Poe, keeping a straight face while trying not to corpse.

'Oh, Poe Black, you really are the living end!' Sorrow exclaimed, in a theatrical manner, sounding not unlike Queen Victoria in her black widow stage.

'Living being the operative word and not the living dead!' Poe replied, hoping to have the final word on the subject.

The best-case scenario for Poe and Sorrow was to find a dream worth chasing, one to break up the nightmare, and that the nightmare ended with a dream.

'Look, a gate,' Poe said, pointing at a black garden gate, although there was no wall attached to the gate. 'I imagine the gate leads to a paradise garden. In Persia, paradise gardens were also known as Black Gardens,' said Poe, in automaton-like fashion.

'Then after you, Mr Black, age before beauty,' said Sorrow, stepping aside so that Poe could lead the way into the latest nightmare, or so she was imagining. Sorrow was imagining looking into an antique glass admirer, one that magically beautified her, turning her from an ugly duckling into a beautiful black swan.

Poe stepped a little nervously through the gate, wondering what was on the other side. In truth, he could see what was on the other side – nothing, other than more trees, but he stepped through the gate all the same, for it seemed the right and proper thing to do. In truth, they both felt compelled to open the gate and step through into what they were imagining was a new world, a parallel world, for it seemed to Poe and Sorrow as if they were inside a giant house and in each room there lay a forest or woods or a garden. Some rooms were big, some were small, some were invisible, as if rooms in the quantum world.

'Now we are out of the woods, metaphorically speaking, I think we should sit and rest a while,' said Poe, having walked through the black gate then after a short walk feeling the need to rest, as walking into a new world had taken away all his energy. Walking through time and space could hardly be called a walk in the park. Poe sat down and rested up against a tree.

'Yes, it would be nice to sit and watch the world go by, although I have no idea anymore which world we are watching go by,' replied Sorrow, smiling on the inside while grimacing on the outside. In dark times, dark humour often rose to the fore. Sorrow sat close to Poe, looking for comfort, using the same tree to rest up against, a silver birch tree. Surely when they fell asleep this time, their dreams would not turn to nightmares.

8

Shadow Puppets

Poe and Sorrow slept in the forest until they were rudely awoken by a shadow, of all things.

'We're surrounded!' Sorrow exclaimed, looking all about her to see they were surrounded by figures, or at least the shadow of figures. The figures appeared to be dancing manically around them as if they were all disjointed arms, legs, hands and feet.

'I think they are dancing?' said Poe, turning around in a circle on the spot as his mind tried to make sense of the latest landscape they were trapped in as once again the forest transformed itself.

'It's the medieval dance St Vitus Dance, a dance which was said to take over a crowd of people, who would end up dancing in a trance, having no recollection later of why they were doing so,' said Sorrow, delving into the archives in her head and pulling out this little fact. This little fact seemed remarkably like a fiction to Poe's mind, as if the fact had been twisted or seen through a bowed mirror.

'Either we have stumbled into a witches' coven or we find ourselves in the middle of a satanic pentagram drawn by devil worshippers and we are to be sacrificed,' Sorrow said.

'Talk about out of the frying pan, into the fires of hell!' Poe replied, with a look of both shock and horror on his face.

'They're not devil worshippers or witches, Poe. They're puppets hanging from the trees like decorations, or they've been put there to scare off the birds like a form of scarecrow,' exclaimed Sorrow, as the fear began to subside and they both saw things in their true light, or at least they imagined this to be the case. What they both could have done with was the Venetian light that Michelangelo used to paint by, for that may shed a light and shine a light on the true nature of their situation. At times in the forest, it was like stumbling blindly about in the dark, and everything looked more frightening in the dark.

'Once upon a time, Alfred Hitchcock said he thought of his actors as puppets whose strings he pulled. Apparently, he didn't like stars,' Poe said, trying to distract himself. 'I wouldn't be a bit surprised if any minute now he makes one of his famous cameo appearances in the form of a silhouette; a short, balding, portly man with a pot belly, smoking a large Cuban cigar.'

'As long as we don't have to fight off a thousand shadows in the form of birds,' Sorrow said, recalling the Hitchcock horror film *The Birds* to mind.

Just as Poe and Sorrow were beginning to breathe a little easier, the puppets opened their eyes, as if being worked by an unseen puppet master. Then the puppets did something quite unexpected; they began to cut their own strings and the strings of the puppets hanging on the same branch next to them. 'Be careful, look out, that's my arm you've just cut off and that's my head. Help, I'm falling!' cried several puppets as the sound of scissors filled the forest as one by one the puppets freed themselves from the branches of the trees, and from the strings they were tied to.

Within a few minutes, all of the puppets were laying still on the ground.

'What just happened?' asked a startled Poe, turning to Sorrow, as she had seen things in a different light to the one Poe was seeing things in. Sorrow simply shrugged, using body language rather than words to convey her reply, for she too was at a loss to find any logical explanation for what had just happened.

'Hold on a minute. I remember now, there were a whole lot of old puppets in one of the tea chests in the attic, gathering dust,' Poe exclaimed, having a Eureka moment of sorts, a twisted one, for no sooner had these words come out of his mouth than the attic appeared. It was as if the words were magical, like abracadabra, hey presto or alakazam.

'We're home!' cried Sorrow, tears of joy in her eyes.

For Poe, these were the magic words, as they took him back to his childhood, when he arrived home with his grandparents from a long holiday.

'Come on, run. I can see the door. We might make it before the vision disappears, the forest regains control and the forest reappears,' Poe cried, grabbing Sorrow roughly by the arm as they both span upon their heels and ran towards where the door of the attic was, as if their life depended upon it. Sorrow was quicker on her feet than Poe and managed to get within a few feet of the attic door before the door began to shrink, or so it appeared. This was an optical illusion, for the door was not shrinking in size. It only appeared to be shrinking due to the door slowly getting further and further away, as the attic began to stretch, so now to the human eye only a dormouse could get through the door of the attic.

'Not so fast, boy. We haven't been introduced. It's rude to leave before you have even said hello,' cried a puppet as it rose to its feet and blocked their way. Poe and Sorrow moved to one side to avoid the puppet, only to find another puppet blocking their way, who uttered the same line. This forced Poe and Sorrow to step sideways once again, only to find another puppet facing them, then another and another. So now there was an army of puppets blocking their route back into the attic and safety.

Poe was beginning to realise that the physics and mathematics in this world was not the same as in his world. Whereas in his world two and two made four, in this weird and not-so-wonderful world two and two made five. It was said spirits often possessed treasured items almost as if they were unable to let go of them, so if you inherited the item, you sometimes inherited the spirit to go along with it. If the spirit was a benevolent spirit, that was fine, but if the spirit was a malevolent one, then you could be in for a world of hurt, as the modern expression goes. Objects from the attic kept on popping up in the Twisted Forest, possibly bringing a spirit along with them for the ride, anything but a joyride if the spirit was a benevolent one, for once in the confines of the forest, the good spirit turned bad, or so Poe was imagining.

The puppets were only a third of the size of Poe and Sorrow, not much bigger than dwarves, and as dwarves were characters out of a fairy tale then once again Poe felt as if he and Sorrow were characters out of a fairy tale. Poe felt like Sleepy and Dozy from the Seven Dwarves, which meant Sorrow must be playing the part of Snow White. This logically meant her shadow was playing the part of Snow Black. Poe could not bring to mind who had written the characters of Snow White and the Seven Dwarves. Was that so surprising? Not really. A lot of fairy-tale characters appeared not to have a creator. It was as if they had appeared out of thin air, as if by magic, the creator lost to the famed mists of time, or lost in a forest shrouded in mist, like the real-life character Major Fawcett in his search for the Lost City of Z/El Dorado.

'Run!' bellowed Poe as he ran for his life. Sorrow was more than happy to comply with these simple instructions, for too many instructions at a time when the brain was having trouble deciphering instructions it was given could only lead to the brain getting mixed messages. Run forward or backwards or perhaps run on the spot was what Poe was asking Sorrow to do, while at the same time she could give her brain a good cerebral workout, and it was a fact that exercise made the brain more active.

Poe took two paces forward and fell flat on his face, as did Sorrow. They both wondered if they had stumbled over an unseen tree stump; that was until they realised the puppets had tied their shoelaces together without them knowing. The puppets were now hanging on to their trouser bottoms, dragging them back into the forest as the attic disappeared into thin air.

After being dragged around the forest several times, Poe and Sorrow eventually blacked out. The next thing they knew, they were hanging from the trees like the puppets had been earlier.

'Shall we cut their strings or cut their arms and legs off?' laughed one of the puppets in manic fashion, as now all the puppets were gathered under the tree as if in a lynching. Poe and Sorrow were hanging off the tree, suspended by ropes, one from each wrist and one from each foot. This made them look exactly like puppets on a string, giant puppets on a string.

'Or we could leave it to the puppet master. After all, the bargain was that he would give us our freedom if we found him two giant puppets,' a puppet close by grunted, tugging against the strings attached to his limbs as the strings the puppets had freed themselves from earlier had now grown back.

'Puppet master, we have done what you asked of us. Now cut our strings and let us free,' begged the puppets as one, bowing down to an unseen puppet master. The puppet master, however, remained in the shadows, as all good puppet masters should.

Suddenly a thunderous voice bellowed, 'Thank you, my children. I will now grant you your freedom. You are no longer my puppets and I would not wish to string you along anymore.'

And with that, the strings of the puppets were cut as they ran free, jumping and dancing for joy, leaving Poe and Sorrow still dangling helplessly from the tree, puppets on a string.

After a while, Poe and Sorrow, so tired from their struggles, fell asleep hanging in mid-air, like flies caught in a spider's web as they wait for the spider to return home. Poe and Sorrow, being the psychic dreamers they were, had the same dream of running towards the attic door, which was ajar. They both heard a voice make the old joke, 'When is a door not a door? When it's a jar.' Neither Poe nor Sorrow had ever found this joke funny. A book entitled *Ventriloquism for Dummies* was, however, funny, although Poe and Sorrow wondered if they weren't much brighter than a ventriloquist's dummy, for they had walked into two traps already, and this nightmare night was still young.

Then just as Sorrow and Poe felt all hope was lost, the ropes tied around their wrists and feet magically untied themselves, or at least the ones keeping them hanging from the tree, as they fell to the ground in a heap, both like rag dolls, not moving a muscle. Poe imagined that the ropes had been untied by some invisible elves. Wishful thinking, my dear Poe. Try again. It appears your imagination is on the blink!

'Thank God!' Poe cried, finally coming to his senses upon seeing there were no elves to be seen, unless they had disappeared into the bark of the tree. Poe saw faces wherever he looked, especially in the bark and trunks of the trees. The more likely story was that, being invisible, the elves were now tying their hair into elf knots!

'Not the puppet god or worse still St Peter with the dark angel, the grim reaper, standing in his shadow,' replied Sorrow, grimacing on the inside.

'You untie me and then I can untie you.' Poe barked out orders, thinking they were now out of the woods, but as Sorrow went to untie the rope around Poe's left wrist, her hand was pulled up, followed by her other hand. Sorrow was now dancing around like a puppet on a string.

'Yes, very funny, Sorrow. Now untie me.' Poe grimaced, feeling a pull on his left wrist as if he'd had a muscle spasm. Then before he knew it, he too was dancing around, exactly like a puppet on a string, in manic fashion.

'Yes, yes, dance, my children, dance.' A loud, booming voice from above laughed as he pulled the strings and his puppets, one named Poe and one named Sorrow, as they danced to his tune and were still dancing to his tune two hours later. Eventually, Sorrow collapsed upon the ground due to exhaustion, followed by Poe, as clearly both were dead upon their feet. However, this dance of death did not end there, for soon Poe and Sorrow were back on their feet, as if sleepwalking.

The dream was a brief one, as it quickly turned back into a nightmare as Poe and Sorrow went for each other hammer and tongs. Poe with the hammer and Sorrow with the tongs as she attempted to extract his tongue without anaesthetic. Poe dropped his hammer on his own foot and Sorrow threw away the tongs as she tried to remove her own tongue and nearly swallowed the tongs. Both these implements had appeared out of thin air, left lying on the forest floor for them to use as weapons. It seemed the devious-minded master puppeteer had thought of everything.

'What are you doing, Poe? You're going to scratch my eyes out. What's got into you? I don't have the strength to fight you, not when half the time I'm fighting with myself and fighting with my inner demons,' Sorrow pleaded, putting her hands up to defend herself but then dropping her hands and putting them down by her side as if giving up. Not that she wanted to give up, but as it was the puppet master pulling her strings, she had no choice.

'I'm sorry. I'm just not myself at times. I don't know my own strength, that and the devil appears to have gotten into me, and I wish for all the world that he would climb back out and leave me be,' whimpered Poe, tears streaming down his face as he slashed at Sorrow's face over and over again with his sharpened nails, nails he had not cut for some time. Sorrow collapsed upon the ground, leaving Poe standing over her like a boxer in a bare-knuckle fight as he raised his hand in victory. But there was no smile, no cries of *I'm the champion of the world*, just a deathly hush. The only winner in this fight to the death was the puppet master.

Poe thought he heard a man's voice cheering wildly in a manic fashion in the background, but this could just as easily have been the voices in his head, goading him to twist the knife in further. In the puppet arena, all the puppets had put their thumbs down, as if to signal that Poe should finish the job, finish Sorrow off. Poe felt no pain. He was dead inside, and being a puppet made of wood helped. It also made it easier to sustain the deadpan expression on his face. As an actor, Poe was wooden. The only part he'd ever got at school was the back end of a donkey in the school nativity.

The curtain of the night fell, ending this particular scene as Poe laid down his head upon Sorrow's lifeless body and fell into a deep sleep. There was no applause, just silence, a silence so loud that it could justifiably be said to be deafening.

9

The Transfiguration

'Where are we?' Sorrow asked, waking first and feeling disorientated, her head still spinning. She fervently hoped she wasn't tied to a Catherine Wheel, the Medieval Torture device. Anything was possible, given the evil and devious mind of the puppet master. Sorrow had given the man pulling their strings this theatrical name, even though the man still remained in the shadows. Of course, the puppet master could easily be a woman? Sorrow wondered if she and Poe were shadows, ghost spirits in the material world. This macabre thought quickly evaporated as Sorrow felt something around her stomach, something tight restricting her movements. She looked down to see a rope tied tightly around her waist that was in turn tied tightly around the trunk of a tree.

'Where are we?' Poe asked, as if repeating the words Sorrow had just spoken, like some kind of *Idiot Savant*, before finishing the sentence with 'We are in hell or at least hell on earth!'

'I feel like Lucy Westenra from Dracula's story, and here I quote from her diary, 17th September – "Four days of nights and peace. I am getting so strong, I hardly know myself. It is as if I have passed through some long nightmare and had just awakened to see the beautiful sunshine and feel the fresh air of the morning around me."' Sorrow felt a kinship with the character Lucy Westenra, for she hardly knew herself. Then it was her good fortune to be going on this journey of self-discovery. By the time Sorrow had reached journey's end, her sorrows would be over and she would know herself inside out. That and hopefully Sorrow would be through the nightmare, for at this moment she was still not sure if she was in or out of the nightmare, or if in fact she was in a dream. There is an expression, "To see through it", which means looking through time, hard times, as you picture yourself standing on the other side of those hard times, mind over matter. One would require more than the mind machine to travel into the future; they would need a time machine, unless there was a portal, say, in the hollowed-out trunk of a tree that led to the future.

Sorrow was trying to picture herself standing at the other side of this particular nightmare but she could not. It was as if she was looking through a black kaleidoscope, one that had been caught in a fire in the attic of a haunted house.

'I'm glad it is all over now,' Sorrow said, hearing the voice in her head of her childhood heroine Coraline echoing through the corridors of her mind.

Could fact eclipse fiction? Yes, it most certainly could. The only trouble at times for the imaginative mind was that it was hard to separate the two, fact from fiction and fiction from fact.

'Wishful thinking, my dear Sorrow, and I think we are about to find out, and I wish for all the world we were not.'

'Wishful thinking indeed, my dear Poe. Wishful thinking won't get you anywhere in this life. In this life, one has to live in the real world. Sometimes, I think you're living in a dream world, or the attic of your mind,' Sorrow replied, trying to avoid two words, nightmare and death, as in this death, not life, and living in a nightmare and not a dream. 'I probably should have gone first in this here fantasy wish list, for I wrote my first bucket wish list when I was seven,' Sorrow said proudly, as if it was a badge of honour to have a death wish at such an early age.

'Seven! Seven! You must have been born old, old before your time like me, and an old head on young shoulders,' Poe sighed, imagining an old man's head on a young man's body, a freak show if ever there was one.

'We're like a couple of peas in a pod, black-eyed peas,' sighed Sorrow.

'Perhaps given the fact this nightmare is about to reach its end, now would be a good time to make a will. However, as we haven't a free hand to write this Will down, I will tell you now that I am going to leave everything I own to you, including the house.' Poe sniffed, trying not to let his stiff upper lip quiver as he tried to maintain his never-say-die attitude, an attitude he would most certainly need if he was to get out of this nightmare.

'It's very kind of you, Poe, but if you don't mind, I'll pass on the house, or should I say pass on the haunted house, the House of many Horrors!' replied Sorrow, grimacing.

'Your funeral. You'll wish you hadn't turned my generous offer down when you're dead, for you'll need somewhere to haunt, and what better place for a spirit than a haunted house. You'll feel right at home!' Poe spat sniffily, for it was clear by the tone of his voice that his nose had been severely put out of joint. In truth, his nose had not but his shoulder had, for whoever had tied him to the trunk of the tree had done it with no concern for his well-being. The fact he was tied to a trunk of a tree and was surrounded by matchwood, this fact was rather obvious. As he was about to be burnt at the stake, a little thing like a dislocated shoulder seemed the least of his worries. One of Poe's worries on his Worry List was that after he was dead and gone, who would feed his black cat, Edgar?

Suddenly the attic started to appear in Poe's mind, as if he had conjured the attic into being, but not in the forest, as Poe searched frantically through the dusty boxes in the attic, hoping he had seen a silver tinderbox in one of them, or at least the attic of the mind, the subconscious. 'Time to reveal yourself. Abracadabra. Hey presto!' Poe muttered under his breath. However, the tinderbox did not appear to him in his mind's eye, which meant there obviously wasn't a tinderbox in the attic.

Poe's mind-over-matter trick seemed to be failing dismally, and as he saw himself walk away from the boxes in the attic, the rays of the moon came shining through the attic window. The sun illuminated the attic so it felt as if a full moon was inside this magical space, which caught something shiny out of the corner of his eye. Poe turned his neck and much to his surprise and delight there was the silver tinderbox, sitting pretty, sandwiched between an old teddy bear that had seen better days and a rag doll, worse for wear.

'Please, God, don't let a magpie appear on the windowsill of the open window and upon seeing the shiny object fly down and carry it off.' Poe wasn't sure if he had left the window in the attic open or closed. It was a nice sunny day; he could well have opened the attic window. Perhaps this wouldn't have been so bad. After all, if the tinderbox vanished from the attic, it would surely vanish from the forest at the same time. The forest and the attic inextricably entwined (quantum entanglement in action, the large entwined with the very small).

In the blinking of an eye, the forest started to fade as the walls, floor and ceiling of the attic began to reappear. Poe could see the old grandmother clock, its pendulum swinging back and forth as the hands of the clock went backwards, anticlockwise. Poe saw a calendar nailed to the wall of the attic, but as the forest was still visible, it looked as if the calendar was nailed to the trunk of a tree. Better the calendar nailed to a tree than him, as the pendulum on the clock began to speed up, or perhaps he was imagining this, the old optical illusion, for it seemed to Poe as if his time was rapidly running out. There was an hourglass in the attic, and as luck would have it, the sand was at the bottom of that hourglass. It seemed The Life and Times of Poe Black was about to reach an abrupt end.

If this was a repeat of all the others times the attic had appeared and the forest had disappeared, then the door of the attic would not stay open long. Poe was no Harry Houdini, the famous escapologist, so he knew he had little chance of undoing the ropes around his waist and wrists in time to make a run for the door of the attic. However, the puppet may fancy his chances, despite his wonky gait. It was a long shot but it may be Poe and Sorrow's only hope of getting out of this nightmare alive.

The forest was now a ghostly image as the attic swallowed the forest up as the months on the calendar on the wall of the attic began to be ripped off by an unseen hand: January... February... March... an old movie trick to show the passing of time. Poe longed for a slow-motion sequence, the ones that often cropped up in a nightmare when being chased by the Big Bad Wolf as you found your feet were stuck in black treacle.

The shadow puppet then magically stepped out of its own shadow to reveal a wooden puppet, one that had not been painted. It was as if the shadow had just given birth to the puppet. If this was not a curious thought, Poe did not know what was. At first, the puppet was unsmiling, wearing a deadpan expression, unless the puppet was wearing a death mask, but as it slowly and awkwardly turned its head, a smile appeared upon its face. Thankfully, the head of the puppet did not spin three hundred and sixty degrees, as it had done to the girl in the old horror film *The Exorcist*. If this occurred, the puppet may well lose its head and then run off in the wrong direction like a headless chicken.

Thankfully, the puppet did not lose its head. In fact, it seemed quite calm as it turned and headed towards the open door of the attic. In Poe's mind, the puppet was as keen to cut its strings as Poe and Sorrow were to cut theirs. At first, the puppet's progress was painfully slow, running like a man with two broken legs as the puppet fell several times as he made a bid for freedom. The tick-tock of the grandmother clock steadily got louder and louder as Poe and Sorrow both found themselves wishing they could stick their fingers in their ears. Once again, this was more wishful thinking that went unanswered. Poe and Sorrow were willing the puppet on, cheering him on, in fact, as if their puppet was in a race against other puppets, a race for life.

This was not the Pinocchio story or Punch and Judy, based upon the Italian punchman story. Only a few moments ago, Sorrow and Poe were wishing the puppet further. Poe even wished it would suffer a rare case of spontaneous human combustion as it went up in flames, until all that was left of the puppet was a pile of black ash. Spontaneous human combustion was very much a Victorian malady, or should I say one dreamt up by writers of Victorian ghost stories.

'Come on, come on, rah, rah. You can do it, you can do it. Show the puppet master you're nobody's puppet on a string!' Sorrow cheered wildly, waving her imaginary black pompoms in the air.

'Yes, just a few more feet and you're there. Don't give up the ghost now. You're almost home, free!' Poe cried, looking at his imaginary stopwatch, convinced the puppet would break the puppet one hundred metre world record. Of course, if the puppet was being worked by a puppet master pulling its strings, it would be disqualified for breaking the rules and the record would be expunged from the record books.

'Run, puppet, run. Run for your life. Run for our lives. Run like the wind. Run like your Forrest Gump being chased by the devil!' Poe wondered if the puppet was possessed by an evil spirit. In truth, if it was possessed by the devil, then right now he wouldn't have cared, for the devil was fleet of foot. Of course, that meant that if the puppet made it into the attic he would have a puppet in his attic possessed by an evil spirit. Poe wisely decided not to add this worry to his worry list, for it was long enough already. Right now, if Poe had to be the devil's cheerleader, then he would gladly do it, and do it with a smile on his face.

Then everything went black… bone-black!

'Hey, who turned the lights out in the forest?' yelled Poe, as if he was watching a movie at home and somebody had pulled the plug on the TV set, probably a mischievous poltergeist.

'Don't worry, Poe. The moon has probably gone behind a cloud. Normal service will be resumed as soon as possible,' Sorrow cried, sounding as if she worked for a television company, and this was a public announcement service due to transmission failure. 'Either that or this is one of those cliffhanger moments, in which case this tree we are tied to is at the edge of a cliff,' Sorrow added, with her tongue so far in her cheek that she was in danger of swallowing it and choking to death. At least Sorrow and Poe still had a tongue in their head and as yet had not had it removed with a red-hot pair of tongs, as many unfortunate souls in the past had.

10

Paranormal is the New Normal

Then light returned to the forest as a spotlight shone brightly upon the door in the attic, which slowly started to swing shut, creaking loudly on its hinges, as in all classic ghost movies.

'See, I told you so. Normal service has been resumed,' cried Sorrow, feeling pleased with herself.

'Abnormal service, if you ask me,' spat Poe, not impressed with the cable station Forest Broadcasting Network FBN.

'Abnormal is the new normal,' Sorrow added, taking a soundbite from the coronavirus crisis when everyone in the media was quoting the line, "The new normal, isolation". At the time, the coronavirus crisis had little effect on Poe and Sorrow. For the most part, they were already in self-isolation; now everybody else was in the same boat as they were. For some, the boat became a Noah's Ark, while for others a Viking funeral boat.

'Paranormal in some folks' eyes is the new normal, and in this abnormal world I would have to agree, although it's not a normal I want to get used to,' Poe added wistfully.

The puppet looked at the tinderbox in its hand as if it did not know why it was holding it. Perhaps it was waiting for the puppet master to give it its instructions to set light to the tree.

Poe felt something sniffing around close by and then out of the corner of his eye, he saw a wolf, a grey wolf. The wolf wasn't a male wolf, for it was smaller. Poe was sure it was a female wolf. Talk about being between a rock and a hard place. Either be eaten alive by a wolf or set on fire. Edgar Allen Poe was alive and living inside the mind of the puppet master, or the more likely tale, living inside the mind of the Forester, the man who had built the house. Poe had a mind to wonder if, like he, the forester was a lover of the gothic macabre tales of Edgar Allen Poe. That would explain a lot. At this moment in time, Poe found himself wishing his hero further!

The wolf began to lick at Poe's wrists, which were tied to the tree, as if it wanted to see if this body tasted good. Might need some seasoning, salt and pepper or some barbecue sauce. If the wolf had any sense, it would wait for the puppet to set fire to the tree and Poe and Sorrow, and its meals would be cooked! Of course, the wolf might not like burnt offerings.

Sorrow could feel the hot breath of the wolf on her hands as it began to chew, but not on their flesh, on the ropes tying them to the tree. The puppet did not sense anything was wrong but then again, being a puppet, no sense, no feeling; in fact, no senses at all, so it could not see or smell the wolf. The puppet master, however, appeared to have eyes in the back of his head, or eyes in every tree in the forest; a twist on the old horror movie *The Hills Have Eyes*.

The tinderbox suddenly lit up as the puppet slowly turned its head and began walking towards the tree then it stopped before climbing up the trunk of the tree. It scampered along the branches, one by one, setting the leaves alight, which then began to spread to other parts of the tree. The puppet then climbed back down the trunk of the tree, but it did not flee or stand and watch with glee. Instead, it held the tinderbox to its head as the puppet began to go up in flames.

'Quickly, the tree is on fire!' Sorrow cried out, as if talking to the wolf.

'Yes, please hurry,' Poe exclaimed, desperately trying to free himself from the ropes, which by this time were frayed due to the wolf gnawing at them with its teeth. A wolf's teeth are extremely sharp; they have to be if they are to survive in the wild.

'I'm going as quickly as I am able. Don't worry, you will soon be free,' hissed the wolf. Either that or this was all in Poe's and Sorrow's minds, which were now running as wild as they had ever done since they had both stepped into the Twisted Forest.

'We're free!' Sorrow cried then helped untie Poe as the flames licked at their feet.

'Thank you, you saved us. I don't know how we can ever thank you,' Poe cried, bending down and hugging the wolf as if it was a long-lost friend. Poe was wondering if this wolf was a friend of White Wolf. He further wondered if this wolf was the spirit of his mother, reincarnated, and she had been watching over him all this time.

Whatever the truth, they were free as the wolf turned, howled out as if in triumph and then disappeared into the forest as Poe and Sorrow once again made themselves scarce.

'We are certainly getting to know the trees in this forest,' said Poe, breathing heavily.

'If we ever get out of this forest alive, I don't ever want to see a tree again for the rest of my life,' groaned Sorrow, shaking her head, for it seemed to her that she and the trees in the forest were getting a little too close for comfort, as if the trees in the forest were invading her space. The thing was, this wasn't Sorrow's space; whom the space belonged to was still in doubt. Perhaps it belonged to the spirit world. This in theory meant that the spirit world was renting this space out to the forest. No doubt the rent collectors in this twisted forest were thin on the ground.

'Oh, I don't know. I can see myself tying the knot with a lovely elegant silver birch tree.' Poe smiled, seeing the funny side of another near-death experience.

'You've got a twisted sense of humour, Poe Black,' Sorrow replied, finding it hard to raise a smile.

'If you never want to see a tree again, that means you'll have to live in a concrete jungle, a nightmare in my book,' Poe added, twisting the knife as if possessed by an evil spirit.

It was an old saying. If bad things happened enough times to a good person, they may begin to turn bad. Sorrow was hoping this was not to be the case.

'And after all that bad news, we have a good-news, feel-good story to end the bad news,' Poe proclaimed, playing the part of the forest newsreader. 'A cat got stuck up a tree in the Twisted Forest today but thankfully the forest fire service, using a long ladder, rescued it. Unfortunately, the fireman who rescued it fell and broke his neck, although I'm glad to say the cat, a black one, is doing fine.'

'It's true there is always a good news story at the end of the news, which is for the most part bad news,' Sorrow said, smiling on the inside.

'Do you want the good news or the bad news? The good news is that this nightmare is at an end, and the bad news is that there is another one waiting for us on the other side of the dream. I know, don't say it, I'm the life and soul of the forest.' Poe laughed, trying his best to cheer Sorrow up, for it was important to lighten the mood whenever possible, for one never knew when the next dark cloud would appear over the event horizon.

11

The Petrified Forest

'The forest has changed again?' exclaimed Sorrow, as once again the forest around them changed. Sorrow was not in the least bit sorrowful at this change, for she hoped this change would be for better and not worse.

'The forest is obviously envious of your quick-change act in the woods back there, although I hope it doesn't change into a giant jaguar. Otherwise, our next nightmare might be trying to get out of the stomach of a giant wildcat!' Poe grimaced.

The forest had never been much of a snappy dresser, only having four changes of clothes in its wardrobe: brown in winter, yellow and green in spring, green in summer and red, yellow, brown and gold in autumn, when it expanded the colours in its wardrobe ever so slightly. In winter, the forest decided its best look was to wear its birthday suit or wear the emperor's hand-me- downs, in other words, his old clothes. Poe thought this rather an odd decision, to go back to nature to become a naturist when the year was at its coldest. Surely that was the time to put on more clothes, not less.

Poe was surprised the trees didn't freeze to death. The fact they made it through the winter was a testament to their hardiness and strength of character. Poe often talked to the trees when he walked through the silver birch forest, and once asked them why they shed their coats of many colours when autumn was at an end. The trees remained tight-lipped, mirroring the po-faced expression that Poe wore morning, noon and night. Then one tree broke its vow of silence. 'You do ask some seriously stupid questions, boy. Didn't they teach you anything at school? May I suggest you enrol at forest school, for traditional schooling has clearly failed you!'

'They say a Russian winter is so cold that even your soul gets frostbite,' Poe said, without a trace of a smile on his face.

'Being Russian, I welcome the winter in with open arms.' Sorrow, aka Yarra, smiled, opening her arms as wide as she could, as if to do just that, as if she had forgotten uttering the line, *If I ever get out of this forest alive, I don't want to see a tree again as long as I live!*

'Be careful you don't welcome the frost fairy in with that winter, or when she leaves, she will take your fingers and your toes with her as a souvenir,' Poe added, being the little ray of sunshine he clearly was, not at this moment in time, any moment in time, Sorrow was given to thinking.

'That sounds grim, like a Brothers Grimm German folk tale, the ugly sisters making sure the glass slipper fits Cinderella by cutting off her toes!' Sorrow shuddered, as if the devil and one of his disciples had just tangoed their way across her grave.

'Yes, the forest has changed, but as they say, a change is as good as a rest. Let's hope the forest doesn't change its mind back again. I've no desire to go back to the forest where we were both puppets on a string,' Poe replied, still half in a dream, half in a nightmare.

'I've got a feeling we still are puppets on a string, being worked by an unseen puppet master, a shadow puppet master who always seems to remain in the shadows,' said Sorrow, her heart heavy, as were her legs, not good when it came to being chased through a forest of nightmares. Sorrow's legs may have been heavy due to all the carbon she had breathed in over the years, which had solidified, petrified like a stone forest, a petrified forest. Mother Nature had breathed in such huge quantities of carbon dioxide that she was finding it hard to get off the ground. Her whole body had become petrified like a heavier-than-air machine, or alternatively a prehistoric elephant bird, so Mother Nature had to create a giant storm to help her fly. Sorrow was more petrified of the consequences of man's destruction of the forests and nature than she was petrified of the nightmare. Even a waking nightmare, like the coronavirus and the isolation it brought. Sorrow did not lose any sleep over it, unlike others, who found they were either awake all night or slept all day. The night and day and the world had been turned upon its head, as if everybody on planet earth at the time felt as if they were living in an upside-down house.

'If you believe philosophers, we are all puppets on a string. Philosophers believe that at the beginning of time, everything was written. God: the ultimate shadow puppet master, the script writer, producer, director and editor of all of our life stories. That's some juggling act, keeping all those puppets going at once,' Poe gasped, blowing out his cheeks.

'Do those trees over there look funny to you? To me, they don't look real. In fact, the trees look like they should be in a stage production of some kind or another, perhaps *A Midsummer Night's Dream*, although Midsummer nightmare would seem more appropriate,' Sorrow said, turning to Poe as once again Sorrow and Poe looked more puzzled than an uprooted monkey puzzle tree that sat at the heart of a maze-like forest.

'Funny in what way? Funny ha, ha or funny looking, as in odd, like you and I,' said Poe, tongue in cheek. 'I mean, a lot of trees, especially old trees, look funny peculiar, odd even. No offence intended, big fella,' Poe added, resting his hand on an old tree, bent over as if it had a bad back or was crippled like the Hunchback of Notre Dame.

'That's true. Once, I stood by a weeping willow tree and somebody at my school said they didn't see me standing there, as if the tree and I were sisters, Siamese twins.' Sorrow sighed, looking a little sorry for herself.

'Insects can disguise themselves like chameleons so they look like leaves or twigs. I didn't get that from a nature documentary, I'll have to be honest, but from the beginning of the book...'

'Coraline.' Sorrow smiled. 'Yes, that is true and it appears I can disguise myself as a weeping willow tree. You couldn't make it up!'

'I always see the weeping willow tree as a ballet dancer doing the dying swan routine in the movie *Black Swan*,' Poe replied, trying to do the dying swan, and in the process almost twisting his neck.

'Yes, so do I. We are now fully paid-up members of the Lyrical Waxing Society,' Sorrow added, as her smile returned on the inside.

'Well, I'm already a member of the Flat Earth Society and the Dead Romantic Poets Society and the Forest Preservation Society. Soon, the only society I won't be a member of is "society". The membership fees of these societies are costing me a small fortune!' Poe smiled as the two new friends made light of their dark situation. The light in the forest appeared to brighten as if the dimmer switch in the forest had been turned up a notch, or the light in the attic, as if an unseen hand had opened up the door in the attic. Once more, the spirit of the forester playing mind games with the occupants of the House of Horrors.

'I'm happy being an outsider. I don't ever want to be a part of "society",' said Sorrow. There was no bitterness in her voice about wanting not to be a part of society, for Sorrow was just a soul who liked her own company and her own space, and what a space nature was. Magical, strange, ever changing, full of both the weird and the wonderful.

'Can't disagree with any of that, my friend of the earth,' Poe muttered, kicking a twig across the forest floor then wondering if the twig was, in fact, an insect, a stick insect. Poe would have to be more careful in future where he was putting his big feet. God knows how many lives he was putting at risk. After all, insects had every much as right to life as he and the animals of the forest.

Then a bedraggled-looking couple came out of a parting in the trees, as if through an old tattered and torn-looking curtain, or perhaps a well-worn moth-eaten carpet would be a better description, albeit a magic carpet. 'Have you seen our child? She's lost somewhere in the forest,' begged a woman with a mournful look upon her face, pulling upon Sorrow's sleeve. As the woman was dressed in black, it appeared as if she was in mourning as a single tear slid down her face which, being dry and crinkly in appearance, resembled a leaf that had fallen off a tree in winter.

'No, no, sorry, we haven't seen any children,' Sorrow replied, trying not to sound unsympathetic.

'You're not my child, are you, all grown up?' sniffed the woman, her eyes full of hope as they temporarily lit up as if fireflies were reflected in them.

'Sorry, my poor wife's mind is full of thick, dark cobwebs. She had a miscarriage, but she has forgotten that, or blanked it out of her mind,' muttered the husband, looking sorrowful as he pulled his sobbing wife away from Sorrow, who was shifting uneasily on her feet, wishing she could tell the woman she was her daughter but knowing that would only make things worse.

'You don't think that doll we saw in the attic was the spirit of their daughter, do you? Perhaps once upon a time they owned your house. Quick, we must catch up with them,' said Sorrow, recalling the nightmare in the attic space.

'You mean, once upon a nightmare. I fear they have gone. They could have been ghosts for all we know,' Poe replied, trying to separate the dream world from the world of reality. For some people, it was hard to separate these two worlds. It was as if the moon was the dream world and the sun the real world. During an eclipse, instead of the two bodies passing across one another, had one somehow got stuck on top of the other? What was reality? Poe and Sorrow were not as sure as they had been before they entered the forest, or was that the attic space? The forest was the sun and the moon the attic, one on top of the other, like two magic lantern slides. One lantern slide was superimposed over the other like in a phantasmagorical trick of a magical light, both the light of the moon and the light of the sun entwined to produce a light even more illuminating than the one in Venice Venetian artists so loved to paint by.

The lines between the dream world and the world of reality were becoming more and more blurred the deeper Poe and Sorrow got into the forest. Even Sorrow appeared to change right in front of his eyes, from Sorrow to Eloise, Eloise

to Pandora, as Poe's kaleidoscopic mind twisted the scope this way and that, trying to get a clearer image of the strange girl he first met in another time and space.

'Look at that tree. If you look carefully, a face will appear in the trunk like in a magic 3D puzzle dot book,' said Sorrow, cheerfully trying to distract herself from what had just happened, which already seemed as if it had happened days ago rather than minutes.

'Yes, yes, I can clearly see the face now,' Poe replied, screwing up his eyes, stepping forward then stepping back until the face appeared to him. 'It reminds me of someone.'

'Whose face is it?' asked Sorrow in trepidation, wondering if the face belonged to an outlaw of the forest, Wanted Dead or Alive. Poe was setting up a joke and she was the straight man/ woman in this comedy act upon the stage, and the joke was at her expense, as she heard a chilling voice in her head laugh, *It's your face, Sorrow. You look like death warmed up. It's like looking in the mirror!* Sorrow could easily imagine a mirror set in the trunk of a tree in the forest, and no doubt one you could step through into another part of the forest, or another forest entirely perhaps, even one in another time and dimension. Sorrow was imagining the tree itself holding out a hand admirer, the old-fashioned word for a hand mirror, as it beautified itself.

'It's the face of the man in the painting *The Scream* by Edvard Munch. It's changing now. It looks like the face of the artist himself, Edvard Munch,' Poe gasped, not sure if his eyes were playing tricks on him or if it was the forest.

'It's probably an optical illusion, delusion more like, another one of nature's tricks walking through the forests of Finland. How many old trees have you imagined as wizened old men or witches or monsters?' Sorrow tried to get things into some kind of perspective, for at the moment they both appeared to be looking through the lens of a warped camera obscura, one that obscured and warped everything around them, or maybe they were looking through a kaleidoscope.

'Look over there. Another face, and it's grinning at me, and over there another one. I'm sure the eyes are following me like in a painting in a haunted house in an old horror movie,' exclaimed Poe, almost jumping out of his thin skin when the bony-like skeletal-looking branch of a tree touched him on the shoulder, as if it was trying to get Poe to back off for invading its space.

'Come over here, Poe. Look, cut into the trunk of the tree, a name and a date and a poem. The tree is like a headstone, and there's another one over here, and here too. It's like we've walked into a cemetery, or the ruins of a giant gothic church. The canopy is the roof of the church, open to the sky, a church where trees have sprung up like in the ruins in the abbey in England where King Arthur and Guinevere were said to be buried,' Sorrow gasped, her ashen white face a picture, a picture of the painting *The Scream*.

Sorrow was going to clasp her hands to her face but, looking deathly pale, she didn't want to look any more like the man in the painting *The Scream* than she already did.

'Do you think the bodies of the dead were somehow put into the hollowed-out trunks of the trees, then over time the trees became petrified, turning to stone?' said Poe, talking out loud.

'I don't know about the trees and the forest being petrified. I'm certainly petrified. I'm sure that tree moved, as did that one over there? They're all moving now, closing in on us. At this rate, before very long, we will be crushed to death!' cried Sorrow, her eyes as wide as two shiny black saucers as she imagined the trees uprooting themselves, sprouting legs as they chased them through the forest, their long bony branches clawing at the air in their desperate attempt to catch them. And when the trees caught up with them, they would slowly squeeze the life out of them and every drop of blood as they twisted their bodies into knots so they looked like the trees in the Twisted Forest.

Sorrow further imagined some of the trees as witches, white witches, or white women, a highland myth of women, drinking the blood of men after inviting them for a dance, a dance of death, women who wore long green dresses to hide their deformed feet. As they say, the devil is in the detail. Sorrow was imagining the devil had gotten into every tree in the Twisted Forest.

'All trees move. It's probably the wind, as clearly some things put the wind up you,' Poe scoffed half-heartedly, as he wasn't sure who he was trying to convince, Sorrow or himself, that this was indeed the truth of the matter.

'Look, that tree is a good foot closer to us than it was a minute ago,' Sorrow said insistently. Poe was half expecting Sorrow to get out her tape measure then set up an instrument for mapping landscapes, just to show Poe she wasn't imagining things. It was clear to Poe that what was needed here wasn't an instrument for measuring landscapes but one to measure imaginescapes.

'It's-it's like the spirit of Edgar Allen Poe has gotten into the forest. It's his story *The Pit and the Pendulum*, the walls of the forest closing in on us!' stammered Poe, now not quite so enamoured with his kaleidoscopic mind as he had been before, for it was clearly lying to him, distorting the truth. Sorrow and Poe now stood rooted to the spot, just like a tree, unable to move a muscle. Another fairy tale (lie), for the trees could move even if their gait was a little stiff, unsurprisingly, as most of the trees in the forest were over a hundred years of age.

The tables were turned, for it was now Poe and Sorrow that were rooted to the spot. Within seconds, Poe and Sorrow were surrounded by the trees, who were giving them the evil eye as faces with wicked grins appeared out of their trunks. Poe and Sorrow closed their eyes, sure it was just a matter of time before they were crushed to death by the trees. Then the trees stopped dead in their tracks and, like Sorrow and Poe, were now frozen to the spot as once again the forest did a quick costume change.

'The trees are frozen. The forest is now covered in ice and snow. It's changed from summer to winter in the blinking of an eye,' gasped Poe, who had felt compelled to open his eyes, even if it meant seeing the glee in the eyes of his attackers as they slowly squeezed the life out of him. Poe was not sure if he should be relieved or not, for now he was shivering and feared that if he and Sorrow were frozen to the spot for much longer, they would both freeze to death. Unlike the trees, who would survive to live another day for they, with their thick protective coats, were made to withstand extreme conditions.

'Yes, an evil eye at that. The forest is playing games with us, toying with us like trees in a model village. If we don't get out of here soon, we will freeze to death I-I already feel like I am turning into an ice sculpture,' Sorrow stuttered, as a jet of cold air streamed out of her mouth, her lips beginning to turn blue with the cold.

'I-I feel like Jack, Jack Frost, and just for-for the record, I'm not all right, Jack, and you can forget the-the giant in the fairy tale *Jack and the Beanstalk*,' stuttered Poe, his teeth chattering like a set of chattering false teeth in a joke shop.

It wasn't long before Poe and Sorrow were unable to speak. Encased within a statue of ice, it seemed here their journey was to end, and end in a nightmare.

12

Beast and the Beauty

Two voices then broke the silence. The first was the voice of a man, for the voice was deep and gruff, as if the man ate gravel for breakfast, all washed down with a pint of turpentine. The other voice was that of a young girl, her voice sweet and as pure as the driven snow. Had Snow White jumped out of the storybook into the real world, for that was what Sorrow was imagining? Poe was imagining this was not Snow White but her evil twin Snow Black. And the gruff voice belonged to one of the three bears from Goldilocks' fairy life story, probably Daddy Bear, with a sore head by the sounds of it.

'Over there, in between that circle of trees, I think I can see two people,' the girl cried, quickening her gait.

'Yes, I see them,' the bear of a man replied, not far behind her.

'You may have to use some of that forest magic of yours, Raspy,' the girl cried, as the crackling of twigs underfoot got louder and louder as the two figures approached. Sorrow and Poe could hear every word, but they could no longer hear their own hearts beat, as they feared they too had turned to ice. People often accused Sorrow of being an ice maiden, like the one in Hans Christian Andersen's tale of the same name, or the Snow Queen from Hans Christian Andersen's fairy tale, icy cool, as if ice was flowing through her veins, her blood as blue as a glacier, superior to everybody else around her, as if she was looking down her long white pointy nose at them. So much so, she sometimes imagined she lived in an ice palace, one built by Iv-Anna the Terrible. The ice palace made of blocks of ice and built upon the Neva River had furniture, a bed and even chandeliers made of ice. The palace sounded as if it should be in a fairy tale. The truth was, it had actually been built for a forced marriage between an ugly maiden and a prince. The couple were told that if they were to survive the honeymoon night in the freezing palace, they would have to make love on the bed of ice. If that wasn't a nightmare, Sorrow did not know what was.

Of course, this was not the case. Perceptions of people were often wrong, especially first impressions. Crippling shyness could often make a person appear distant or aloof when the truth was that they were just uncomfortable around others, often more comfortable in their own skin. Some of these people suffered with autism, Asperger's syndrome.

'All they need is some good old-fashioned body warmth,' the big bear of a man named Raspy growled, picking Sorrow and Poe up as if he was a giant, uprooting trees from the ground. The truth was, the man was a giant of a man, like a brown grizzly bear, in fact, as he was wearing bearskins. When Sorrow first saw the man mountain, she thought he was a grizzly bear and the forest had turned from the Petrified Forest into a forest in New England, or the Rocky Mountains, or the territory known as New Finland in the Arctic Circle.

'R-Rasputin?' Poe stuttered, turning from the colour blue to red then back to the non-colour white, so much so that Rasputin imagined Poe to be an albino, or perhaps a ghost from the spirit world. Rasputin looked at Poe with curiosity, not sure if the boy was simply frozen stiff or was wearing a death mask.

'Are you still alive? You both look as if you've seen a ghost. More than one, in fact.' Rasputin laughed heartily, slapping Poe on the back with one hand and Sorrow with the other hand, helping to restore them to rude health, as the old expression went.

'I-I think we are both still alive, just.' Sorrow coughed, rubbing her hands, icy cold hands, together to warm herself up.

'My name's Anastasia and this is my friend Rasputin,' the girl named Anastasia said politely.

'B-but you're dead, you were poisoned, shot, beaten over the head, drowned,' Poe stuttered, unable to believe his bloodshot eyes or his senses. Poe imagined this girl to be an ice sculpture as her skin was so translucent, brought to life by a tree witch, one with a finger like an ice pick, one she would use to pick the lock of Poe's icy heart. And if this ice princess failed to unlock his heart, then she would simply stick her icy finger through it, and in doing so, the icicle would snap off, thus lodging itself in his heart, turning it as black as a shrivelled prune.

'Dead! I might be dead tired, dead on my feet from traipsing through the snow, through this endless forest, but I can assure you I am very much alive!' Rasputin laughed, beating his chest like a gorilla as a great jet of hot air shot out of his mouth as if he was a fire-eater, hot air which appeared to warm Sorrow and Poe up.

'We faked our own deaths. It was the only way to get out of the Russian Revolution alive, I'm afraid,' Anastasia said, as a pear- shaped teardrop slowly rolled down her pale cheek, almost turning to ice as it did so. 'I'm afraid my family did not escape, nor did the brave souls that offered to play the part of myself and Gregory, doubles, almost the splitting image of us, so like us, in fact, that they even fooled our own friends and family. For years, our doubles lived with us in secret, hiding in the cellar or the attic whenever anybody came calling, learning all our ways and habits. It was like looking in the mirror, a dark mirror, I admit, a looking glass that in the end cracked like ice on a pond, a mirror pond.'

'There, there, child. Waste no tears on the dead. It's the living we must save our tears for. The dead are in a better place. I fear hell may be a better place than here, for there at least it would be warm. I'm sure the devil would welcome me in with open arms.' Rasputin smiled as he rested his large hairy hand upon the slender shoulder of Princess Anastasia.

Sorrow could not help comparing Anastasia and Rasputin to the characters in the fairy tale *Beauty and the Beast*. And, like in the fairy tale, the beast had a heart, and not a black heart as some had said. Historians had painted Rasputin into a dark corner that he hadn't a hope of getting out of, although it appeared the mad monk, as he was known, had one more trick up his sleeve, the Lazarus trick, coming back from the dead. Rasputin had escaped with Anastasia and disappeared into the mists of time. What better place to hide than in the cracks and shadows of history? According to historians, the only survivor of the Bolsheviks' massacre of the Romanov family in 1918 was Alexi's pet spaniel named Joy.

Was this fanciful dark fairy tale such a hard story to believe, Rasputin and Anastasia frozen in time like two woolly mammoths? It wasn't impossible; nothing was impossible. That was the mantra of all quantum physicists. Russia and Finland were within spitting distance of one another, and you could easily disappear into the giant forest that was Finland.

If Princess Anastasia and Rasputin had somehow escaped from Russia, the Winter Palace, the House of Romanov and the Yellow House, where the Romanov family had been assassinated during the Russian Revolution. Princess Anastasia and Rasputin may have crossed the border into Finland, entered this house, the attic or the space that the house was built in. If so, in theory, they could have entered another dimension, for many people had suggested there were such doorways and places on earth, even if to most these tales seemed far-fetched. It wasn't stretching the imagination at all to believe in such weird and wonderful happenings. After all, the weirdest and most wonderful happening of all was the universe. Life, our earth and everything else paled in comparison to the grandest design of them all: the cosmos.

13

The Forest of Fire and Ice – Part 1

'What on earth is that?' Anastasia cried, holding her hands up to stop the light blinding her.

'It's not from this earth. It looks like a giant ball of ice, one that's on fire,' Rasputin replied, protecting the princess by shielding her with his giant frame.

'It's history repeating itself again, the Tunguska Event!' Poe exclaimed, for in his head Poe had matched up the flaming fireball that tore through the forest with a black and white image he had seen in an old book, a book he had found in the attic. The book was entitled *The Tunguska Event*, an event which had happened back in 1908. A fireball was said to have crashed into the forest, leaving it looking as if giant charcoal matchsticks were sticking out of the ground. There were many stories of what actually had occurred; some believed it was a

UFO, a flying saucer that had crashed in the forest. Scientists told a different story of this famous event in history, saying it was a fireball which had exploded just above the canopy of the forest, causing a forest fire to sweep through the forest.

'Yes, I think Poe could be right. I saw the book in the attic space when I was looking for Poe,' Sorrow said, and as the words left her mouth, for a brief moment, the attic appeared to them, at least the walls and the floor. The ceiling had a giant gaping hole in it where the asteroid had torn through it. Poe could see the stars as clear as day, and the moon a crescent moon as a shower of shooting stars fell from the sky, creating a celestial fireworks display. The vision did not last long, that and the fire in the forest burnt so brightly that night had turned into day. However, this day light was soon extinguished, as day turned back to night, a giant black cloud of smoke covering the forest like a giant vampire's cloak. At least this was what Poe and Sorrow were now both imagining.

Poe could hardly believe his eyes, for just above his head there was a vortex spinning like a spiral galaxy, as a blast of blinding light shot out of it like a giant solar flare. Poe imagined this to be one of the many dimensions that quantum physicists said were spinning unseen above our heads. Except this one could be seen. A blinding flash of light forced Poe and Sorrow to draw back and cover their eyes. Out of the vortex came what appeared to be two ancient flying machines piloted by two ancient Argonauts, which flew out of the vortex and into the forest.

It soon became clear that Poe had not quite imagined this correctly, so he was forced to re-imagine this extraordinary happening. One of the pilots of the flying machines was the wicked prince from the fairy tale by Hans Christian Andersen, and the other was King Ludwig II, otherwise known as the dream king. Poe could only re-imagine that two worlds had collided; the wicked prince from a dark fairy-tale world of nightmarish happenings had collided with King Ludwig II from the dream world. This had caused a third world to be created out of this chaos. However, the world was too unstable due to a dream and a nightmare being incompatible. The two characters, one real and one fictional, had been expelled from that world into this world. It appeared that Edgar Allen Poe's dream within a dream theory wasn't such a kooky theory after all, or at least not if one twisted the theory, say, someone with a kaleidoscope mind.

The two flying machines chased one another through the forest, the wicked prince firing bullets from the peacock eyes that were painted onto the sides of the flying machines. The flying machine driven by the wicked prince was being pulled by fifty vultures and a murder of crows, a twist in itself, for the machine was normally pulled by eagles. The dream king's flying machine was being pulled by seven magnificent giant white swans with orange beaks and seven black swans with red beaks. The dream king was sure he was having a bad dream, but so used to flying in his dreams was he that he had no trouble flying his machine skilfully between the trees, avoiding crashing into them by a hare's breath. 'Give me more power. I must have more power if I am to win this death race!' cried the wicked prince to his shadow crew. In truth, his crew thought the prince had more than enough power already. However, the prince was the sort of man who always wanted more. He was never satisfied and thus never happy.

'You're flying like a dream, my beauties, keep it up!' cried the dream king, trying not to imagine this was a nightmare, for if he did then the dream would turn bad as he and his beloved swans fell into a nightmare. If that happened, the king would turn into a giant swan and defy the rules of the nightmare by breaking through the fabric of the bad dream into the real world. One of his many monikers was the Swan King, so this was not another case of wishful thinking on the king's part. Unfortunately for the king, the real world was often like a waking nightmare, having to deal with his courtiers and his unruly kingdom. The king was a man who liked to live in a world of his own, living in his fairy-tale castle built on the very top of a mountain. There he was at his happiest, but the dark clouds were circling, as were his enemies, determined to have him certified as mad so they could take his crown away from him.

Suddenly a crowd of people appeared out of the forest, cheering wildly, and it soon became clear they were characters out of a fairy tale. Little Red Riding Hood, the Little Match Girl, Big and Little Claus stood side by side with the likes of Rumpelstiltskin, the Snow Queen and the Big Bad Wolf, without any hint of bad blood.

The death race continued at a pace until on the third circuit of the forest, the death race suddenly came to an abrupt halt as the two flying machines crashed into one another and burst into flames. Now it looked as if two fireballs had entwined and become one great giant fireball, twisted machinery meshed together. The terrible sound of scraping metal on metal filled the air. A billowing, twisted plume of black smoke trailed behind the flying machines like a giant windsock. Molten metal began to drip from the red sky, which turned into a blood-red sunset.

Eventually, the king and the wicked prince and his crew of shadowy figures emerged from the burning wrecks, their faces as black as coal. The wicked prince's shadow army marched through the trees, following the prince, who as usual was marching to the beat of his own drum.

The shadows were like ghosts as they disappeared through the trunks of the trees as if they were not there, and as they did so, the trees died. The forest turned from green to black as summer turned to winter, the silver birch trees turning into Judas trees, as if the forest had died of a disease that spread throughout the forest like wildfire.

Poe and Sorrow stood watching this terrible sight, unable to speak, unable to move, as if in a nightmare, feeling compelled to watch the whole thing as it played out in front of them. The dream king then reappeared overhead in a ghostly-looking flying machine, a luminescent shell boat pulled by fourteen giant white ghostly swans. Another vortex opened in the sky, although it could just as easily have been the ceiling of the attic. The light was so bright that it was blinding, yet they were unable to turn away. It felt to Poe and Sorrow as if they were staring directly through a telescope at the sun, unable to turn away, although they knew if they did not, they would go blind. The ghostly-looking shell boat pulled by the fourteen giant ghostly swans with the dream king at the helm, who soon found himself in a death spiral he could not pull out of as he was sucked into the vortex and disappeared.

Poe and Sorrow looked at one another, shaking their heads in disbelief, as if they had just awoken half in and half out of a nightmare.

'It was probably just a bad dream, one conjured up by the Dark Energy, the forester who built this house, his evil spirit doing its worst. Come on, Poe, look, a sheep. It must have got separated from the flock, for sheep follow one another like... well, like sheep!' said Sorrow, skipping over to the sheep to stroke it, as if she imagined she were Little Bo Peep.

'You'll scare it off. You know how easily sheep get spooked.'

'I know how easily you get spooked,' Sorrow spat, ignoring Poe, who she felt was becoming a little annoying at times, picking holes in everything she did or said. It felt to Sorrow at times as if Poe was a sibling, her brother more than a friend.

All brothers and sisters fought, while also fighting the other's corner when someone picked on them.

'See, look! It's not running away. It can see I mean it no harm. I'm a friend, not a foe. Just call me the sheep whisperer,' Sorrow said, and although she was unable to smile, Poe pictured a great big grin on her face and one he was more than happy to see, for he had no desire to upset her. He just wanted to protect her, be her shield and her guide through the dark forests of life. All humans suffered at times of not being able to see the wood for the trees, and Poe had a feeling in the pit of his stomach that this was such a time. Thankfully, he did not bring the pendulum to mind from Edgar Allen Poe's dark tale of horror *The Pit and the Pendulum*. Poe saw something in the sheep's eyes, eyes that were bloodshot, eyes that were shifty, and one now shining brightly as if it was eyeing Sorrow up, but what for? Perhaps the kill, if this sheep was one of those black sheep of the family.

'Sorrow, I think you need to take a step back. Make that several steps back,' said Poe in a husky voice, as if the fear had already overtaken him. Poe tried again to warn his friend, but this time his voice came out so raspy that he wondered if Rasputin had now possessed his mind, body and spirit. It would not have come as a surprise if this had been the case as Rasputin, according to the history books, had died a century ago.

'Don't be silly. There's nothing to be afraid of,' Sorrow said, turning to Poe then turning back to the sheep, as if talking to both of them at the same time. Poe could see Sorrow was too close to the object to see things clearly. She could not see the wood for the trees, either that or her kaleidoscopic mind, like Poe's earlier, was twisting the truth.

'Oh, there is every reason to be afraid,' the sheep cried, as it threw off its sheep's clothing to reveal a large grey wolf.

'A wolf in sheep's clothing!' cried Anastasia, placing her hands over her face as if she was nothing more than a one-dimensional character from a fairy tale. But then Anastasia took everyone by surprise, even the wolf, as she picked up a branch from a silver birch tree and with all the strength she possessed hurled it at the wolf. The wolf had no choice but to leap out of the way. This gave Poe the opportunity to rush forward and pull Sorrow from harm's way. Rasputin sprang into action like an animal defending its young as he ran full tilt towards the wolf, snorting like a bull. Poe was not picturing a bull; she was picturing Rasputin as a large brown bear, and one with a sore head, or more likely a hangover if you believed everything you read in the history books, which Poe did not. This caused the wolf to turn tail and run for the hills, for through the eyes of the wolf, it must have looked as if a grizzly bear was chasing him. There was no doubt Gregory Rasputin was a great big bear of a man, dressed in bearskins and wearing a hat made from wolfskin. No wonder the wolf ran in fear of its life, for by the look in Rasputin's eye, if he had caught up with the wolf he really would have skinned him alive.

'I-I don't know what happened. My woman's instinct, my sixth sense gave me no warning of danger,' sighed Sorrow, shaking her head as she wondered if somehow her strength of mind and woman's intuition were being drained away from her by an unseen force. In truth, she was only a young woman, so her sixth sense was not as strong as it would become when she reached her prime.

'The forest has powers not even I fully understand. The Norse people believe the trees have souls and that the forest is a living entity,' said Rasputin, resting one giant hand upon Sorrow's shoulder and one upon Poe's shoulder, as if they, like Anastasia, were now his children. 'I'll tell you a little fairy tale. Once upon a time, a powerful man, Nicholas II, rode into a golden kingdom, St Petersburg, in a coach made of gold, the city that was later to become known as "The City Built on Bones". So much for Peter the Great's Dream. For most of the peasants, the dream city was built upon a thousand nightmares.

'The tsar was not on his own, for beside him in the coach was his princess, the Tsarina Alexander. Both were dressed in the finest threads and jewellery, which made the peasants look even more dowdy. In the sky, a golden sun shone down, one shaped like a giant egg which was also made of gold. The tsar's subjects, who according to the Bolsheviks had been subjected to terrible hardships, came out to greet him as if he were their saviour. The people did not see the tsar as the wicked prince in Hans Christian Andersen's dark fairy tale. As the tsar passed his subjects, he stood up and waved at the people, who threw themselves to the ground and kissed his shadow.

'Later, the landscape changed from summer to winter. The winds of change were bitter in more ways than one, and not even a giant could stop these bitter winds turning the tsar and tsarina and their children into sculptures of ice. The Romanov family were now encased within a giant winter palace made of snow and ice, their only hope that a mountain giant wielding a sword of fire and ice would appear out of the landscape to set them free.

'Sorry. That's all I've written so far. You'll just have to stop at the forest library if you want any more fairy stories,' said Rasputin, not finishing the tale, for he knew it had a terrible ending. 'So what do you think of my little tale? It had me in tears. In fact, while I was writing it, the paper was so stained with tears that I could hardly read my own writing by the end of it.' Rasputin sniffed, then a big broad smile appeared on his face. 'As you can see, I am no Hans Andersen or a Grimm Brother. I think I'll stick to cutting down trees. At least this way the storytellers of this world will have enough paper to write their tales upon. I hope they never run out of stories, and I hope the forest never runs out of trees,' Rasputin added, in one of his brief moments of contemplation, for he was more a man of action than a man of deep thought, even though as a young man he had studied at a monastery. The trouble with Rasputin was that he was impatient and felt he could learn more from life than from books, travelling as far afield as the Middle East, Constantinople and India to learn from the teachings of wise men. Upon these travels, he spun tales of his own, made predictions of future events that came true, healed the sick and quickly became thought of as a mystic, a man of magic.

Rasputin wasn't as thoughtless as some had made him out to be. Many, many stories had been written about this giant of a man. Some had made him out to be taller than a giant redwood tree and wider than a mountain, as if a god, not a mortal man made out of flesh and blood, indestructible, a superhero before superheroes had even been thought of. And perhaps in part this was true, for he was still standing, standing tall and erect, as large as life and twice as ugly, the beast to the beauty of the fairy tale princess that was Anastasia, or the wicked prince as in Hans Andersen's dark fairy tale.

Poe wondered if the forest was taking away Sorrow's powers and adding it to its own power, as it had done to all those who stepped into the forest. If this were true, it meant the power of the forest was growing while their powers were diminishing. Soon they would be powerless to stop the forest. It would overwhelm then crush them as it squeezed the very lifeblood out of them, like sap out of a tree. Poe and Sorrow were imagining just this, as their imagination ran wilder than it had ever done before.

It was Poe's belief that in life you had to have the ability to be able to see through people, like the man in the classic sci-fi B movie *The Man with the X-Ray Eyes*. For you would meet people on your journey through life who were not what they appeared to be, tricksters who were able to pull the wool over your eyes and the rug from under your feet as easily as a magician can pull the magic carpet from under you. You would encounter many wolves in sheep's clothing, and occasionally a sheep in wolf's clothing, as Sorrow had almost found to her cost. Poe and Sorrow were not the kind of people to follow others like sheep, unless they were black sheep, as they both saw themselves as the black sheep of the family.

Sorrow wanted to tell Anastasia the full story, although, as she did not know the full story, she decided it was better she did not. Even if she did tell Anastasia what she perceived as the truth, Princess Anastasia would not believe her, and what was the truth? There could be many versions of the truth, as many as there were in the history of the world. The story Poe and Sorrow were living through may well be an alternative history of life, and the universe a parallel universe. Anastasia and Rasputin may have entered another time and dimension through a door in time, or even through the door of an attic. They may all have fallen into a black hole, a vortex in time, all ending up in the same place, a magical place, or space, upon which the forester-cum-explorer felt compelled to build his wooden house. A necromancer, an evil spirit who could talk and conjure up the dead, could be the man pulling the strings in this world. Or alternately the forest itself, for that too was within the circle, one that time and space seemed to ripple through like quicksilver upon a lake of mercury.

The House of Horrors held many horrors but no more than the House of Horrors the Romanov family had been murdered in.

Poe had no desire to confront Rasputin with the truth, not that he thought Rasputin couldn't handle the truth. He could clearly handle most things, even royalty and those within its circle. Poe was more concerned with Rasputin's fearsome reputation for having a quick and fiery temper; he might take Poe as a jester, trying to make him look a fool. Or Rasputin may think he had finally gone mad, living up to his nickname the Mad Monk. The more likely tale from a whole host of unlikely tales was that Rasputin may well think Poe was mad and had escaped from a lunatic asylum nearby, perhaps one on the edge of the forest. The lunatics were taking over the asylum, or taking over the forest if the asylum was in the heart of the forest!

14

The Forest of Fire and Ice – Part 2

Suddenly Rasputin spun upon his heels in balletic fashion as, out of the corner of his eye, he saw something move. In truth, it was not easy to imagine Rasputin in the Bolshi Ballet, unless he was playing the part of a brown bear. Rasputin's senses were like those of a wild animal protecting its young. Sorrow was picturing Rasputin lifting up Anastasia as if she were a feather. Poe was imagining Rasputin as part of a group of Cossack dancers, big burly men with beards, dressed in billowy white ruffled silk shirts with a large fancy red, or purple, waistband, black trousers and black boots. The men all stood in a line with their massive arms tightly entwined around each other's shoulders, twisting and turning their bodies first to the right, then to the left and back again, before squatting down then springing up as if out of a Jack-in-the-

Box. Poe could also imagine these men as paper-cut figures, all linked together hand in hand, ones fashioned by the skilled paper artist Hans Christian Andersen.

'What is it, Gregory? What did you see?' exclaimed Anastasia, as she attempted to see through the eyes of her protector.

'I saw a shadow, I'm sure I did. The trouble is, I've been seeing shadows ever since we escaped from Russia, both real and imaginary,' sighed Rasputin, before a great big beaming smile appeared on his ruddy-looking face, for nothing could keep this giant of a man down for long. Sorrow imagined most folk would be scared of Rasputin. In fact, most folk were even scared of his great shadow, a shadow which appeared twice the size and even three times the size of the great man himself.

'I also saw the shadow!' exclaimed Poe, pointing wildly at a tree, or the shadow of a tree. For once upon a time, it wasn't Poe's imagination running wild, as a shadow stepped from behind the tree and out of the shadows. At first, it looked as if this figure did not have a body, a shadow of its former self, one Poe pictured as the character the Shadow out of Hans Andersen's fairy tale.

It soon became clear this was not quite the truth according to Poe, for the shadow spoke, although, unlike Rasputin, Poe sensed it would not speak its mind, for this shadow was used to being in the shadows and found the harsh light hurt the eyes. A young man stepped out of the shadows as if his shadow had been protecting him. In truth, Poe felt both the fire of the giant's breath and the icy cold stare he was giving him, which made it feel as if he had an ice pick sticking in his heart. But faint heart never won fair lady, either in or out of the dark fairy-tale winter wonderland that was Russia. It was time, time to step out of the safety of those shadows as the young man spoke as if he wasn't even sure of his own name. 'My-my name is-is Ivan—' the figure stammered hesitantly.

But before the young man could spit whatever he wanted to spit out, he was cut short as Rasputin spat, 'Let me stop you right there, for if your surname is Terrible then may I suggest you turn right around and disappear back into the shadows and never darken our doorstep again!'

'My-my name is Ivan VI, Tsar Ivan VI,' the young man stuttered nervously, clearly not sure of the reaction this statement of fact would bring. The fact that he was not Ivan the Terrible should at least buy him some time, or so he hoped. Rasputin was thinking this was not a statement of fact but a fairy tale, in other words, a lie he had in mind, Hans Andersen's tale of the wicked prince, whose only thought was how to conquer all the nations on earth and make his name a terror to all mankind. Rasputin imagined this was a trap to find another member of the Romanov family tree in this dark neck of the woods, another lost soul. The odds were a million to one. Ivan was not in the same league of terrible gentlemen as Ivan the Terrible. Ivan VI was born a prisoner and died a prisoner, as if his own mind and body were a prison. Being born in the time Ivan was born meant he was a marked man from his first breath. Ivan may not have been terrible but he did have a terrible life and a terrible death. The young man was put to the sword when he was only seventeen, the same age as Sorrow and Poe were now. This was after a rescue attempt and coup failed to free Ivan from his prison cell.

Sorrow knew the history of this poor, unfortunate young man, who was certainly not poor in monetary terms, for he came from the Romanov Dynasty. This meant young Ivan would inherit a large fortune when he grew up, but he never enjoyed the lavish lifestyle and comforts that most others in the Romanov dynasty enjoyed. Ivan never got the chance to grow up in the palatial surroundings of the Winter Palace. In truth, it was as if the poor boy lived all his life in winter, such were his awful surroundings, those of a dark, dank prison cell. Ivan's own change in circumstances was changing one prison cell for another. As some writers of a poetic nature wrote, the poor boy swapped a gilded birdcage for one made of iron, as the iron fist of the Russian Royal Family. The Romanovs crushed his mind, body and spirit as if the boy were indeed a bird but one that was made of paper. Sorrow had always imagined Ivan as a fragile bird in a cage, as in the simple Victorian magic trick made with paper of the bird in and out of the cage. The bird had flown its spirit now, flying free, or so Sorrow imagined, and such was the poor boy's life that she was sure in the end he must have been glad to have been released from the birdcage made of iron. Being released from the dark prison of his mind and his emaciated body, Ivan's spirit was finally released to fly wherever it wished.

It was hard to believe how cruel man could be to his fellow man. Perhaps that was why the forester, the man who built the house, was so cruel. During his lifetime, the forester had been treated cruelly; it was as if the forester, who clearly had a mirror-like mind like Poe and Sorrow, was now turning that mind on others. He was holding a mirror up to society, holding society and those in it to account for the way he had been treated.

Sorrow and Poe had both been treated badly by society and the people in it because they were different and they were Jewish, which to some made them even more of a target. Sorrow knew that Alexander III of the Romanov family was said to have had Anti-Semitic views. Poe and Sorrow hoped these bad experiences in life did not twist their minds to the point where they in turn treated others badly, which was sometimes the case. One would have imagined that if somebody had been treated badly by their parents, the very last thing they would do is treat their children badly. Sadly, this was not always the case. It was a sad reflection of our society that anyone who was different was treated differently, and for the most part that meant being treated badly.

While imprisoned in the forest, Sorrow and Poe had time to think, time to reflect on their lot, and both were of the same mind, that there was no danger that the forest or the forester would kill them with kindness.

Standing before them was the young man named Ivan, who, it appeared, had escaped from his prison and his jailers, as had Anastasia and Rasputin. Rasputin believed he was indestructible but was not sure that this frail, thin-looking boy was strong enough to have escaped a prison. It was an unlikely story, even more unlikely than Rasputin's own dark fairy life story. In truth, Rasputin's story was more like a tall story than a fairy story.

'The lost tsar, is that who you are claiming to be?' Rasputin barked, challenging the figure calling himself Ivan IV as he stood with legs apart, hands on hips. The imposing figure of Rasputin, who towered over most men, would have anybody in their right mind trembling in their boots. The figure that had come out of the shadows was but a mere slip of a man, almost boyish in his appearance despite his dirty face and dishevelled appearance. In truth, the young man was so paper-thin that it really was as if he were made of paper, a silhouette, a black silhouette, a shadow of a man. Sorrow imagined the bird cage with the shadow of a bird in it, or the shadow of death, or a dark angel as she pulled the string that made the bird disappear then reappear in the cage, or at least the one pictured in her mind.

'I-I am who I say I am,' stuttered Ivan, as he nervously took a step forward when he felt like taking three steps back. This would have taken him back into the shadows, the protection of the forest and back into history. Ivan had fallen through the cracks, not so much in society, as the old expression went, but through the cracks in history. The more time passed, the more cracks appeared in that history. Sorrow and Poe were imagining history rewriting itself right before their very eyes, a clever conjuring trick from the puppet master standing in the shadows, rewriting his story and the history of all the many puppets he had dangling on a string. Sorrow, upon hearing the young man's name, imagined that this Ivan may be the young guard Ivan Skorokhodov at the Yellow House, who was smitten with Maria Romanova. Ivan was caught by other guards in a compromising position with Maria and was dismissed and sent to prison.

Poe hoped this shadow of a man, whoever he was, had performed the same trick that the shadowy character the Shadow had done in Hans Christian Andersen's tale of the same name. The Shadow had taken the place of the man, and it was the man who was now languishing in prison as the Shadow had taken on his appearance, taking over his life, even dressing in his clothes.

'So, we have the lost girl and the lost tsar. We should clear the forest and have ourselves a fairy-tale wedding. What do you say, Anastasia? Is this the lost prince? Not a match made in heaven if he turns out to be the wicked prince from Hans Christian Andersen's dark fairy tale, or worse still Ivan the Terrible, a worse character than I!' Rasputin laughed, not far shy of laughing himself to death.

Poe pictured a babe in arms in his cot armed to the teeth, for it was written that when Ivan VI was born, a babe in arms had inherited the throne. Ivan became a puppet from the day he was born, powerful puppeteers all fighting over him to as who should pull his strings. One puppet master snatched the puppet from another's hands, who snatched it back, as a tug of war over the puppet tsar raged. Eventually, the puppet was pulled apart limb from limb as its limbs lay strewn upon the floor like the leftover parts of a doll in a toy factory.

Poe had imagined all this in the blinking of an eye as his mind put various images together, cutting and splicing them up until they fitted together. Poe did this by using the information and pictures he had stored in the library in the attic of his mind of Ivan VI, then his imagination went to work. Or should that be working overtime like a manic storyteller, editor or producer of a film, until he was happy with the end product? It was all a little rough and ready, rough around the edges, it has to be said, like Gregory Rasputin himself, but it would do in the meantime. Later, Poe would edit these ideas, whipping them into shape for his journal, his dream journal. For, after all, when all was said and done, all this was simply a dream, a bad dream wrapped inside a dark fairy tale, Poe Black's mind up to its old tricks again, blurring the fantasy world with the real world as folk who suffered from the neurological condition aphantasia did.

15

One Last Fairy Tale for Old Times' Sake

In the blinking of an eye, everything changed from winter to summer, like in a time-lapse nature documentary, or so it appeared to Poe and Sorrow. However, as Poe and Sorrow were quickly beginning to realise, appearances can be deceptive. In truth, being the people they were, different, they were already well aware of this.

'What happened to winter? Not that I want to say goodbye to it. Good riddance to bad rubbish. I'll-I'll be glad to see the back of winter; chillblains, frostbite, chapped lips, colds, flu, and that's just the tip of the iceberg,' stuttered Poe, his teeth still chattering. That was despite the warmth of the sun upon his face. It was as if his mind still pictured the forest in winter. 'Perhaps the gods Summer and Winter fought out a bloody battle, Summer putting Winter to the sword, using its powerful heat rays to pierce Winter's thick, white icy coat of amour,' Poe added, as he imagined Mother Nature tearing a tapestry of winter and summer in two with her bare hands.

'Never mind what happened to winter. What happened to spring and what happened to Anastasia and Rasputin?' exclaimed Sorrow, looking all about her to see they were nowhere to be seen; they had disappeared like the snow. Sorrow had always loved snowflakes; they were unique as was she, but not all snowflakes were beautiful works of art. Some of the patterns thrown up by Mother Nature's whirlwind approach to sharpening the landscape were misshapen. However, the snowflakes still had a beauty, the beauty of imperfection, the beauty being in the eye of the beholder.

Sorrow missed the Beauty, Princess Anastasia, but she did not miss the Beast, Gregory Rasputin, even though he wasn't the devil some had made him out to be. Anastasia was indeed a beauty, a princess from a fairy tale, dressed all in white lace with the pale complexion of an English rose. At times, Anastasia looked more like a ghost than a girl made of flesh and blood, so white was she, made even more ghost-like by the floaty cream and white-coloured lace dress she wore. Anastasia was one of Sorrow's heroines, and she was just getting to know the girl rather than the myth Anastasia had become over time. The lost girl trapped in a royal bubble made of frosted glass, the sort one may have seen if they looked through the window of one of Queen Victoria's palaces hanging from a Christmas tree, so tall that it almost touched the ceiling. Sorrow could certainly picture Anastasia as a snowflake, as she could imagine Anastasia wearing a dress made of snowflakes, or if you want the truth over the fairy tale, a white lace dress designed in the pattern of a snowflake.

'We should go back and look for them,' urged Sorrow, insistently turning back in the hope of catching a glimpse of the illusive ghostly figure of Anastasia, followed by a giant brown bear on a long silver chain. In truth, Poe was picturing Anastasia with a silver chain around her pretty little neck as a bear led her away into the forest of silver birch trees. Chains, even ones made of silver or gold, were still chains if they tied you to someone or something you wished to be free of. Sorrow knew of the history of the Royal family the world over; in Denmark, Germany, Holland, England and Russia. She also knew the princesses and princes were puppets hanging from silver and gold chains being worked by royal puppeteers, the puppet master being the kings and queens of these powerful royal families.

'Excuse me, we are lost. Could you tell us where we are?' Poe asked, as an old lady appeared out of the wooden door of a thatched cottage on the edge of the forest. But Poe was not imagining the house as a thatched cottage; he was imagining it as a giant wooden Russian doll. Poe then refocused the kaleidoscope in his mind as the giant Russian doll transformed into a dolls' house, one belonging to the child of a giant. Sorrow, on the other hand, was imagining the cottage as a giant bejewelled blue oval egg, a Fabergé egg on hinges, the top of the egg, or roof, lifted off, for when it was stiflingly hot in the summer months, the egg turned into a summer house.

'Why, of course. It's nice to see young folk. It reminds me of when I was young,' the old woman replied in a Russian accent, welcoming these strangers into her world with open arms.

'It's like looking in an old mirror, a bowed mirror,' whispered Sorrow, not entirely making sense, as she turned from the old lady to Poe with a look on her face of both wonderment and surprise.

'She does look familiar, but I can't picture where I have seen her face before,' hissed Poe out of the corner of his mouth, as he screwed up his face, as if trying to bring the face and the name to mind. It appeared that Poe needed to stoke the steam-powered search engine in his head, as clearly it was only working half steam ahead.

'I can. I think, I think it's Anastasia, Anastasia Romanov,' Sorrow replied, her eyes as wide as those of the Big Bad Wolf when he first came across Little Red Riding Hood.

'But she's an old woman,' Poe retorted, not even bothering to suspend his disbelief, as all characters in wonder tales were asked to do from very early on in the storybook.

'It's in the eyes, look into her eyes,' hissed Sorrow insistently, digging Poe in the ribs.

'I'm not sure I want to. I'm beginning to picture her as the Big Bad Wolf, with teeth as sharp as broken glass. She appears almost too welcoming. I'm sure I can smell something burning.' Poe grimaced, picturing the old woman first as a wolf in sheep's clothing, and then the old witch out of the Hansel and Gretel story, for she baked children in the oven.

'If this is Anastasia, the older version, then perhaps we have also turned from young people to old folk in the blinking of an eye,' Poe replied, looking at his hand, hoping he hadn't got old hands that resembled the bark of an old tree or a cracked leaf in winter, or worse, a neck like an old turkey.

'Well, I'm still young and pretty as a picture of... *The Scream*. It's true I could do with some more white make-up. I do look a little pale. But I'm not at death's door yet, unless this really is the Hansel and Gretel story,' laughed Sorrow, bending down and peering at her reflection in a pond in the front garden, although a smile still did not appear on her face.

'Yes, me too. Not quite the picture of health, more the pallid looks of Dorian Gray before he became old and grey,' Poe replied, breathing a huge sigh of relief.

The cottage was fairy tale-like, old-worldly, and one he could easily picture in a book of fairy tales. It was funny how the cottage appeared to pop up out of nowhere, as if it were a giant pop-up book. Perhaps this forest was full of giants; after all, giants must have children, and children must have books, pop-up books! Poe was wondering if this was a fairy tale or a fairy tale. In other words, a fairy-tale story of a princess trapped in time and space, a magical space, an enchanted forest. Alternatively, it was a fairy tale as in a lie, and this enchanted forest was, in fact, the Disenchanted Forest, masquerading as an enchanted forest, as the forest was indeed a master of many disguises. The forest seemed to have the ability to get inside the mind and consciousness of everything in the forest; trees, animals and humans alike.

Once inside the mind, it was able to deceive the mind's eye, or so Poe was thinking, not sure if this was indeed the case or just a case of his own mind twisting things. Perhaps the forest was a living entity, a changeling that could twist and untwist itself into any form it liked, changing from a small wooded area to a vast forest then into a rainforest or a swamp.

Poe's mind started to do what it always did: twist things until they no longer bore any resemblance whatsoever to the original object he had been looking at. At times, you could be too close to an object and thus could not see the wood for the trees. At other times, you were so far away from the object that it was as if you were looking in the wrong end of the telescope. This made the object look like a model. When the mind did not have the full story, like a storyteller, it made the rest up using past life experiences, including stories fed into the brain over many years.

'You are in the Black Forest,' the old woman replied, smiling warmly, yes, too warmly for Poe's liking. It was as if she was already picturing Poe and Sorrow baking nicely in an oven, then taking them out and laying them on the table like giant gingerbread men, both burnt to a crisp.

16

A Fairy Tale is a Lie in My Book

'Come in, come in, make yourselves at home,' the old woman cried, trying to tidy the place up as she hurriedly put things away.

'I think she is trying to hide something. She's spinning us some old fairy tale, well past its sell-by date. A fairy tale is a lie in my book, at least in a thesaurus under the word lie is written the word fairy tale,' Poe hissed, talking out of the corner of his mouth, which made it appear as if he had a facial disfigurement to match the one Sorrow was born with.

'I agree she has got a secret and I think I know what it is. Try and distract her then I can nosey around,' Sorrow hissed, also talking out of the corner of her mouth. It was as if Poe and Sorrow had both turned into snakes. 'If I'm correct, her surname is Andersen. Anna Andersen, the woman that was said to have died on the 12th of February 1984, Grand Duchess Anastasia – the lost girl Anastasia. That was what most of the world thought, although some others said she was an imposter, a fake, a Polish peasant girl who imagined she was not a pauper but a princess. It was only when the bones of the Romanov family were dug up and their DNA tested that it was confirmed that Anastasia had died along with the rest of her family. Unless there is another twist in this story we do not know about. We only have half of the fairy tale in our minds, the end is still to be written.'

'Andersen... that name rings a bell,' replied Poe, looking puzzled, for he could not think where he had heard that name before.

'Of course, it could be Eugenie Smith, the Polish woman who claimed she was Anastasia,' Sorrow added, picturing the two women, one mirroring the other, or perhaps as they were, older, in a bowed mirror, one covered in dark cobwebs.

'What are you two whispering about? You're as thick as thieves. I hope you're not thieves come to steal my life savings. If you are, you're out of luck. They were stolen years ago,' sighed the old woman, although clearly from her tone she did not mean that her life savings were stolen but her life. The old woman then stumbled over a broom and nearly fell over. Poe, playing the part of her knight in shining armour, rushed to her aid, steadying her and pulling up a wooden chair for the old lady to sit upon.

'My knight in shining armour.' The old woman smiled, blushing a little as she brushed her long silver hair with a silver hairbrush. 'I hope you're not a black knight.' She smiled, although her smile resembled a grimace, but the twinkle in her eyes was still there.

'Why don't we go into the sitting room? It's more comfortable, more homely than the kitchen. Oh, sorry, how rude of me. Where are my manners? I haven't introduced myself. My name's Babushka, or at least that is what the faeries at the bottom of my garden call me, although I suppose the bottom of my garden is a forest. My real name is Anna.' The old woman smiled as she stood up, as Poe helped her walk shakily into the sitting room. Poe was relieved to be leaving the kitchen and the old stove oven. The further away he could get from the kitchen, the better. The Hansel and Gretel story had always given him nightmares.

Well, that was obviously a fairy tale, a lie. Poe wondered how many other lies this sheep in wolf's clothing would spin him on the spinning wheel in her mind. Poe was picturing the old woman as a cross between the Big Bad Wolf out of the fairy tale and the sheep dressed in old woman's clothing from the wonder tale *Alice Through the Looking Glass*. Perhaps, being so old, she could no longer tell the difference between a truth, a half-truth and a fairy-tale lie. Poe knew he shouldn't be so judgemental, for after all he was having great difficulty telling the difference between a dream and a daydream, a nightmare from a waking nightmare. Poe's mind was spinning one way; the old woman's mind the other, one clockwise, the other anticlockwise. The question was, which mind was spinning which way? It was like the theoretical physics thought experiment of two twined atoms spinning millions of miles apart, one atom spinning clockwise, the other anticlockwise. Was it possible for two twins to be the polar opposite? Yes, quite possible. Anything was possible in this weird and wonderful universe, even the impossible.

'Yes, good idea,' said Sorrow, pretending to follow but then hanging back, which gave her a chance to look through the kitchen drawers and cabinets in the kitchen. Sorrow could not believe the woman's name was Anna, now surer than ever that this was the woman who claimed to be Anastasia the lost princess. But then a darker thought struck her, like a blow to the back of the head. Could this old woman be Empress Anna, the second woman to rule Russia, who was said to have a cruel streak in her? Some had nicknamed her Iv-Anna the Terrible, as if she were the twin of Ivan the Terrible. Sorrow's mind was racing; she had to concentrate on the here and now. The history lesson\fairy tale could wait. Sorrow was sure the old woman had stuffed a silver frame into one of the drawers when they had first entered the house. It didn't take long before Sorrow came across a photograph, sepia in a silver frame. Holding it up to the light, she was amazed to see it was a photo of the Romanov family. Sorrow was more convinced than ever that this old woman was Anastasia, all grown up. In truth, the old woman may just have admired the Romanov family. Anastasia may have been one of her heroines.

The old woman could have played the part of Anastasia, inhabiting her character like an actress does in preparing for a role, and doing it so thoroughly that eventually she began to believe she was Anastasia. The woman even had fake pictures of the Romanov family, or perhaps the picture was not faked. Perhaps she had bought it at auction? Perhaps dementia was the reason she believed herself to be Anastasia?

Was it possible that Anastasia and Maria had escaped the nightmare with the help of one young guard named Ivan Skorokhodov, he who had taken a shine to Maria, even smuggling a birthday cake into Ipatiev House, as was said to have happened? After all, many men and women have died for love, risking their lives simply to be with the one they love, more than life itself. And there was nothing more powerful than young love.

Anastasia, said to have been the last one to die in the massacre, was said to have given out such a heart-wrenching cry before she was killed that some of the soldiers wanted to spare her life. Perhaps they did. Given the fact most of the soldiers were drunk on vodka when they carried out the assassination, it was a wonder they didn't shoot one another. Another strange but true fact was that the children had sewn diamonds into their underwear, which acted like a bulletproof vest, diamonds they intended to sell when they escaped this nightmare. It was said that many bullets bounced off Anastasia, as if she truly were bulletproof. In the end, the commander Yakov Yurovsky was said to have shot her in the head. The rest of the details on the assassination were so gruesome that Sorrow had understandably blanked them from her mind.

But what about the bones found in an unmarked grave of her and her entire family? What if Anastasia had escaped, got married, had children? Would they want to be thrust into the public eye, especially given what their ancestors had gone through? Could it be that the Romanov family still had some friends in high places and were able to pull some strings, the pathologist asked to fake evidence so Anastasia and her children could live out the rest of their lives in peace? It seemed like a highly unlikely story but given the nature of cover-ups over the years, perhaps not as unlikely as it may sound.

Sorrow rifled through a few more drawers with a growing sense of excitement at what else the old woman was hiding, but she could find nothing there, other than some silver cutlery and an embroidered napkin. Sorrow lifted the napkin and underneath it she found an egg, a hen's egg. That was funny, keeping a hen's egg in a cutlery drawer. Perhaps Anna had picked it up from a henhouse, the hen had died and, because it was winter, she had put it in the drawer. Later, she had wrapped the egg in a napkin, hoping it would one day hatch and, hey presto, as if by the magic of nature fluffy chicks would appear.

The more likely dark fairy tale was that the old woman was fast losing her mind, dementia cobwebs of the mind, bats in the attic as some of a less sensitive nature describe old age. Sorrow looked more closely at the egg. It wasn't a hen's egg; it was a Fabergé egg made to look like a hen's egg. The egg could be described as a gold hen dotted with rose-cut diamonds, picking a sapphire pendant out of a jewelled basket. This was a gift to the Empress from her husband, Alexander III. Sorrow knew enough about Fabergé eggs, due to her love of the Romanov family, to know a Fabergé egg when she saw one. This Fabergé egg was scratched and some of the diamonds were missing and the paint faded, but it was definitely a Fabergé, a miniature masterpiece and not a fake. Apparently, in 1922, the hen's egg was taken to the Sovnarkom Salesroom in Russia, and there the hen was separated from the egg and, like several other Fabergé eggs during the Russian Revolution, was lost to the mists of time.

Sorrow carefully picked the egg up and placed it on the palm of her hand, so gently that it was as if she really believed there was a chick in the hen's egg. Then she caught sight of something out of the corner of her eye; it was a shadow, or two shadows, like a double negative on an undeveloped roll of film. Sorrow felt as if something evil was watching her every move. Perhaps this was the infamous Evil Eye, or Eyes in this case. But shadows could do no harm. After all, they were just shadows. Of course, it wasn't the shadow you had to worry about but the persons or persons unknown that were casting those shadows.

'You must be hungry now. I feel a little better. The cobwebs covering my eyes have melted away like the early-morning mist. You must have the magic in you. Forest children are born with forest magic in them. They carry invisible wands around with them, crafted out of the silver birch tree.' Anna smiled for it was clear she was still very much young at heart and had a twinkle in her eye. Anastasiya had been given the nickname of "Little Mischief". It was said she loved a good practical joke. Perhaps if this really was the real Anastasiya Nikolayeva Romanova, Grand Duchess of Russia, she still had that mischievous streak in her.

Don't let the birch tree goddess hear you say that. She may think you imagine these children of the forest are using the bones of her children to make wands from dark magic indeed, Poe heard a voice in his head say, but thankfully the words stayed in his head, for he did not want to give the old woman nightmares, or any more nightmares, for if this woman called Anna really was the lost girl Anastasia Romanov, then she had already had more than enough nightmares for several lifetimes. Of course, if this Anna was Empress Anna, the one who had been nicknamed Iv-Anna the Terrible, then it had been her who had given nightmares to her subjects. This was hardly the sort of gift one wants to receive: *Here, my disloyal subjects, is a nightmare for you, all wrapped up in stinging nettles and poison ivy. Don't say I don't give you anything.*

Poe did not know as much about the Russian Royal family as Sorrow did, so it did not occur to him that this may be the fearsome Empress Anna who had ruled Russia with an iron sceptre. This was understandable as Sorrow was of Russian descent and Poe of Finnish descent. Finland and Russia were hardly blood brothers. In truth, they were more like giant brothers in an armlock, or Siamese twins. Finland had always stood in the shadow of its big brother Russia.

'It's a feast for a King and a Queen, a King and Queen of the forest. In England, they call royalty of the forest the Oak Queen and the Oak King. Shakespeare named them Oberon, the King of the Fairies, and Titania, his Queen, in his play *A Midsummer Night's Dream.* If it had been set in a forest in

Russia, Titania would have been the fairy, but an old one with tatty wings like the ones I imagine I hide under my clothes,' laughed Anna as her eyes sparkled like the diamonds in the Fabergé egg she kept hidden in her cutlery drawer. Sorrow was no thief so put the egg back under the table napkin. She would keep the old woman's secret and take it to her grave if necessary.

The smile quickly faded from Anna's face as if something she had said had pricked her conscience, or her sub-conscience.

'Yes, a feast, and one a beauty and a beast could happily share,' Poe said, imagining the older woman sitting down next to an even older man who looked like an old brown bear, grey bear now, due to extreme old age. If the woman was not who she appeared to be, a changeling of the forest, the Black Forest, she may well be a wolf in sheep's clothing, a grey wolf. If this was the case, Sorrow and Poe would be the meal on the table, the meat on the bone, as the grey bear and grey wolf polished them off in double-quick time. After which they would not let their skeletons go to waste, using their bones for knitting needles and their balls and sockets as clubs. Their skulls would look good on the table as ornaments or illumination to hold candles, so the grey wolf woman and the grey bear man could read without straining their bloodshot eyes.

Poe was not imagining a feast, for his mind had twisted the meal on the table from bread, cheese and wine to poisonous toadstools, deadly nightshade, all washed down with a flagon of blood or weedkiller! Poe was so hungry that he could have eaten a unicorn. His stomach felt as if his throat had been cut; not the sort of thing one wants to think of before they sit down for a meal. It made him sick to think about it. If this meal really was an illusion, toadstools and deadly nightshade made to look like bread and cheese, it would surely make him sick. He would die a slow, agonising death! Poe imagined

the wolf woman and the bear man would enjoy sitting back in their old flea-bitten armchairs, watching Sorrow and Poe writhe around on the floor in agony.

'I've a bad feeling in the pit of my stomach,' said Poe with a grimace, under his breath, as he held his stomach tightly.

Sorrow was imagining things slightly differently as she sat at the dinner table waiting for the old lady to finish thanking the good lord for what they were about to receive.

'Thank you, that was delicious,' Poe and Sorrow cried as one, their stomachs full, their hearts even fuller.

'It's my pleasure. It's been wonderful having such lovely company. I'm just sad to let you go,' Anna said, as a tear appeared in the corner of her eye. For a moment, she looked lost, as if she was about to say something but had forgotten what it was, then a star-like twinkle appeared in her eye, as if she had remembered what she wanted to say. 'I have a secret and one I'd like, I need, to share with someone, and as I rarely get visitors, and you young people seem trustworthy, I would like to share it with you, if you don't mind listening to the ravings of a mad woman. I want to tell you a story,' Anna said, and for an hour Poe and Sorrow were spellbound, as if she were not an old woman but an old fairy out of an attic, spinning tales on her storytelling spinning wheel.

Anna told them a story they found hard to believe, but coming from the woman's mouth they believed every word. 'I can assure you every word I told you is true. I was not spinning you a yarn, although the fairies in the attic of my mind, the one filled with cobwebs, may well have been.' It appeared the old woman could read minds as well as being a clairvoyant who could read the tea leaves.

'Yes, yes, I can hear a little voice in my head asking me to tell you the story about me meeting the dream king, King Ludwig II. The king, a more handsome and charming man you could not wish for, took me for a ride on his shell boat, the one pulled by seven giant silver swans. These magnificent creatures glided across a lake of silver and then took off as we flew high over the Black Forest, over the mountain and over King Ludwig II's fairy-tale castle. The castle had been built upon the top of a mountain by a team of giants, or so the Fairy King informed me, and who was I not to believe his tale? After all, he believed all of mine, and we were home in time for tea… Oh, the fairy in the attic in my mind says I should tell you it was black dragon tea, one sip from a cup and you can fly. That bit I should probably tell you was a fairy tale or a dream, not sure which. You can tell too many fairy tales, to the point where nobody will believe a word you say. It's a bit like the story *The Boy Who Cried Wolf*, but with a twist.' The old woman laughed, her silver-grey hair tumbling around her shoulders. This made her look every inch the fairy-tale princess, even if she was a little frayed around the edges, as were her fairy wings.

Then a loud crash was heard in the kitchen, which made Poe and Sorrow almost jump out of their skins, both rushing out to see what had happened. Perhaps one of the gingerbread men had broken out from his prison, the oven, as their imaginations ran wild! When they got to the kitchen, there was nobody there, although the kitchen drawer was open and the back door was wide open.

17

The Lost Fabergé Egg

'Somebody's taken the egg!' Sorrow cried, clasping her hands to her horror-stricken face, which made it appear to Poe as if she had seen a ghost.

'Was it made of gold?' Poe quipped.

'Yes!' Sorrow replied, starring dangers at Poe as she then gave Poe the full story of the egg, the Fabergé egg.

'Perhaps it was a replica,' Poe said, trying to make Sorrow feel better, although in truth he may well have been correct in this assessment. Auguse Dupin, the great detective, he was sure, would agree with him, and although Poe knew Dupin was a fictional creation, for the life of him, he could not recall who the author was who had created the character.

'Perhaps somebody has handed it in to the Lost and Found Department in the forest,' Sorrow quipped, trying to lighten the mood.

'What was it, the ghost of the past finally leaving me in peace?' Anna smiled.

'Just the wind. It blew the door open and the broomstick fell onto the floor,' Sorrow replied, telling a fairy tale of her own, in other words, a lie. 'We loved your true-life fairy story, which made Anna Andersen's autobiography *My Fairy Life Story* seem dull by comparison,' Sorrow added, this time meaning every word she said as she looked up towards the ceiling as if it were heaven, in case Anna Andersen's ghost, now a ghost writer, was still hanging around.

'Anna, pretty name, although I have never read any of her fairy tales,' Anna replied, with a wry smile upon her face.

In truth, Sorrow wondered if she should be looking down towards the fires of hell, for as Poe said to her once upon a time, 'If you went to a party in heaven, you would be bored because all the best people had not received an invite,'

'We both swear on our lives, cross our hearts and hope to die a terrible and painful death at the hands of Ivan the Terrible and Iv-Anna the Terrible that we will not tell this story to anybody. We will both take it to our graves,' Sorrow said, looking at Poe for confirmation that he agreed with this pact. Sorrow was now certain this was not Eugenie Smith or Anna Andersen, both said to be imposters by the media and historians, but the Princess Anastasia. The fact that the woman did not recall meeting her and Poe in the forest with Rasputin and Ivan VI did not seem to deter her in the slightest from this belief. Clearly, the woman was old. No actor, however brilliant or however great their make-up artist was, could pull off such a disguise. It was also clear that the old woman was very forgetful. If they had indeed met in the Twisted Forest, it had clearly happened over sixty years ago. How time flies. Well, as Albert Einstein said once upon a time, 'Time is an illusion.'

'Yes, what Sorrow said goes triple for me, three being the magic number, taking out the part about a terrible and painful death at the hands of Ivan the Terrible or his terrible twin,' Poe said, still very much under the spell of the fairy tale and the Fairy Teller. Poe was now imagining the old woman as an old fairy, riding an adapted spinning wheel around the house in manic fashion as if it were a wooden penny farthing. The fairy appeared to be in a race against other invisible fairy folk riding upon spinning wheels until she eventually fell off but came up smiling. Poe imagined that whatever life threw at this old lady, whether she was Anastasia Romanov the lost tsarina, or simply a fantasist lost in a world of her own making, she came up smiling in the end. Her infectious personality and smile had rubbed off on them, as had the fairy dust she was covered in from head to toe. Whereas before, when they first arrived, the old woman named Anna seemed slow of movement and slow of mind, she now seemed as light as a feather, as was her heart. Her visitors had put the spring back in her step and lifted her heart and spirits so she believed she could fly.

Poe and Sorrow could easily imagine the woman flying around the forest, not on a broomstick like some old witch but on the back of a giant white swan, a swan rider, perhaps even riding the swan side saddle or holding on to the back of the Swan King, King Ludwig II, as if in a dream. They could also picture her doing a pirouette upon a music box and on the kitchen table, or on the ceiling for that matter. She was so graceful that she appeared to glide around the house like a prima ballerina who once upon a time was a member of the famous Bolshoi Ballet.

As the story the old woman had now ended, Poe and Sorrow embraced the only lady calling herself Anna and began the next part of their story. And they did it with renewed vigour and energy, with a spring in their step, for it felt to them as if wintertime had been replaced by springtime. For Poe and Sorrow, there was always a light at the end of a dark tunnel. Now all they had to do was find it.

As they left the Black Forest, Sorrow looked back, half expecting the fairy tale-like cottage to have melted into the background or simply melted in the heat of the day, it being a gingerbread house. 'There's a shadowy figure in the attic of the old house,' Sorrow exclaimed, pointing at a raggedy-looking shadow that backed away from the window as if the person did not wish to be recognised.

'That could be any number of characters that have disappeared into the forest of history. I know it was a shadow but to me it looked like the shadow of an old woman, Anne Frank's shadow,' Poe said, smiling on the inside and on the outside, for he, like Sorrow, was determined to write Anne Frank out of the nightmare into the dream, by the way from the Disenchanted Forest into the Enchanted Forest. For Ann and Anastasia, their deaths threatened to overshadow their lives, but over time, their personalities lit up the darkness as the dark shadows were transformed into a magical moonlight shadow, the light of which would shine like a dead star for centuries to come. In the end, the lives of these two remarkable girls overshadowed their deaths, as it should be.

The entire Romanov family, Tsar Nicholas II, his wife, Tsarina Alexander, and their five children, Olga, Anastasia, Maria, Tatiana and Alexi were canonised, elevating them to saints, by the Russian Orthodox Church – the Church of the Saviour on Spilled Blood in honour of all Saints, in Yekaterinburg, St Petersburg.

Anne Frank's House and Museum in Amsterdam, the Netherlands, have inspired hundreds of thousands of young people, some of whom have gone on to achieve great things themselves. The spirit lives on.

Anne Frank's fondest wish for her future was to become a writer which, due to her diary, she did. Sorrow was sure Ann would have loved somebody to write her into a fairy tale, even a dark one, as long as that fairy tale had a happy ending. Poe and Sorrow were still searching for that fairy-tale ending they still believed was out there waiting for them.

Anne Frank may have lived some of her life in a small attic space but, thanks to her imagination, she was able to transform that small space into a larger space, a magical space. When Anne was in the attic looking out at the stars through the open window, no doubt she was imagining flying free, as if in a dream, escaping the darkness of her world, swapping it in fact for another dark space, that of the universe. Standing upon a magic carpet, a star cloud bejewelled in a million tiny diamond-like stars, as Anne was treated to a magical mystery tour of the wonders of the universe, care of her imagination.

In recent dark times, that of the coronavirus, a dark energy that seeped into every attic of the mind, it was only the imagination that kept us all from losing our minds. The imagination transformed the small space into a palace, a palace made of crystal. For Sorrow, this had been the case. Most of us got through those dark times. However, some did not, but their spirits live on. Poe and Sorrow believed that to be true. More wishful thinking perhaps, perhaps not.

'I imagine all of the Romanov family, including the lost tsar, Ivan VI, trapped in a giant glass house like the Crystal Palace in Victorian England, covered in frost and snowflakes, no, not trapped, protected; a winter wonderland, a Kew Gardens. This crystal winter palace that not even the terrible twins, Ivan the Terrible and Iv-Anna the Terrible, with an army of thousands will be able to smash or tear down,' said Sorrow, smiling on the inside, for this image made her feel warm inside. Sorrow found herself wishing that in her fairy-tale ending, if she ever found it, there would be an image included of her with a smile upon her face.

'That is a lovely thought, Sorrow. I take it there is no room in the giant snow dome for the Snow Queen,' Poe replied, trying to force a smile upon his face, for he did not wish to tear Sorrow's fairy-tale wonderland down no sooner than she had dreamt it up.

We all wished this imagining to be true, that somehow Anastasia had escaped her fate worse than death, escaped the nightmare. But all the wishful thinking in the world could not unwrite what had already been written, for this dark fairy tale had not been written in fairy dust; it had been written in stone and written in blood.

Poe smiled to himself as he reached out and took Sorrow's hand. He could see Sorrow as a character out of a fairy tale, Snow White, and could see that he and Sorrow were destined to one day marry in the fairy-tale wedding to end all fairy-tale weddings. No sooner did the name Snow White fall over the edge of the black waterfall of words and images that his mind churned up than the snow in the fairy-tale forest turned to black ice. Poe turned from a prince into the wicked prince, as Sorrow, in the guise of Snow White, slipped over and broke her pretty little neck, leaving Poe heartbroken. It was the name Snow White that had killed the fairy tale stone dead, had ended the fairy-tale romance even before it had a chance to blossom. You see, Poe was imagining the bride in a glass coffin as the tale of Snow White, her face pale as if wearing a death mask, rather than a fairy-tale princess standing at the altar with a smile upon her face. It was as if Poe had crossed out all the happy parts of the fairy tale from the giant book of fairy tales, leaving only the dark bits.

It was grim, all right, brother. It was grim. 'It is just as well I am leaving the Enchanted Forest for the Disenchanted

Forest, for my soul is unwell,' sniffed Poe, who was dressed in a long dust jacket, his long nose in the air.

The spring in Poe's step had lasted exactly three paces; a few more paces and hopefully a trap would spring up and he would be snapped in half. Or alternatively a giant spring-up children's book of fairy tales would spring up. He'd fall into it. The cover of the book would snap shut and he would be crushed to death. Poe started to hum the words of an unhappy tune: 'Always look on the bright side of a grim fairy-tale ending. It's only being so miserable that keeps me going, bah humbugs!'

18

Pandora's Playhouse

Poe and Sorrow walked through another curtain of weeping willow trees to find themselves in another part of the forest.

'Where on earth are we now?' Sorrow replied, waking up in another part of the forest, as if she and Poe had been sleep walking. The forest was so vast that at times it seemed like she was in another world, as if she were a character out of the Jules Verne novel *Journey to the Center of the Earth* or *The Lost World* by Arthur Conan Doyle. Yes, this vast space was in fact inside a tiny space, that of an attic, although as all attics were magical, they had the ability to expand like the universe and the imagination.

Sorrow had travelled quite a bit in her young life, unlike Poe, whose travels for the most part had been restricted to the imaginary world and his small world, that of the old wooden shack-house. Sorrow had visited the Impenetrable Forest in Uganda, the Black Forest in Germany and the Rainforest in South America.

At times while she was in these vast forests Sorrow really felt as if she were in another world, that she had dropped off the face of the planet, where mobile phones were of no use because you could not get a signal. It felt good to step out of the straitjacket of the modern world and step into these magical worlds of many wonders, leaving so-called technological wonders and wizardry far behind you.

Sorrow rubbed her eyes, for she could see what appeared to be a giant box in the heart of the forest. She walked towards it and the closer she got, the bigger it became. Finally, she arrived to see that the box was in fact a house, a box house. Sorrow had to rub her eyes again, for she was sure there was a nameplate on the house. But as she got closer, the name of the house disappeared. Sorrow imagined it must be because she was tired, her eyes playing tricks on her, or her mind.

Sorrow closed her eyes tightly as she took a sharp intake of breath, trying to clear her mind, and as she did so, the name of the house became illuminated in her mind. It was like an afterimage caused by a bright light on the retina of the eye – Pandora's House, or was that the House of Pandora, in which case it should have a blue plaque on it with *Pandora Lived Here* and the dates she was born and died. No doubt Pandora had just stayed here overnight on her travels around the world, and as she probably couchsurfed, there were no doubt thousands of houses, flat, apartments and even gypsy caravans with blue plaques stating that once upon a time Pandora lived here, a likely fairy tale, or so Sorrow imagined as her mind wandered. Wanderlust had got her under its dark magical spell, or was that Wonderlust?

Sorrow wondered if someone had built this house for her. Perhaps it was her birthday and for a present the forest had built her a house. After all, one of her middle names was Pandora.

Pandora walked cautiously towards the house, for the door was invitingly ajar, almost as if the house was inviting her in with open arms. 'Take a step back, you silly goose. Your name is Sorrow, I mean, Yarra Eloise. Pandora is only one of your middle names. You have not stepped into Pandora's shoes or Cinderella's glass slipper, although you may well have stepped into the glittering ruby red shoes of Dorothy Oz.' Sorrow did not imagine there was a shoe shop in the forest high street, because the high street had been decimated, like the forests of the world, thanks to the coronavirus and the ever-changing landscape, which included the cyber landscape. Sorrow heard her own voice giggle in her head, like that of a little schoolgirl.

Sorrow wondered what it looked like inside the house; probably small, poky, the opposite to what would normally happen in a storybook, the house being small on the outside and large on the inside. Gingerly, and with more than a little apprehension, Sorrow pulled the door open, hoping there was not an ugly-looking witch with a wart on her nose on the other side. Sorrow half expected the wooden door to make a creaking sound, as in all haunted houses, but it did not. It swung open with ease. Sorrow felt at ease, and why wouldn't she? After all, this was her house; it had her name written all over it. Once inside, she would choose the best and biggest bedroom she could find as she was tired. She would be able to rest her weary bones and her even wearier head on the pillow, stuffed, undoubtedly, with the feathers of a golden goose. Or, as this was Pandora's House, as she slept, the pillow would be whipped from under her head and stuffed in her mouth, causing her to be asphyxiated. Presumably, Pandora's ghost did not like anybody sleeping in her bed.

The house was nothing special; it was certainly not a palace. Inside, nothing extraordinary, just ordinary, like any other house in any other street in any other forest!'Dream on, Pandora. You'll be laughing on the other side of your face.' The voice cackled as Sorrow felt a shiver down her spine.

'You're spineless. All ghosts are. Yes, I'm talking to you, that's right, Pandora's ghost. Go back into the shadows where you belong before I give you what for,' snapped Sorrow, her voice echoing around the house until it eventually died.

'Oh dear, what's become of me? I'm talking to the voices in my head as well as myself. I must be going doubly mad. I really must get some sleep. I just hope an evil wicked prince does not sneak in while I'm asleep and he becomes my jailer as my house turns into a prison.'

Sorrow flopped onto the bed like a giant moth-eaten rag doll, not even bothering to turn back the sheet, and soon she was in a deep sleep.

*

'Where on earth am I?' Poe exclaimed, seemingly lost inside the forest, or the attic of the mind, his inner compass spinning wildly. 'Ask a silly question, get a silly answer. I'm in the Middle of Nowhere! Still, if I'm in the Middle of Nowhere, that means I'm not at the Beginning of Nowhere, or at Nowhere's End. I suppose that's something to be grateful for at least. I should count my blessings. Look up ahead, there appears to be a house, although I cannot see a roof or a chimney. It looks more like a giant box than a house, a black one, as if burnt in a fire. Perhaps it is a four-storey house. After all, if I am sleepwalking, my subconscious may well have dreamt me up a fairy tale or four. Box houses were all the rage in the seventies. They all looked the same, as if made of ticky-tacky!' Poe mused, whistling an old-time song in which the lyrics said just that.

Poe walked towards the house in dream-like fashion, as if on autopilot, for he was so tired that he felt he may well be sleepwalking. If he came across a wolf dressed in Little Red Riding Hood's clothes, Poe imagined he may well be eaten alive as he walked out of the dream straight into the jaws of a nightmare. The house now looked like a giant toy box with windows and a door.

'Nice house. I wonder who it belongs to,' muttered Poe, and then no sooner had the words left his mouth than he added, 'Pandora. This is the house that belonged to Pandora. Nice touch, subconscious mind. You've outdone yourself this dream time.' Poe smiled, imagining the house winking at him, the same imagining he'd had when he said goodbye to his grandparents' old house. To Poe, it seemed he'd left his grandparents' house and his past behind him several reincarnated lifetimes ago, another time, another magical space. It appeared to Poe that small space had expanded as he felt as if he was still trapped within it, unable to outrun the ripples of time. Everybody had their own time. For some, it was a short time; for others, a long time. Eventually, the ripples would stop as your life ended.

'The door is ajar, I see, as I would expect it to be. No surprises there,' Poe said, raising his eyebrows, hoping there were no nasty surprises waiting just around the corner, or on the other side of the giant book he was imagining belonged to a giant girl named Pandora. Here, it was clear that Poe was bringing the story of Pandora's Jar to mind, the original title of Pandora's Life Story before the story went through a metamorphosis, turning into Pandora's Box. 'Now, subconscious, I hope you're not thinking of turning this dream into a nightmare, or should I say this dream home into a home full of nightmares? I do not want this house to turn into Pandora's Box, a box full of nasty surprises. I hope I've made myself crystal clear, although if Pandora's House turned into a crystal box house, then I would not mind one iota.'

The house was silent, not a creaking door or floorboard in sight; too quiet, thought Poe. This silence was soon shattered by a whistling sound. Poe looked nervously around but could not see anybody then realised it was his nerves which had set off a Newtonian chain reaction which in turn had caused his tinnitus to start playing up. Poe began to hear music in his head. Unfortunately, it wasn't a sweet soothing lullaby but the film music from the horror film *Interview with the Vampire*.

'Nice place, nothing too ostentatious.' Poe coughed, trying to drown out the whistling in his ears and the horror soundtrack in his head as he continued to poke around the house. Poe was too tired to climb the stairs and, logically, if he was sleepwalking, he did not want to fall down the stairs and break his neck. It was a well-known fact that more people died while climbing the stairs than died in any other manner. Or was that more people died after getting out of bed in the morning when they were half in and half out of a dream then fell down the stairs, a dream that turned into a waking nightmare? The next thing you knew, you were a ghost walking through a shut door, so Poe wisely decided to sleep on the settee downstairs. This was infinitely better than sleeping rough like the Little Match Girl, or sleeping in a glass coffin like Snow White, or sleeping on a bed of nails like a snake charmer.

Poe was soon away with the fairies. Only time would tell if in this dream the fairies were good or bad. If it was a dream, they were probably going to be fairies with a good nature, and if it was a nightmare, then it followed that the fairies would be bad to the bone, not so much bone collectors, more fairy collectors, or dark fairies, ones who liked to collect nightmares.

Poe had no idea that Sorrow was asleep in the room directly above him, and Sorrow had no idea that Poe was sleeping directly below her. If they really were both psychic dreamers, then they would undoubtedly cross paths in the dream world.

19

Pandora's Jar

'What pretty wings you have. I think I'll pull them off. Another thousand wings and I'll have enough for a quilt for my bed,' giggled a giant girl by the name of Pandora as she held up a glass jar to her face. Inside the jar was a moth with raggedy- looking wings and a butterfly with silky smooth wings. Both moth and butterfly appeared to be asleep.

Poe felt as if he were having an out-of-body experience, Sorrow mirroring Poe's every thought as she experienced the same thing. Was this a dream inside a dream or a nightmare inside a nightmare? Poe could see that he was the moth in the jar and Sorrow the butterfly as they both fluttered their wings in a manic fashion, bashing into the glass in a panic to get out. Poe imagined he was Moth from Shakespeare's play *A Midsummer Night's Dream*.

The air in the glass prison was now so thin that it was becoming hard to breathe. Sunshine from the window streamed through the glass jar, bending it as it did so. Dust motes floated around the jar as if in slow motion. This was not fairy dust, so a fairy did not magically appear as if by magic inside the jar, although Sorrow and Poe had both imagined this happening. This could well have been down to the lack of oxygen in the jar causing the mind to hallucinate. By this time, Poe and Sorrow were exhausted from their exertions in attempting to get out of the glass jar, so much so that they settled down at the bottom. Poe had just enough strength left in his frail-looking body to cover Sorrow with his moth-eaten-looking wings, as if they were an old blanket. Sorrow did likewise, covering Poe with her silky smooth wings as if they were a satin sheet made of silk.

'Wake up, it's not time to go to sleep yet, wake up. I say, my little beauties, you know I might try an experiment, extract DNA from a butterfly and a moth and create a hybrid: half butterfly, half moth. Imagine how much such a rare winged specie would fetch on the black market!' cried Pandora, shaking the glass jar, waking Poe and Sorrow from their beauty sleep. Pandora held the jar to the light as her diamond black eyes stared wildly at Poe and Sorrow. Pandora tried to smile but it came out as a scowl. Pandora then scratched her sharp, cracked glass-like nails down the glass, causing scratch marks on the side of the glass jar. From the inside of their glass prison, Pandora's face looked distorted, as if looking into a bowed mirror, but then glass distorts images. To Pandora, they probably also looked misshapen, like freaks only fit for a freak show.

'That should wake you up. It's not time for you to die yet. I haven't finished playing with you,' Pandora said, dropping the jar from a great height several times before rolling the jar along the floor, which then rolled towards the staircase and then fell down the stairs and broke. The glass shattered into hundreds of tiny fragments shards, so sharp they could cut you to ribbons.

Poe and Sorrow were free, but their joy was short-lived. They could not fly free for their wings were broken; they could hardly move for fear of being cut to shreds. The house now towered above them. It was almost like a gothic cathedral inside the house. They could not be sure if this was because they had shrunk or because the house had grown, as if it were a living and breathing thing. Perhaps Pandora was the same size as Poe and Sorrow were before they transformed into insects. At least they hadn't transformed into cockroaches, which had happened to the main character in the story *Metamorphosis*. Perhaps if the house shrank, then the giant girl Pandora would shrink too. The only trouble with this theory was that Poe and Sorrow would disappear into thin air, or they would appear no bigger than an atom.

'Oh dear, I must call my nursemaid. She will fix your wings good and proper. After all, when I sell you to a Butterfly Collector, I want you both to look your best. I mean, you cannot expect a collector to buy you with broken wings. How will they be able to pin your wings to the board? You must look your best for when you're displayed in a glass cabinet.' Pandora giggled in manic fashion but her face stayed as straight as the lid of a coffin as she arrived at the bottom of the stairs of the house. 'Although I do hear some collectors like to display their butterflies upon the walls of their houses like miniature works of art. I guess it takes all sorts to make up a mad world.'

Poe and Sorrow held their breath as Pandora stood hovering over them with a fixed expression of puzzlement upon her face. It was as if she did not know what she should do next. Picking the butterfly and the moth up meant she might well cut herself. Poe and Sorrow hoped she tried; she may cut her wrist and bleed to death. More wishful thinking from the butterfly minds of Poe and Sorrow, leaving out the moth minds for the time being.

'I could press you in a book of flowers, call it *The Butterfly Press Book*, although the pages would be stained in blood, but they would make good ink stains. Once upon a time, my maker sent me to a child psychologist and he asked me what I thought about ink stains, and I said they looked like black dried blood. The poor man fainted upon the floor. I don't think he'd ever been that close to pure evil before.

'My creator said it was not my fault that I was evil but his for creating me in his image. I imagine my box is a giant coffin, one covered in cobwebs. These are not the sort of images a child should have in their head, are they?' Pandora sniffed as a small opal-shaped tear slid down her face, causing a deep track in the thick white make-up her face was caked in. No wonder Pandora didn't crack a smile. If she had, her face would have cracked into a thousand pieces. The tear fell down Pandora's face in super slow motion before it hit the foot of the stairs. This created a small waterfall in which Poe and Sorrow were swept away, out under the door into the forest.

'Come back, I didn't mean to drive you away. You are my only friends. This house has become a prison and I am my own jailer, my own worst enemy!' Pandora cried, bursting into a flood of tears which filled the house. Pandora tried to get out of a window, but as there were now iron bars over the windows, she could not get out. Pandora shook at the door handle furiously, but the door was locked and the key had dropped out onto the doorstep. Pandora could not swim and she quickly drowned, her dead eyes appearing at the window as a moth and a butterfly flew happily by, without a care in the world, or perhaps they were broken angels, once fallen, now restored to their former glory.

20

A Viking Funeral

Poe and Sorrow saw a black gate in the middle of the forest –
it was not attached to a house – then stepped through it into
another space, not sure if this space was in another time and
dimension from the space they had just come from. Poe and
Sorrow were equally unsure as to whether this door would
take them closer to or further away from the world they had
been born into.

'A Viking boat! What on earth is a Viking boat doing in
the middle of a forest? It's a funny place to park your boat,' Poe
exclaimed.

'Waiting for a Viking funeral,' Sorrow replied, matter-of-
factly.

'Or waiting for the Vikings to return so they can plan
our funerals. I knew we would never make old bones,' Poe

said with a grimace, not wishing to come face to face with a Viking army. 'Whoever dreamt this nightmare up is really pushing the old boat out. It looks like we are not out of the woods yet.'

'We are never out of the woods, as you say, until we die, and for the Vikings it seems not even then. During coronavirus, I must have heard that phrase "we are not out of the woods" a million times. It has been said that Vikings were like a virus that spread like wildfire throughout Europe.'

'The Viking Virus is still spreading. You only have to turn on the television to see that, both in fact and in fiction,' spat Poe, seeing Thor and Vikings wherever he looked.

'It seems you're channelling your inner Viking, Poe, and, after all, most of us have a little Viking blood in us.'

'Then I'm all for the practice of blood-letting!' Poe retorted, imagining opening up a vein and letting only the Viking blood out of him.

'It's good to see you haven't lost your sense of humour, Poe. I'm sure you are aware of this fact, but a few decades ago, they discovered five Viking ships buried in a Fjord, all of which are now in a museum in Denmark,' replied Sorrow, as if she was imagining she was the tour guide for this sequence of the nightmare.

'I thought I saw something move in the trees, a shadow,' Poe said, looking up at the trees.

'It's probably Thor, the God of Thunder, about to crack open our heads with his giant hammer,' Sorrow replied, fed up to the back teeth with exclaiming or crying out at every shadow she saw.

'I'm being serious. Something up there moved, and it wasn't the trees before you say anything, like I'm scared of my own shadow,' Poe snapped.

'Then perhaps we should move on to the next nightmare.

I don't like the look of this one,' Sorrow said, quickening her pace in an exaggerated manner.

'Vikings,' Poe exclaimed, pointing up ahead as a group of shadowy figures appeared before them.

'You don't know that. All we can see is a group of shadows. They aren't exactly very big. Vikings are normally big-boned men, with legs and thighs as wide as tree trunks and skin like armour. These shadows are all thin, there's barely anything of them,' Sorrow replied, taking one pace forward to get a better look as Poe took one step backwards.

'As Pandora was created out of clay, I imagine the Vikings were born out of the forest, fashioned out of the same timber they built their warships out of,' Poe said, recalling the Viking legend of trees having souls. However, this thought soon died to be replaced by another one every bit as strange. 'Skeletons,' Poe gasped, as the cry got stuck in his throat.

'A skeleton crew. Not sure which is worse, a Viking skeleton crew or a crew of sixty Viking oarsmen with an axe to grind,' Sorrow said with a grimace.

'I'd prefer a ghost army of Viking fighters, for I fear that against this lot we don't stand a ghost of a chance,' Poe grimaced.

'They're coming down from the trees. It's a trap, they've been waiting for us,' Sorrow cried, finally finding her voice.

'We're surrounded. It's official. It's a nightmare,' Poe exclaimed. 'Here,' Poe said, picking up a branch from a tree and passing it to Sorrow.

'Really, a willowy-looking branch from a tree is going to protect us from a hoard of angry Vikings, unless this is a magic wand made of willow.'

'Angry dead Vikings. I wish you'd get your facts straight,' Poe retorted, arming himself with a branch of a tree, 'and yes and no to that question. No, it's not exactly a magic wand, but it is a silver birch tree, which makes it magical in the right hands, of course.'

'You're making all this up as you go along, aren't you?' snapped Sorrow, standing back to back with Poe as the Viking army moved closer.

Poe and Sorrow fought the Viking attackers off, who were using bones from their fallen comrades as weapons, along with some razor-sharp jawbones from animals that had died in the forest, bones that were positively prehistoric by the looks of it. Sorrow fought like a banshee, channelling her inner Joan of Arc, while Poe channelled his inner Viking, what he had of it. Both drew on the strength of the magical silver birch branches they were wielding, as if they both held Excalibur in their hands. Two Excaliburs, well, as Poe and Sorrow were standing back to back, mirroring one another's actions, then whyever not?

Then a giant shadow appeared; a misshapen figure with a slim waist, thunder thighs and thin, spindly legs. In truth, the shadow did not appear to have any feet. The shadow also appeared to have two heads, so Poe imagined this giant shadow had escaped from a freak show, or a nightmare, or his imagination. Poe was not sure what the truth of the matter was.

'The skeletons are being cut to ribbons,' Sorrow said, hardly able to believe her eyes, and not for the first time, and she imagined probably not for the last either.

'Not sure you can say skeletons are being cut to ribbons,' Poe said, back to his pedantic worst.

'It's a giant pair of scissors!' Sorrow exclaimed, looking up to see a giant pair of scissors towering over them.

'It's the scissor man,' Poe exclaimed.

'Who?' Sorrow retorted.

'The scissor man. He lives in my house, or should I say my attic, or should I say the attic of my mind. He's out of one of my nightmares,' Poe replied.

'Please tell me this character isn't out of one of your worst nightmares,' Sorrow said with a grimace.

'I'd really like to tell you that, Sorrow, I really would, but if I did, that would make me a liar,' Poe replied, grim-faced.

The skeleton Viking army, what was left of them, as most of their skeletons were scattered upon the floor of the forest, as if in a giant game of Operation, boarded the Viking warship and started to row out of the forest. The scissor man hadn't finished with the Vikings yet and stabbed at the boat, piercing it so that if it ever did make it into a body of water, it would surely sink. Poe imagined the Vikings, or what was left of them. Their souls had not been given a proper Viking funeral, a burial at sea, the ship set alight with their dead bodies aboard.

Many ships and their crews had received a Viking burial but not by choice. Fire ships were common in sea battles employed by the British Fleet against the Spanish Armada, setting the Armada ablaze, making it easier for the British ships to win battles. All these facts came to Poe's mind as it jumped from one thing to another. At times, it felt to Poe as if he had a quantum computer in his head, one side of his brain doing one calculation, the other side another, and then the two sides of his brain came together, producing the answer. This, however, did not work quite so well when it came to the science of sleep. The subconscious mind was not so easy to figure out. The same could be said of dreams and nightmares.

'What's he doing now?' Sorrow said, turning to Poe for answers.

'What, because he came out of the attic of my mind, I'm supposed to know his every move?' Poe spat.

'You've created this monster. He's your monster, a monster from out of your dark mind, and as such you are responsible for his actions,' Sorrow snapped back, as the giant pair of scissors continued to snip and snap furiously at the Viking boat, cutting it to pieces in no time at all, as if it were made out of balsa wood.

'It's as storytellers always say. You create a character, give it shape and form and then it takes on a life of its own,' Poe said, defending himself and his nightmare creation. In truth, Poe was not sure if the scissor man was his nightmare creation or somebody else's. He could be the forester's nightmare creation, as could everything inside the attic. After all, he created the monster house, so Poe was now thinking, although he kept this thought to himself.

'The Viking boat is on fire, set alight by the snapping of the scissors. Together, they've created a spark,' Sorrow said, pointing to the burning ship.

'The Vikings are collecting up the bones of their dead and putting them into the burning boat,' Poe said, giving a running commentary, when perhaps running away from the scissor man may have been the best course of action. Perhaps as this was a nightmare then Poe could not run anywhere, his feet stuck in the mud, or black treacle, as often occurred in a nightmare. One was forced to look upon something truly terrifying when the natural instinct was to turn and look away, or run away as fast as was humanly possible.

'Look, it's flying. A flying Viking boat. It's heading for the stars. It looks like the Vikings have finally got their wish for a Viking burial, ashes to ashes, stardust to stardust,' gasped Poe, his eyes as wide as saucers, or was this an illusion, as often seen in the Bermuda Triangle, otherwise known as the Devil's Triangle? Ghost's ship appeared on the horizon, so from the land it appeared as if the ship was floating upon air, an optical illusion created by a weather system of hot and cold air colliding.

If this were the case then Poe wondered what else lay in store for him over the next event horizon. Of course, this mirage could well be one of the mind. The last meal Poe and Sorrow had eaten was mushroom soup. If the soup contained magic mushrooms this may well have been the case. Alternatively, the forester was up to his old tricks again. It was beginning to feel to Poe as if this madman was projecting an old black and white movie onto the attic walls, a horror movie inside which Poe and Sorrow were trapped.

The scissor man snapped at the air above the Viking ship as if he believed they were holding the Viking ship aloft, as if the ship was being worked by a giant puppet hiding in the shadows. But try as he might, he could not, as the Viking boat, rowed by a skeleton crew of Viking warriors, continued its journey towards the stars.

'Where's the scissor man?' Poe cried, fearing that now the Viking boat was no longer in the picture, he and Sorrow were easy targets.

'He's disappeared back into the shadows, I hope,' Sorrow replied, thinking that if she believed this to be true then it was true. The trick was to make Poe believe this was true, if the scissor man was indeed Poe's worst nightmare and his own creation.

'Wishful thinking, I would imagine.' Poe grimaced, trying to blank the scissor man from his mind.

'Please don't dream up any more nightmare characters until we are out of the woods,' said Sorrow, staring daggers in Poe's direction.

'Don't lose any sleep over it, Poe. It's only a nightmare,' whispered two Siamese shadows as one voice into Poe's ear, ones he imagined were sleep whispers. Poe twisted the kaleidoscope in his head and the nightmare turned into a dream… a bad dream.

21

Shadows of the Mind

'You're a shadow!' Poe exclaimed, looking at Sorrow, who he imagined was but a shadow, cast in her image by the moon's silver rays. The moon goddess was a shadow caster of great power, who could cast any number of shadows in any number of places, and all at the same time. Sorrow and Poe had a dream where they dived off the edge of the world and into the moon, a giant white pool of light. They swam across the pool and when they got to the other side, they pulled themselves out and found their bodies had turned to gold. Not pure gold but white rolled gold. Other times, the moon transformed itself into silver and thus when they swam across the moon, their bodies had turned to silver.

'Of my former self, I'm not surprised this journey into the unknown has taken a lot out of me, so much so that all that is left is my shadow. I'm now a one-dimensional paper-thin character out of a children's fairy tale, little more than a silhouette. Still, it's hardly my worst nightmare.' Sorrow smiled, sure that Poe was playing the forest court jester as she patted herself down in a theatrical manner.

'No, you're just a shadow and so am I, and as you say, I've had worst nightmares,' Poe replied, looking into what he first imagined was Sorrow's soul and then into a black mirror, as if he were mirroring everything Sorrow did, as if they were Siamese twins, or Siamese shadows.

'The trees are shadows, so are the creatures and birds, and the moon is a shadow moon, or a new moon, or a Black Moon, as is seen in the Orient,' Sorrow replied reflectively. 'The Forest of Shadows, I thought it was simply a myth, a dark fairy tale,' replied Sorrow, unable to read Poe's face, for being just a silhouette without eyes and lips, there was nothing to tell whether he was happy or sad. However, the tone of Poe's voice at least gave her some idea of how he was feeling, but even that was not easy, for the tone of Poe's voice was often flat, without much emotion. Some said that listening to Poe's voice was like listening to a robot or an automaton. Sorrow had not told Poe this, for she did not want to make him feel bad.

'I would imagine the silver birch forest is so magical that it has no need for shadow magic, so it casts its shadow away, thus creating the Forest of Shadows,' said Poe, explaining science fiction and fairy tales as if they were science fact. In truth, quantum physicists spun their quantum wonder tales as if they were facts, when most people knew they were little more than fairy tales. If Plato was right and we are living in the shadow realm, perhaps that may not be so far from the truth.

'I did not realise we have entered a fairy spinning circle, Poe. Black shadows move across landscape, so make it appear as if they are moving. It's an illusion, nothing more?' retorted

Sorrow, raising her eyebrows and a smile, not that Sorrow could smile but that was fine, for neither could a shadow, and that was a fact, 1,OOO%! 'If you had a silver shadow, Poe Black, would you cast it aside as if it were not worth more than a silver shilling?'

'A Shadow Circle or Circle of Shadows spun by a giant spider, I hope not. If this was the real world, I might agree with you as say that was a highly unlikely fairy story, but this is an unreal world. As such, I am no longer sure what is and isn't possible,' Poe replied, as in his head spun a thousand and one different versions of reality. The question he was now asking himself was which one to choose.

'I've always believed we are all puppets, but now it appears that we are all shadow puppets, how are we to tell the good guys from the bad guys?' exclaimed Poe, looking all about to see if his shadow had a shadow, and perhaps his shadow a shadow, like in a hall of black mirrors.

'Perhaps that is no bad thing. After all, we judge people on their appearances and do so in double-quick time, and more times than not, our first impressions are wrong. Now we are all in the same boat. In the shadow realm, the colour of your skin is immaterial. If only that was true in the real world,' Sorrow replied, as she momentarily had a flashback to the Black Lives Matter campaign in her world.

'What the remains of a Viking funeral boat burnt black so its little more than charcoal floating in the Black Sea. It's true we are all in the dark, a dark parallel world, a dark tunnel with no light at the end of it,' said Poe, sounding woebegone, although once again this was not discernible by the sound of his voice. Poe wondered who the puppet master was in this world and if they would ever reveal themselves. There were times in life when the puppet worked the puppet master without the puppet master realising this was happening. If Poe and

Sorrow could find a way of smoking the puppet master out, who they believed was the forester who originally built the house, then perhaps they, the puppets, could manipulate the puppet master and turn the tables on him.

'Why do you always have to look on the dark side of life?' said Sorrow, for even she was getting a little fed up with Poe's downbeat approach to life.

'Try looking in the mirror. Oh, that's right, the only mirrors in this neck of the woods are black mirrors!' Poe replied, without raising his voice, but it was clear by his tone that he felt Sorrow was being somewhat hypocritical, for she also looked on the dark side of life before eventually looking on the brighter side. Poe, on the other hand, only looked on the dark side of life, which at this point in their lives may be the only side they were able to look upon. Thankfully, Poe's eyes had become accustomed to walking around in the dark, while Sorrow's clearly had not, as she stumbled blindly about, almost tripping over a tree stump, or the shadow of a tree stump. Despite being a little miffed, Poe took Sorrow by the hand as they walked deeper into the Forest of Shadows. Poe appeared to have night vision, or inferred vision, like wildlife documentary film cameras were fitted with so they could capture images of wildlife in their nocturnal habitats at night.

Poe loved carrots, ate them with most of his meals and for snacks, his favourite cake being carrot cake. He joked he must have been a rabbit in a previous life, a black rabbit, not the White Rabbit in *Alice in Wonderland*. If Alice's shadow was starring in the shadow play *The Forest of Shadows*, she would imagine this to be either the film *The Nightmare before Christmas* or a twist on *Alice's Adventures in Wonderland, A Nightmare in Wonderland*, a winter wonderland if the snow was black or it was set on a pond of black ice.

'I wouldn't say it's pitch-black in this forest, more bone-black,' Poe said, just managing to avoid walking headfirst into a tree, as black as night, one that looked as if it were a skeleton, or at least the shadow of a skeleton. 'Look over there. Over there's a shadow!'

'Yes, but whose shadow is it'? Sorrow exclaimed, still in the dark as to what was happening, as if she had suddenly gone blind. In truth, when you are but a shadow, you have no eyes to see, ears to hear or lips to speak. Although clearly this was not the case for Poe and Sorrow. Poe wondered if there were other human figures in the forest and if the same could be said about them.

Poe hated the thought of being blind, being in the dark for the rest of his life. Imagine the horrors of being on your own in an old house, hearing all the creaks and groans as your imagination ran wild. It would drive you to the nearest madhouse. Poe would rather be deaf and dumb than blind. He could hear a little voice in his head which said, *You already are dumb and blind so you may as well be deaf as well!*

Poe imagined he was wrestling with his own conscience, or a shadow from the Shadow Cabinet, as Poe's imagination played forest politics. In truth, as usual, Poe was wrestling with his own shadow, who was clearly a giant. This giant shadow twisted Poe this way and that, tying him into knots which left him looking like a black balloon in the hands of a twisted magician performing magic at a children's party.

No doubt this party was being held in the *Village of the Damned*, the old black and white horror movie from the 1960s. In this film, it was the children who held all the power and the adults whose minds were twisted to the will of the children. The dark mirror image of the real world, or so Poe thought, looking on the black side of the dream, a bad dream. That was the downside of watching horror movies. They gave you recurring nightmares, yet still we watched them as if we felt compelled to do so.

Poe heard a loud high-pitched scream that almost made his ears bleed; it was his tinnitus playing up again. Whenever Poe got stressed he heard whistling sounds and repeated tones in his head, as if he were picking up a signal from an alien race.

'Whose shadow? Taking an educated guess, not being an expert in the study of shadows, I'd say by his height, small, and stocky banded legs, Rumpelstiltskin, the Return of Rumpelstiltskin. And over there, a tall, shadowy figure, no doubt the wicked prince, or it could be the Shadow from the fairy tale written by... by... no, I can't recall the author. No, no, my apologies. It's neither of these shadowy figures. It's the shadow of a weeping willow tree. Oh no, I don't like the look of that shadow over there one little bit. Wouldn't want to meet that shadow down a dark alley!'

'Who is it? Tell me, tell me. Don't keep me in the dark, I beg of you,' Sorrow exclaimed, as all sorts of dark, shadowy figures crept into her mind, from Attila the Hun to the "Bloody Countess" Hungarian noblewoman Elizabeth Báthoray de Ecsed, from Ivan the Terrible to the wicked prince, as Sorrow pictured a giant children's Victorian pop-up book. But instead of colourful characters standing up straight, there were only black silhouettes, some in crouched positions as if turning from man to beast. Poe and Sorrow had already experienced their own shadows going through changes from human to animal. Sorrow's shadow had transformed itself into a jaguar and Poe's a night hawk and a raven, among the many shadows they had cast since entering the Twisted Forest. Or cast out, for as yet they had never cast the same shadow twice, other than their own shadows.

It seemed with every new forest they entered that the forest went through its own metamorphosis, casting shadows of its own as if it had a thousand and one shadows to cast whenever it felt like it. Or alternatively cast off the shadows like a forest shed its coat of many coloured leaves, from winter to spring, spring to summer and summer to autumn. And then back to winter again. Perhaps these shadows were the cast-offs of the forest, ones the forest no longer needed, like a snake repeatedly shedding its skin. Or perhaps the forest was casting off souls, ones it had collected or gathered over the centuries; men, women and children lost in the forest, draining their minds to add to its own, souls that it used as its fuel to drive it. And when these souls had served their purpose, they were cast out to become ghost shadows of their former selves. It was fair to say that Poe was a young man who did rather overthink things!

'The shadow appears to be a friendly sort. I think I may have misjudged this shadow,' Poe said, waving back at the shadow, who was now waving at him. He was hoping it really was friend and not foe posing as a friend, for shadows were masters of disguise and ones that in all cultures brought more fear than joy.

'How can you tell? It may be the shadow of any number of shadowy figures from history,' Sorrow retorted, looking puzzled, or at least that's how she pictured her shadow looking, her face in the shape of a piece of a puzzle of the sky at night.

'The shadow is waving at us. I'm afraid I cannot read people's shadows any more than I can read people's faces, or read tea leaves,' Poe sighed.

It was true that people who suffered from Asperger's Syndrome (Autism Spectrum Disorder), as it was called nowadays, found it hard to read facial expressions. Most people found it hard, if not impossible, to read what was going on inside the mind of a person who was autistic.

Poe was trying his best to sound cheerful, but it did not come naturally to him, nor did acting. He was to acting what

Pinocchio was to acting; wooden, unexpressive, no better than a tree. If Poe was ever to get into the world of the theatre, it would be as a tree, as background scenery, and even then he would be a bit wooden, according to the critics, or so Poe imagined.

'It's a shadow of a Queen. Which Queen? A fairy-tale Queen Titania from *A Midsummer Night's Dream*, or a member of a Royal Family? And that could be both a dream and a nightmare,' Sorrow said, not sure whether to bow or curtsey or run for her life if it was one of the shadowy figures from the Russian, German or Austrian Royal Families. Empress Anna of Russia from the Romanov dynasty was said to be somewhat of a tyrant. Some called her Iv-Anna the Terrible, as if she and Ivan the Terrible were twins.

'No, it's my tinnitus playing up again, due to stress. It's bad enough I'm hearing voices without hearing a drummer boy with a tin whistle sending me off to war with a ringing in my ears!' sighed Poe, peering round a tree to try and get a better view of the shadow, which seemed to dart about from one place to another as if it were made of quicksilver. Perhaps the shadow was made of quicksilver moonlight, in which case if they followed it, they may come to a part of the forest bathed in silver moonlight. How this would help them, Poe did not know, for they would still be shadows, just shadows made of quicksilver, but every cloud had a silver lining, which meant at least they would be able to see one another in each other's reflection.

'I've been hit. I'm bleeding?' Sorrow cried, holding her stomach as a shadow of an arrow flew through the air and pierced her body.

'Can a shadow bleed? We've got no form. No, look, Sorrow, the arrow went straight through you without leaving a scratch. Look, the arrow is still going. I imagine it will end up stuck in a tree. Either that or stuck in the wall of the attic, not unlike when I play darts in my bedroom, although I don't use the blow darts that I found in a tea chest in the attic,' Poe said, trying to explain the unexplainable, something that annoyed people, especially the children at his school who liked the mystery and did not want the mystery to be explained. No swamp beast, no Loch Ness Monster, no mystery in the Bermuda Triangle, no ghosts, no flying saucers, no Ancient Aliens, no nothing apart from science. Pseudo-science can stay in the shadows, along with the vampires, for they cast no shadow.

The Law of Poe, or the Law According to Poe, did, however, allow for parallel worlds, which was good, for it was clear as day that they were in one now. Although it could just as easily have been the spirit world they were in, especially if they were already dead. And if they were already dead then that would explain why the arrow passed straight through Sorrow's body.

'Thank God for that, or should I say thank the gods that are happy to remain in the shadows,' Sorrow exclaimed, breathing a huge sigh of relief as she imagined a giant shadow man in the shape of a pair of scissors flying through the forest, cutting everything down in its path; trees, animals and, yes, a gruesome thought indeed but even... even people!

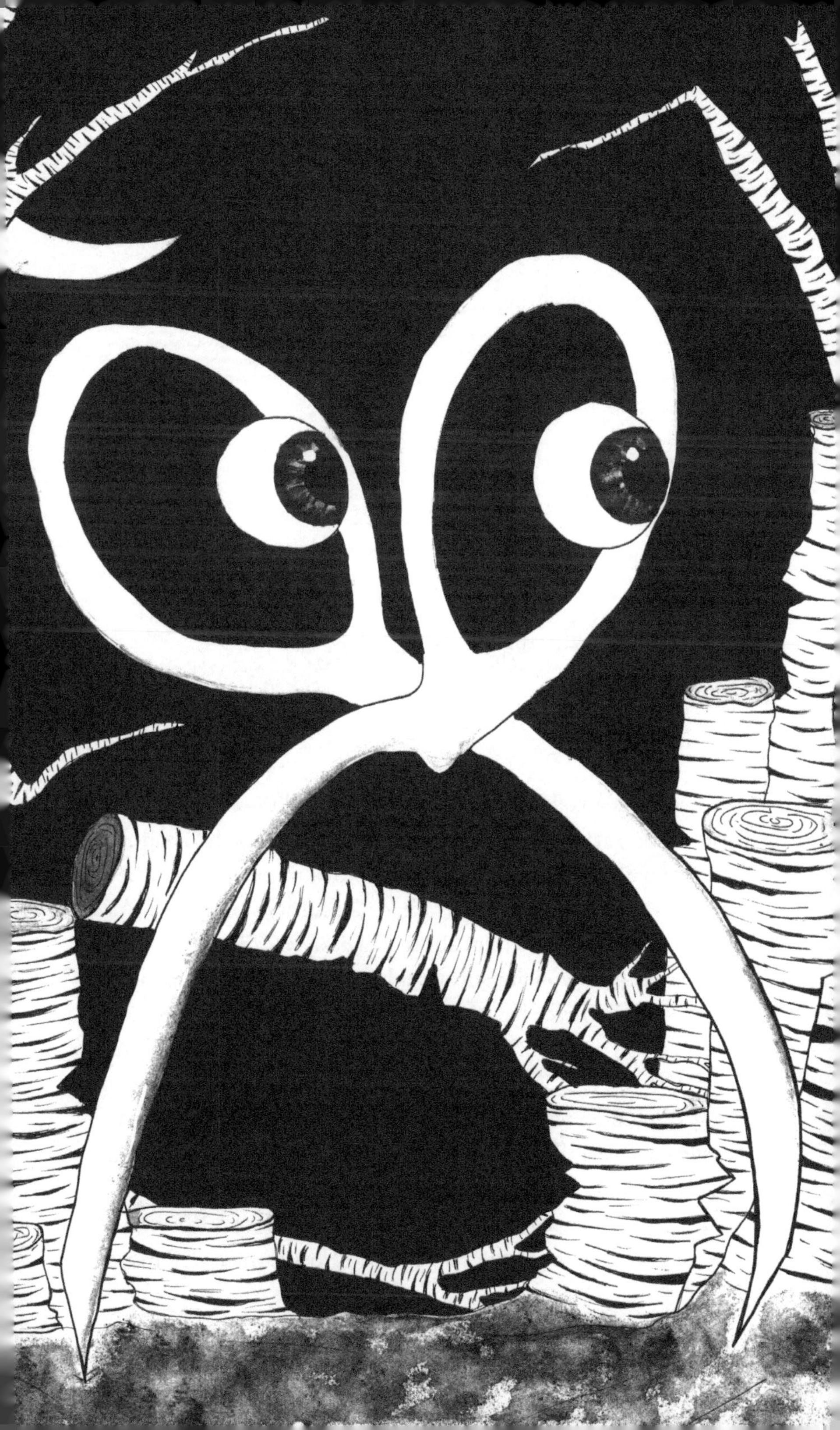

22

The Scissor Man

Sorrow was awoken by the commotion and upon seeing Poe was being sat upon by a shadow, jumped upon the shadow, as if playing the old Victorian game of jumping on another person's shadow, often a friend's, or a brother's or sister's. As Sorrow was an only child, she jumped on her own shadow, a game she never won but she never lost either, which is probably why she never, ever fell out with her own shadow. They were inseparable, like Siamese twins, in fact. 'Unhand my friend or you'll be sorry!' Sorrow cried, wrestling with the shadow.

'What are you doing?' Poe cried, although it could just as easily have been Poe's shadow that made this remark. After all, a shadow was a master of disguise. Poe imagined his shadow had turned into a tiger, hopefully, a paper tiger. Otherwise, he may well be more than a shadow of his former self, more like shadows of his former self as the shadow tiger tore him to pieces.

'Don't listen to him!' Poe's shadow cried once again, although once again it could just as easily have been Poe who made this remark. Now Sorrow was confused; she did not know if she was doing right or doing wrong. Then Poe's shadow transformed itself into a giant raven and began to peck at Poe and Sorrow as they ganged up on the bird. Poe picked up a branch of a tree and Sorrow did likewise. 'Get back, I tell you. Get back, shadow!' Poe cried as he struck out at the shadow, and with each blow of the branch it was not the raven that felt the blow but Poe. 'Stop, stop!' Poe cried, realising that once again he was beating himself up.

'But why?' Sorrow cried, still hitting out at the shadow of the raven, which was still pecking at them both, flapping its wings furiously. This caused twigs and leaves to fly all about. Of course, the twigs and leaves were just shadows, which made it appear as if moths were flying about here, there and everywhere in a manic fashion.

'Because I'm the one feeling the blow, not the raven. I'm the punch bag!' yelled Poe, wrestling the branch out of Sorrow's hand, as Sorrow and Poe were now wrestling one another upon the ground. The raven stood back and watched with curiosity then flapped its wings and flew off into the forest.

'Hey, come back, you've stolen my shadow!' Poe cried, not sure what in fact he was saying, as if he imagined the bird was a thieving magpie rather than a raven.

'Are you all right?' Poe asked Sorrow as he got to his feet, offering Sorrow his hand and pulling her to her feet.

'Yes, yes, I think so. I'm a little rough around the edges but I'll survive,' Sorrow replied, brushing herself down. 'And you?'

'Yes, although I feel a little piece of me has died, if that makes any sense. I feel more than a little rough around the edges, but then all shadows are a little rough around the edges,' Poe replied, straightening his shadow, or his appearance; he was not quite sure which. Being a shadow of your former self took a bit of getting used to. Poe was wondering if his grasp on the science of shadows was not quite as good as he had imagined it was, then he heard a sound he wished he had not heard. It was the sound of a pair of scissors cutting at the air, as if needing to find something, or someone, to cut to justify its existence.

'What was that sound?' Sorrow said, turning to Poe.

'Don't look back. Keep running, run for your life. It's the scissor man, the one who lives in my attic. He's come back for revenge. I tied the scissors up in wire to stop the scissor man cutting me to pieces in my sleep, a nightmare, or a waking nightmare. I could easily imagine both at the same time,' cried Poe, having looked back to see a giant pair of scissors cutting down everything in its path. If this was a game of rock paper scissors, and he was but a shadow, a silhouette, a paper-cut figure, he needed to find a rock to hide behind, or to befriend. Could an inanimate object really have a soul like some religions believed? Poe was having trouble believing his eyes, although funnily enough he could believe his ears as the snapping, snapping sound of metal on metal made him shudder.

The sound of scissors snapping together had always given Poe the creeps, and grated far more than fingers down a blackboard. Perhaps this was why he had never taken to art, especially the Nordic national obsession for paper art.

'Scissor man, scissor man, cutting the shadows to pieces as fast as you can!' a voice laughed out in manic fashion, a voice so cutting that Poe and Sorrow felt it cut through them like an icy wind.

This whole nightmare experience from beginning to end – of which he hadn't reached the end yet, unless the scissor man cut him to shreds, that was – was all a delusion, a psychotic episode. But how he could be sure, he could not know. Poe knew he had a bright mind, and one that had a tendency to look upon the dark side of life. It also had the ability to twist things, so things he believed to be true turned out not to be true. In the circles of mental health, this was known as paranoia. On the other hand, playing devil's advocate just because you were paranoid did not mean people were not out to get you. The scissor man was out to get him and get Sorrow, as the voice cried out again, 'Scissor man, scissor man, cut off their heads as fast as you can.'

'Help!' cried Sorrow, as the scissor man caught up with her and cut her head off, followed by a leg then an arm then another leg and finally an arm. Sorrow was lying on the floor, having been cut to pieces, but at least her sorrows were over. Poe was speechless; he could not believe what he had seen. Sorrow's shadow, a silhouette in black paper, had been cut to pieces by the scissor man. Perhaps he hadn't seen it right; perhaps he had seen it in the wrong light. After all, there was that old saying, "A trick of the light". The eyes and the mind were often deceived. Poe bent down and picked every last piece of Sorrow up, or what was left of her, hoping that if he had all of her, he could put her back together again. 'I'm not sure if I can piece you back together again, Sorrow, but I will try,' said Poe, with grim determination on his face. 'Perhaps I can if I can channel Grandfather's spirit. After all, once upon a time, he was a magician, and in his act he used to cut up pieces of paper and throw them up into the air, as if confetti. And when they came back down again, they were made whole.

Poe had seen modern street magicians bring flies back to life, but he knew that was just a trick, the fly in semi-hibernation as the warmth of the magician's hand gradually wakes the fly up. Poe knew he held Sorrow's life in his hands.

He needed some serious forest magic, and he needed it badly. Poe carefully closed the palm of his hand around the pieces of paper, as if he was holding a butterfly. Then he blew on his hand as if he had two dice in his hand in a game of craps, hoping for a lucky seven; four and three. 'I'm not big on wishful thinking, but I wish Sorrow back to life,' said Poe, trying to believe this was possible, for he was sure the trick would only work if he believed. *Storybook nonsense!*, a voice in his head said with a laugh, a voice he tried his best to ignore.

Poe closed his eyes, threw his arm into the air and opened the palm of his hand as he did so, as if releasing a dove. Snowflakes fell all about him, snowflakes that in this case were not unique but all the same, or so Poe imagined. But that was not the trick. He was not trying to create a snow woman or recreate the frost fairy but a girl, or at least the shadow of a girl. 'If you really are a changeling, Sorrow, now is the time to change,' Poe said, then holding his breath he turned his back, hoping that when he turned back around, his friend Sorrow would be standing there. Poe slowly turned around, opening one eye at a time, his face screwed up like a piece of paper he'd thrown in the rubbish bin. If this trick failed to work, when he got back to the real world, Poe would throw his childhood magic set into the rubbish bin. Poe's heart sank as his eyes were greeted by shadows, but only the shadows of the trees in the forest.

Then one of the trees moved, another trick of the moonlight or the wind blowing through the forest? But no, the tree was moving, and moving towards him. 'Sorrow, is that you?' Poe exclaimed, not sure if this tree was friend or foe. Perhaps this was a Tree Witch about to turn him into a giant horny-backed toad.

'Do you know any other girls who look like elegant silver birch trees, Poe Black? I bet you do. I bet you have a whole harem. No wonder you spend so much time in the forest,' laughed Sorrow, as she embraced a rather amazed and slightly red-faced Poe. Two shadows embracing was a most unusual sight, so two night jars who were sitting on the branch of a tree thought as they flew off into the night. When you were a shadow, it was easy to hide your embarrassment.

'What just happened?' Poe asked Sorrow, with a look of puzzlement on his face, or at least he felt that was the expression that should have been on his face.

'You must have been reading my mind, as I was about to ask you the same question,' replied Sorrow, sounding puzzled by her tone of voice.

'Well, I certainly wasn't reading your body language,' Poe said laughingly, as the relief of seeing his friend again overshadowed all other emotions.

'Look, the shadow we were following earlier has reappeared. It's over there, but it's changed its appearance. The shadow is no longer a simple shadow. It's transformed into a shadow of moonlight. Moonlight shadows are magical; they can move like quicksilver and transform into all sorts of magical forms. I imagine that one to be a mermaid with a silver tail, or a knight in shining armour,' cried Sorrow in an excited manner, as Poe imagined she had turned into a child before his very eyes, which meant her shadow was now only half the size.

'Let's follow it before the scissor man makes another unwelcome appearance in this latest nightmare, one I'd like to cut up so it ends up on the cutting-room floor,' Poe said with a grimace. Poe tried to recall what a pair of scissors represented in Sigmund Freud's book *Interpretations of Dreams*. Scissors probably represented dreams being cut down to size, along with the dreamers of those dreams. Some people seemed to delight in making cutting remarks as they cut your dreams into tiny little pieces; the first cut and the last cut were the deepest. Poe felt Sorrow had cut him to the quick when she had disappeared out of his life shortly after she had appeared out of the shadows. If the scissor man had cut out Sorrow's heart, he may just as well have cut out Poe's at the same time, and then he really would have been a paper tiger.

Poe and Sorrow then joined hands so it looked exactly as if they were paper-cut figures fashioned out of black crepe paper, and ran towards where the moonlight shadow had been standing.

Sorrow and Poe had the child in their eyes and they probably always would, along with a child-like behaviour that all those who suffered with autism had. The transformation of the shadow may have had more to do with the fact that Sorrow's shadow had shrunk so she looked like Thumbelina's shadow and Poe looked like the Little Match Girl. If Sorrow had a match, would she strike it and set Poe alight then watch him go up in flames, ashes to ashes, embers to embers? I would not imagine so, for they were still attached to one another in more ways than one.

'Look, now I've got a moonlight shadow too,' cried Sorrow, her heart as light as paper.

'As have I,' exclaimed Poe, for that was all they had, a shadow, but still, if your whole being is reduced to a shadow, what better shadow to have than one made out of moonlight?

Paper was actually the name of an anniversary for those married a year. At times Poe and Sorrow felt as if they were an old married couple tied to one another, while at other times they felt like best friends and at other times brother and sister and at other times virtual strangers. Relationships changed like the seasons. Sometimes we grew together, sometimes we grew apart, and sometimes we were torn apart, or torn from one another, whether we liked it or not.

A moon as blue as the ocean appeared out of a cloud, and Poe and Sorrow were pulled towards it and soon disappeared into the moon's silver glow.

23

The Twisted House

'A kissing gate, how romantic,' Sorrow cried, upon seeing the old-fashioned kissing gate, not realising that she and Poe were no longer moonlight shadows, their fairy-tale flight of fancy over for the time being at least. In truth, neither of them could recall this incident; it was as if their memories had been wiped.

The kissing gate was not attached to a fence or cordoning off a piece of land or property; it was as if it was either a prop from a movie or it had been there so long that the fence had been lost to the mists of time. There was an old wooden sign nailed to a tree which read - *The Disenchanted Forest This Way*. Neither Poe nor Sorrow appeared to see this sign for surely if they had, they would have walked a mile.

'I've got a feeling that we are about to fall out big time, so may I suggest we kiss and make up to get ahead of the game, or nightmare in this curious case,' said Poe, getting a lot ahead of himself, as was his wont. Poe was wondering if this was a trap, for kissing gates were legendary for snapping back and catching a person's hand or leg in the gate.

'Like before with the black garden gate we went through, I feel compelled to go through it,' Sorrow replied, as if in a trance as she walked towards the kissing gate.

Poe and Sorrow walked on through ankle-twisting terrain up and down a series of hollows until they got to a higgledy-piggledy-looking house built with the help of a Cyclopes by the looks of it. This was a Cyclopes who Poe imagined had stolen other folks' houses and dumped them one on top of the other on the instructions of an architect with a twisted mind, junkyard-like, another twist and we have the Twisted House, another twist from the kaleidoscopic mind of Poe Black and the House of Fun from an old fairground takes its place, and the kissing gate is the turnstile to which you enter the House of Fun, Poe was thinking to himself, or at least he thought he was until Sorrow piped up.

'You got all that from a twisted house, I'm impressed,' said Sorrow, blowing out her cheeks. In truth, Sorrow was impressed by whoever really did build this house, for it was a work of art, one that belonged in the Tate Modern, thought Sorrow.

'Yes, but it's not a patch on the Upside-Down House in England, or the Endless House in America,' Poe replied, not seemingly bothered or surprised that Sorrow could read his mind. Poe twisted his head first one way then the other, trying to see the house in its proper light. Poe was unsure what the proper light was for this house; perhaps it would be better if it stayed in the shadows, as to his mind it was ugly.

It brought to mind the House of Usher, although the title was the Fall of the House of Usher. Poe could not bring the author to mind. However, Poe could recall how the main character in the story felt when he first came upon the house, saying he felt a sense of melancholy, foreboding sorrow even, and that the shadows were crowding in on him. The man in this dark tale wondered whether remodelling the house would make it more pleasing to the eye and less gloomy. By the looks of the house, the owner was the type of man who got bored easily and instead of moving house remodelled it himself, as if it were a toy house. That and the owner was obviously as blind as a bat; he was probably a bat, a vampire bat. That way, he could move the separate storeys of the house around without having to risk his life climbing a long, shaky ladder.

If there was a giant in this nightmare, and one enslaved by the owner to do his dirty work, then it was the giant who was blind as a bat. A giant vampire bat did not bear thinking about; the giant could be a Cyclopes, and an old Cyclopes, poor of sight with a shaky hand. 'The moonlight would no doubt show the house in a better light,' Poe added, as finally his kaleidoscopic mind stopped twisting the image of the house this way and that.

'I'm going to walk around the outside of the house to see which is its best side,' said Sorrow, walking slowly round the house, examining it as if she were an art critic or an estate agent. 'Yes, I think the Twisted House would look perfect on Elm Street,' Sorrow added, producing a sketchpad seemingly from out of thin air, like a magician, and some artists were magicians.

'Are you sure this house has a best side?' Poe retorted, screwing his face up like a piece of tinfoil, and as he did so, the house shook as if it felt that a great sleight had been done to it. Poe imagined the house would fall on top of him just to spite him, even if it meant the house was destroyed.

'What are you doing?' spat Poe, looking in wild-eyed horror at Sorrow, as if she'd lost her mind.

'Isn't it obvious? I'm painting the nightmare, or should I say I'm sketching the nightmare, or the Nightmare House, or House of Nightmares depending upon which angle you look at the house. Vincent Van Gogh used to paint his dreams, not while he was in them, you understand, but when he woke up. The only difference is that I am painting the dream while still inside the dream, or nightmare in this case, thus making the painting more vivid. Being a Dream Analyst, I am sure you are aware that once you leave the dream world for the real world, the vivid images immediately begin to fade, losing their colour, as you are at this very moment,' Sorrow replied, as all the colour drained from Poe's face, or what little colour there was in it. For the most part, Poe's complexion was the mirror image of the figure in the painting *The Scream*.

Then everything changed as day turned to night as a giant blood-red moon appeared in the heavens, one that Poe imagined was dripping blood, for now it was raining.

'What just happened, where on earth are we now?' Sorrow exclaimed.

'We are in the back garden of the house, one full of black roses, except the owner seems to have his own personal cemetery. I hope the owner isn't a serial killer,' Poe replied, looking all about him nervously to see they were surrounded by black marble headstones. The headstones were so mirror-like in the moonlight that you could see your face in them. Poe imagined that if he stared into them for long enough, he would see his own death. But that wasn't exactly the truth, for the black marble gravestones were not gravestones, in fact, but black mirrors. Sorrow was seeing the cemetery in its true light, a magical moonlight, as the graveyard itself went through a sort of metamorphosis as the black marbled gravestones transformed into looking glasses.

'I look like death warmed up, and my hair is a terrible

fright. Talk about a nightmare. I'm certainly having a bad hair day,' Sorrow laughed, slicking her hair down as the rain plastered her hair to her head. 'I've never seen a looking-glass graveyard, very poetical, I must say. You could even say the graveyard looks like a modern work of art.'

'My dear Sorrow, a graveyard has always been a work of art, albeit a dark one. You know, the way we look, I think we could even scare the living dead. It's funny how it always rains when there's a funeral,' Poe replied, as Sorrow and Poe continued their stand-up routine in the graveyard that would have even the most downbeat souls dying of laughter. Yet there was a deathly silence in the cemetery, so it seemed this double act had just died onstage!

'Let's hope this isn't our funeral, a joint funeral. We've died on the same day and will be buried in the same grave, perhaps even the same coffin,' Sorrow replied, grimacing.

'Let's hope we are dead then. I for one don't wish to be buried alive,' Poe said, mirroring the look upon Sorrow's face. In truth, both looked as if they were wearing death masks.

'No, that's not on my bucket wish list either. Hopefully, there will be a bell in our coffin if this is a Victorian funeral,' replied Sorrow, recalling the fact to mind that the Victorians put a small bell into the coffin in case you were buried alive.

'I was going to look in the looking glass, but as I don't wish to see my own death, I think I'll give it a miss,' Poe grimaced.

'Good idea. I've had enough nightmares to last several lifetimes,' Sorrow replied, mirroring the look upon Poe's gaunt face.

'Sorrow, over here. A gravedigger, perhaps the owner, has just popped his clogs,' Poe hissed, pointing wildly at a ghostly figure who appeared to be digging a grave.

'We shouldn't disturb him. Perhaps he's digging his own grave, or if he's a ghost, he imagines that's what he's doing,' replied Sorrow, as she spun the spinning wheel in her head and the fairy tale changed direction.

'No, look, he's a grave robber,' Poe exclaimed, peeking out from behind a crooked-looking headstone.

'I don't think he is. Look, he's got a black bag. He looks like a doctor, Dr Death by the looks of him. It looks as if he's on his last legs,' said Sorrow, wiping the rain out of her eyes.

'Dr Sawbones!' Poe exclaimed then wished he had not, because the figure looked around, and if looks could kill then they undoubtedly would have.

'He's got a pair of bellows in his hand. Now he's taking some glass jars and a pair of tweezers out of his coat. Surely he's not performing a magic act in the cemetery,' said Sorrow, imagining a travelling freak show had entered the cemetery, and, after all, there was the graveyard stand-up routine, a magic act. It wouldn't be long before the sword swallowers and the jugglers and the harlequins turned up, all dying to get in on the act.

'I've seen this shadowy figure before in my nightmares. It's the nightmare catcher. He's extracting nightmares from the dead, one presumes souls that have not left the body,' hissed Poe, as his mind took him on a walk on the wild side of the cemetery.

'He can gladly extract my nightmare any time he likes,' Sorrow said, re-imagining this dark character as a dentist. She soon wished she hadn't, as the character she was picturing in her head had a sadistic streak, as he extracted the teeth without anaesthetic.

Then a giant cloud, shaped like the wing of a raven, covered the moon. The next thing Sorrow and Poe saw was the sun as it appeared on the horizon, as if in a time-lapse film, unless this wasn't the sun but the blood-red moon.

Sorrow and Poe continued their walk around the house, seemingly unaware of what had just happened.

'Come on then, follow me, slowcoach. Last one in buys the knickerbocker glories,' Sorrow cried, imagining that a part of this house used to be in a funfair, the House of Fun, and the stairs were an old helter-skelter.

'I'm coming but if this dream home falls down around our ears, don't blame me,' retorted Poe, glaring at Sorrow, or the back of her head, as Sorrow had already started for the steps of the front door, so reluctantly he followed her into the Twisted House. Once inside the house, it was exactly as Sorrow had imagined. The bottom floor was a house of fun and the twisted spiral staircase a repurposed helter-skelter, with steps that led to the top of the house.

'Its most disconcerting, discombobulating, I would say, although I could never spell the word in a million months of iced Sundays,' Poe wailed, his legs feeling like a plate of live jellied eels as he nearly slid down the stairs, as if in the blinking of an eye the stairs had been replaced by a slide. In his mind's eye, Poe was seeing the Ames Distorted Room, a psychological experiment set up to trick the mind. One wall was taller than the other and the floor slanted downwards. Standing against one was what appeared to be a very tall, thin lady. In the opposite corner of the room stood a very small lady. The truth was that both women were exactly the same weight and height. It is said the eye is like a camera and the mind like a photographic laboratory, but that is untrue, for a camera cannot lie, whereas the mind can and frequently does. The Twisted House appeared to be defying gravity, like the Leaning Tower of Pisa before it was straightened. However, in straightening the Leaning Tower of Pisa, it lost its character and its title. The Tower of Pisa, now no longer leaning, had lost its main selling point. Not that Poe wanted to sell the Leaning Tower of Pisa. Besides, the Florentines would not like it any more than the English liked it when the Americans bought the old Tower Bridge in London and rebuilt it in America.

'I'm done in,' Poe said, stopping for a breather, not sure if he was halfway up the twisted staircase or halfway down it.

Then he heard a deep, gravelly voice say, trying not to laugh, 'Done in? Not yet, my boy, but give it a little time and you will be!'

'Did you hear that?' Poe exclaimed, looking all about him, wild-eyed now, trembling at the sound of his own voice, which echoed up and down the staircase as if they were now in a gothic cathedral. Poe felt it was just a matter of time before he saw a spirit carrying its own head under its arm.

'I only heard the wind whistle through the walls, along with a few ghosts,' replied Sorrow, trying not to corpse.

'I wish there weren't so many stairs!' Poe moaned, sounding like a ghost saddled with carrying a ball and chain with him for the rest of his afterlife.

'Your wish is my command,' a disembodied voice boomed, as the stairs turned into the twisted trunk of a tree covered in ivy and vines. The tree then began to twist in an upward spiralling motion like a drill as splinters flew everywhere.

'Strap yourself in, I think we are in for a hell of a ride,' Poe cried, tying himself to the tree with a vine and some ivy. Ivy is one of the strongest weeds known to man other than Japanese knotweed. Both are almost impossible to kill off; they cling to walls long after they appear to be dead. Poe feared that by the time this journey was over, they would either be dead on their feet or just plain dead, or spirits, ghosts, having entered the spirit world.

'Hell is the other way,' Sorrow replied, also strapping herself to the tree rather reluctantly, for she recalled the time she had been tied to a tree by a puppet. Sorrow could not help feeling that in or out of the nightmare they were puppets on a string, and if they did not make it out of this nightmare alive, shadow puppets. This made her think their strings were indeed made from ivy, probably poison ivy at that!

'Repairing the hole in the roof of my house is going to put a massive hole in my savings!' Poe sighed, as he pictured his house split in two, both halves having fallen over so the house looked like an open book. Poe had never been called an open book; a closed book, yes, but never an open book.

The tree continued to spiral upwards as if boring a hole into the very sky itself, cutting through clouds, noctilucent clouds and then star clouds, which from earth made it look as if the tree were a giant spike that paper bills were spiked onto, for the clouds from earth would appear as if they were made of paper. Shooting stars shot by them like fireworks. Poe felt he could reach out and touch the stars, and tried until Sorrow put him straight: 'You'll get your fingers burnt if you're not careful!'

'It wouldn't be the first time,' Poe grimaced, quickly pulling his hand back as he felt the blazing heat from the star.

'Well, may I suggest you make it the last!' Sorrow snapped.

'It was an experiment I was carrying out. They say you cannot feel pain in a dream. If I had burnt my hand, at least we would know this is real and not simply a bad dream,' Poe said, as usual trying to explain the unexplainable.

'If this is real then it would be a waking nightmare, for you would have been burnt to a cinder, leaving poor old Cinders out of this nightmare,' Sorrow replied, trying not to look down for she, like Poe and like most people, wasn't overly fond of heights. The trouble was, the mind could not help itself. It was as curious as a child, and soon they both found themselves looking down at a tiny house no bigger than a faerie dolls' house.

'The House that Jack built and the giant's house in the fairy story *Jack in the Beanstalk* are not a patch on this house in the star fields. What a view, not sure about the neighbours, though, too many giants for my liking, Orion, Perseus, and the pond at the end of the garden contains a giant sea creature, Cetus, Hydra the water snake, not to mention Draco the dragon,' Poe exclaimed, forgetting the nightmare, as this seemed more like a dream, and a wondrous one at that, seeing the wonders of the universe from the best seat in the house. Poe wanted to untie himself from the tree so he could fly, or at least float, for if this really was space then they would not be tied to the earth's gravitational field.

'What on earth are you doing, have you gone mad?' Sorrow exclaimed, as Poe began to loosen the ivy and vines tying him to the star tree, as Poe was imagining the tree. If the tree was a magical silver birch tree with its white and silvery bark then was this imagining so far-fetched? Yes, but not so far-fetched as to make it a complete stretch of the imagination.

Talking of hot seats, the worst seat in the house was the one the Chinese Emperor fell out of, according to oriental stargazers, that giant seat being known as The Chair as it is turned upon its head as it moves across the sky; another optical illusion, as Poe was imagining this dream to be an optical illusion.

'I wish you hadn't mentioned Draco the dragon, Poe,' Sorrow sighed, as no sooner had the words left Poe's mouth than a giant black dragon made of stars popped up out of thin air, or as Sorrow was now imagining it, a giant Victorian stargazer's pop-up book. The giant black dragon was now circling the tree in menacing fashion, breathing fire, which set a part of the tree ablaze.

'I'll huff and I'll puff and I'll blow your tree house down,' spat the fiery dragon, or at least these were the words coming out of the mouth of the dragon that Sorrow was hearing in her head.

'I wish I hadn't mentioned there being too many stairs in this nightmare house of many horrors,' sighed Poe, and as he did, the house stopped spiralling upwards and began to spiral back down towards the centre of the earth.

'Hopefully, the spinning motion will put the flames out. Otherwise, we might find ourselves being burnt at the stake, and a very big stake at that!' exclaimed Poe, hearing the words in his head, the exact same words Sorrow was now hearing herself utter.

Draco the dragon had been sucked into the tree and was then violently spat out again as stars, dust and matter were sucked into the vortex then spat out again just as quickly and just as violently. The star giants were either sucking in their breath as they consumed suns and stars as if they were food, energy ones that made them even more powerful, or as if they were trying to put out the giant twisted fire stick, or a giant tinderbox, as Poe had re-imagined the tree.

'It's like being inside a giant twister, inside a spiralling galaxy, inside a giant black kaleidoscope, inside a supermassive black hole,' Poe cried, seeing so many stars in his head that it was as if every universe in the multiverse was now inside his head. If that wasn't a weird way out, thought Poe, he did not know what was.

'A world inside a world inside a world, or alternatively, and here I think I can top that fantastical imagining, a twister inside a black hole inside Pandora's black box,' cried Sorrow, her mind now a fiery twisting mass like the inside of a black hole. Sorrow felt as if her mind, body and soul were being sucked out of her body through her nose. The pain was agonising. If they had really been sucked into a black hole, at least it would have been quick. Sorrow imagined that after this misadventure, too weird for both words and pictures, her mind would be black, like the universe at the end of time and space.

'I would say welcome to the Twisted House, but you are not welcome. In fact, you are most unwelcome. I hope you wiped your feet on the cork mat. If you didn't, I'll wipe the floor with you. Now I do hope you liked your first nightmare, bespoke, especially for you, by yours truly, the nightmare catcher at your disservice. You can thank me later if you survive all the nightmares,' a voice at the end of the room said coldly.

There was an old rocking chair at the end of the room, facing the opposite way. The figure was dressed in black, unless the figure was a shadow. There was a large mirror on the wall and as they grew close, they could see a shadowy figure in the mirror, but they could not tell if the figure was a man or a woman or a beast dressed in a black shawl, like the sheep in the rowing boat in the old shop in *Alice Through the Looking Glass*. The shadow figure then walked over to a spinning wheel and started to spin a story, a story Poe and Sorrow imagined to be their dark fairy life stories. The spinning wheel was turning in an anticlockwise direction so fast that smoke was rising up to the ceiling, creating a small dark cloud that Poe imagined would soon hang over them, perhaps forever. Was this shadowy figure spinning a tale or re-spinning a tale, re-spinning their life story?

'Come closer. Don't be shy, I've been dying to meet you,' the shadowy figure said, stretching out a long bony-looking finger, one that looked like a branch of a tree.

'Well, you've changed your tune. First, you were pulling the unwelcome mat from under our feet, and next, you're welcoming us in with open arms, welcoming us into your nightmare, perhaps that is why,' Poe said, not moving any closer. 'I can't be sure but I think we may be inside someone's head, the attic of their mind, so to speak,' said Poe, not making any sense, but as he appeared to be mirroring the house and the owner, then that didn't seem to matter.

'If we are, I wish they would have a light-bulb Eureka moment,' said Sorrow, dryly.

'I'm being serious. I think we are in the mind of the nightmare catcher, in his twisted mind, by the looks of the state of this place. It looks as if it hasn't been cleaned for years, cobwebs everywhere you look.' Poe coughed, swallowing a large cobweb and God knows how many large spiders. Still, perhaps his bad luck had changed and some of those spiders were money spiders.

'So, I take it that last horror show was only a nightmare. It wasn't real, it was an illusion, although I can't believe I said only a nightmare,' Poe said, talking to the back of the figure's head.

'What is real and what is unreal? You of all people, Poe Black, a young man who loves the quantum world with a passion bordering on obsession, should know nothing's that black and white.'

'Help, I'm sliding sideways!' Poe cried, as the house started to tilt.

'I think we are unwelcome guests who have outstayed our welcome. I think you've upset the owner of this house of horrors. a house of horrors inside a house of horrors,' Sorrow cried, as in her head she pictured Russian dolls' houses, one inside the other, getting smaller and smaller, and all this Sorrow imagined as she and Poe slid across the room in slow motion.

'If we are inside the mind of the nightmare catcher then we should fall out of his ear any second now!' Poe exclaimed, trying to hang on to a cabinet or curiosity but only managing to grab an old birdcage on a stand. Thankfully, there wasn't a bird in the cage, unless the bird in the cage was a ghost bird!

The house leant so far over that it almost touched one of the trees growing close by the house.

'Jump!' Sorrow cried, as she jumped and fell into the branches of a large weeping willow tree.

'I'd rather not,' Poe spluttered, hanging on for grim death to one of the window shutters, which flapped so violently that in the end he was shaken off and he fell, and as he did so, Poe found himself wondering if this was another of those cliffhanger moments. In the end, he decided this was not the case, for he had fallen off the edge of a house and not a cliff. It was good to get things in perspective as you fell to your death, good to get your house in order before you came face to face with the grim reaper!

24

The Edge of Reality

Poe was sure he was falling to his death, but thankfully a tree told him otherwise, for it was a tree that broke his fall and it appeared he did it without breaking any major bones, apart from his bonehead. It appeared that not for the first time Poe Black had over exaggerated his own death, and probably not for the last time.

'How come the tree saved you and dropped me?' bemoaned Poe, picking himself up off the ground as he removed a twig that was sticking out of his ear, which made him look like a scarecrow.

'Couldn't say, perhaps I'm just lighter boned,' Sorrow sniffed, as she gave the tree that saved her life a great big bear hug.

'Are you saying I'm big boned?' snapped Poe indignantly,

popping his nose back into joint, as clearly it had just been put out of joint by Sorrow's snide remark.

'Big boned, am I saying that? Yes, yes, you know, I think I am saying that. It's not your fault. You probably come from a long line of giants, it happens. You see it all the time on reality TV, a family of dwarves, excuse my language, little people, give birth to a person of normal size. Although what's normal and what's abnormal, I'm not sure anybody can tell one from the other. The lines are so blurred that it's hard to tell the normals from the abnormals,' Sorrow said, twisting herself up in so many knots that it would take Harry Houdini a week to untie her.

'Cheek of the girl, this is my life story, not yours. You're just along for the ride,' Poe retorted, huffing and puffing, wishing he could blow this nightmare house of horrors down like a house of cards.

'A nightmare ride on a never-ending rollercoaster ride, which just keeps going round and round and round. The next time you need a friend, Poe Black, to go on a journey with you, please don't ask me, for I'll be permanently out to lunch!' snapped Sorrow, crossing her arms across her chest and turning her back on Poe.

'When you've finished flouncing out of the nightmare, I think we'd better get out of here,' Poe said, trying to get back into Sorrow's good books. There seemed little chance of getting back into the nightmare catcher's good books, for all the books in his small library were bad books: *Bad to the Bone* by A Bonehead, *How Not to Mend your Bad Ways* by E Ville and a small selection from *The Library of Nightmares*.

'In hindsight, looking back through the nightmare, I probably shouldn't have borrowed that gold antique diamond-studded pocket watch on the mantelpiece. It's not my fault, you know. I'm a kleptomaniac, it runs in the family. I come from a long line of kleptomaniacs. Still, it could have been worse. I could have come from a long line of pyromaniacs!' Sorrow smiled, or at least she imagined she was smiling.

'I don't normally condone theft, but in this case I can make an exception, as it may stop the nightmare catcher breaking into my dreams, standing over my bed as he tries to hypnotise me into following him into a nightmare,' Poe smiled. It appeared for the moment at least that Poe and Sorrow had finally buried the hatchet. Better still, they had achieved this without burying that hatchet in either one of their thick wooden heads.

The Twisted House, covered in cobwebs, was within spitting distance of a large tear-shaped pond, draped by weeping willow trees. Poe had already imagined the pond was created by the tears cried by the willow trees, for this dark place seemed draped and dripping in sadness.

'You mean the nightmare we are still in?' Sorrow replied, as she stepped shakily into the rowing boat that was tied to the jetty by the pond as Poe followed her lead.

'Yes, the nightmare we are still in, although we've been in so many nightmares that it's hard to keep up. I'm no longer sure which nightmare we are in,' Poe said with a sigh, scratching his head.

'I would imagine we are inside the nightmare inside the forest inside the attic, as I'm pretty sure we are no longer inside the nightmare inside the mind of the nightmare catcher,' Sorrow added, also scratching her head as two nits popped out to say hello and goodbye.

'How sure are you percentage wise?' asked Poe, turning to Sorrow as they sat in the rowing boat, each with an oar, slowly starting to row across the pond.

'One hundred per cent,' Sorrow replied, dropping her oar to point at a giant shadowy figure that had appeared out of the door of the Twisted House, which was now running towards them, shaking its fist violently.

'That's nine hundred per cent, shy of my new quantum figure of one thousand per cent!' Poe exclaimed, trying not to imagine Pythagoras twisting and turning in his grave.

'That's because you're looking in the wrong end of your kaleidoscope,' Sorrow spat, shaking her head in a sorrowful manner, thinking that not only was Poe no Einstein but he was no Pythagoras either.

'Ah yes, I see clearly now. I blame my kaleidoscopic mind. It clearly seems to enjoy twisting things. No wonder I can't see the wood for the trees,' replied Poe, as he appeared to screw up his face so it looked as if a moth-eaten handkerchief or a cobweb was now covering his face.

'Because we just stepped into this nightmare without an end, I'm not sure how we are going to get out. We don't have a map,' Sorrow said, trying out a bit of Poe thinking, or overthinking in Poe's case.

'I think the woods are just the other side of the Twisted Forest,' Poe replied, as if indeed he did have a map of every nightmare that had ever been written.

Poe and Sorrow set off in search of Nightmare's End, as if their very lives depended upon reaching the end of the nightmare. The nightmare catcher did not give chase; it appeared he had better things to do than scare the living daylights out of two such sensitive souls. The catcher went looking for a new challenge, leaving the spirit of the forester to take up the slack, or the nightmare in this case.

Poe and Sorrow reached the shore, escaping the clutches of the nightmare catcher, Dr Sawbones and the scissor man, although they did not imagine for one moment they had escaped from the nightmare itself. At least this nightmare had a happy ending. So, Poe and Sorrow walked on through the forest, knowing it was just a matter of time before the forest once again changed, hoping all the time that it would be a change for the better and not for the worse.

25

The Impenetrable Forest

'There is no one here. The silence is deafening,' Sorrow said, looking downcast.

'It's a forest of ghosts, ghost gorillas,' said Poe, mirroring the expression on Sorrow's face, for a blanket of mist hung over this forest, except to Sorrow and Poe it felt like a giant shroud.

'Unless they're hiding deep within the forest, using the mists as a giant cloak of invisibility,' replied Sorrow, thinking out loud.

'Or they have disappeared back into the mists of time, like Rasputin and Anastasia,' said Poe, wondering if they too were ghosts and did not realise it. They had both come so close to death so many times that it would not have come as a surprise if this was the case. It was the classic Victorian ghost story where the ghost believes himself to be real until they realise the terrible truth. Still, being dead was not so bad; you no longer had to be afraid you were going to be killed in some terrible nightmarish way. Yes, every cloud had a silver lining.

Poe and Sorrow could not see any silver lining to losing the fantastical beasts that were the silverback gorillas that lived in the famed mists of the Impenetrable Forest in Uganda. This forest, like so many others, had begun to shrink so that now from Google Earth it looked no bigger than a forest on a model railway set, or a wood in a model village.

Poe sometimes pictured the silverback gorillas huddled together in a tiny forest, frozen in time under a glass Victorian dome. The mist was dry ice. Other times, he pictured the silverback gorillas playing in a fake forest, like the one at Helsinki Airport, being gawped at by passengers on their way to catch their connection for their flight. The gorillas in the mist were vanishing fast and doing it before our very eyes. Now you see them, now you don't; a conjuring trick gone bad, for the gorillas never reappeared. Dian Fossey was one of Sorrow's heroines, a woman who lived among the gorillas, her life story made into a film, *Gorillas in the Mist*.

'Hey, look, Poe, gorillas. They are not extinct after all!' Sorrow cried, and for once these were not tears of sorrow but tears of joy.

'I think your eyes and your heart deceive you, these are but ghosts,' Poe said, not moving as the gorillas charged towards him at great speed.

'Get out of the way, for God's sake, get out of the way, Poe, or you'll be killed!' exclaimed Sorrow, her tears of joy short-lived.

'I cannot be harmed by ghosts. It's the living we should be more afraid of. Besides, even if these gorillas were real, for the most part, they are gentle beasts and would not harm a fly, unless attacked,' Poe replied calmly, smiling as the beasts were now almost upon him. Poe was picturing any number of naturalists on TV sitting happily with the beasts, as if they were their children. Sorrow could sense that Poe could not see the wood for the trees as the gorillas stampeded towards Poe and ran right over him, as if they were not interested in him but the prey they were chasing, or imagined they were chasing. Perhaps the gorillas, like Poe and Sorrow, were chasing ghosts. Poe looked dead to the world, or perhaps he was simply playing dead in the hope the gorillas would leave him alone.

'Poe, Poe, speak to me,' Sorrow cried, holding Poe's head in her hands as she wept uncontrollably.

'Parting is such sweet sorrow, Sorrow,' said Poe, his voice little more than a whisper as he lifted his head and quoted Shakespeare, although not before he winked at Sorrow theatrically before delivering the killer line, 'And if I am to continue this conversation from the afterlife, I may need a necromancer to speak on my behalf. I think a parting may suit me, like the Victorian artist Aubrey Beardsley, who also died before his time.' Poe smiled weakly as if it pained him greatly to lift his head.

'You beast, you absolute beast. You're a monster, a little monster, how could you! How could you let me believe you were dead!' yelled Sorrow, instantly letting go of Poe's head, which hit the ground with a thud as Sorrow's sorrow turned to anger and the red mist descended.

'I'm dead sorry, will that do?' Poe said with a grimace, realising a little late that his head now hurt like hell. 'Ow, that hurt. You're no Florence Nightingale, more like Florence "Deadly" Nightshade!' Poe grimaced, wondering if he was turning not into a werewolf but a gorilla. 'Did you know that once upon a different time, Florence Nightingale said,

"Outside my hospital, some men are princes, some men are paupers, but inside my hospital all men are princes."'

'What happened to the princesses?' Sorrow scowled as if her feminist heroine Florence Nightingale was not quite so big on women's rights as she imagined her to be.

'They, like a lot of Victorian women, were invisible,' Poe replied, po-faced. 'Doctors and nurses are real heroes, don't you think? I know they were portrayed that way during the coronavirus, and rightly so. In truth, they have always been the unsung heroes, like those who work for the fire service.'

'True,' Sorrow replied, stopping her rant long enough to consider the real heroes of life and death. 'Stop trying to sidetrack me. I'm still mad as hell,' Sorrow snapped, glowering at Poe, and if looks could kill, they certainly would have done.

Poe was going to utter the old wives' tale, *If the wind changes, you'll be stuck looking that way*, but wisely bit his tongue. Poe was so hungry, for his exertions in the forest, running away from nightmares and battling with devils and demons made you ravenously hungry. Poe would have eaten his own tongue if it were not for the fact he would no longer be able to tease Sorrow. To Poe, and to most men, a woman's mind was as impenetrable as the Impenetrable Forest, a tangled mess of twisted thoughts, every bit as tangled as Medusa's hair of vipers, their twisted logic impossible to untwist.

To Sorrow, and to most women, men were Neanderthals, beasts who predominately lived their lives in their man caves.

'I'm dead sorry. Will that do?' Poe sniffed, feigning an apology. Sorrow was not impressed; she could see right through Poe's sorry excuse for an apology.

'I'd like to say I feel your pain, Poe, but the only pain I feel is for the silverback gorillas, and if I had my way, I'd put your head on the top of a spike, like Attila the Hun used to do to his victims.' Sorrow huffed, crossing her hands across her chest as she turned her back on her friend, her-ex friend as she was now seeing things.

'Don't you think you're being a little bit melodramatic, a little spiky?' Poe sniggered, trying to make light of his near-death experience, 'and please don't flounce out of the forest, for if you do, you'll get lost, which means I'll get lost trying to find you.'

'Sorry, I thought I heard a voice. No, I must have been mistaken. It must have been the long-since extinct call of the Man Beast, the one that became extinct around the same time as the dodo and the lesser-known bird, the speckled Poe,' huffed Sorrow, crossing her arms across her chest, falling short of falling into teenage speak, *You're dead to me!* or *I hate you, I hate you, I hate you.* In truth, Sorrow preferred Victorian speak to teenage speak, which she found even more theatrical and melodramatic than Victorian speak. If the gorillas were watching this scene play out in the forest, they would have found it quite entertaining, for when Sorrow and Poe were engaged in a conversation, it appeared as if they were a Victorian couple.

'You left the corpse bird off your list of extinct species,' Poe added playfully. 'Besides, I thought it would be good practice to play dead. It may come in handy one fine day if we find ourselves in the Land of the Living Dead. In all honesty, I thought I played the part of the dead body as well as any wooden Hamlet or Romeo, ones who looked as if rigor mortis had already set in while onstage, waiting for Juliet to kick the old bucket. I feared I might corpse, but no, I managed to play the role of the stiff with great aplomb. Here's your chance to get your own back, Sorrow, your line is... over my dead body.'

'Standing over your dead body would give me no satisfaction. Standing over your body while you were still alive, while you were being buried alive, well, that would undoubtedly bring a smile to my face. Now if you would like me to arrange your funeral, I would be happy to do so. If you could give me a list of funeral songs, I could start making the arrangements!' spat Sorrow. It was clear that she was in no mood to kiss and make up, as she was picturing Poe as a dead man walking.

'I'm sorry,' sniffed Poe, uttering what he thought of as the magic word.

'You will be if you ever do anything like that again,' snapped Sorrow, speaking out of the back of her head, or this was how it appeared to Poe.

'Come on, Sorrow, I want to get a closer look at the gorillas now they are out of the mist, before they vanish again,' Poe said, leading the way through the mist, deeper into the forest.

'You have just seen the gorillas up close and personal. How much closer do you want to get? Put yourself in their place, get under their skin,' Sorrow retorted, still not ready to let go of her anger.

'Let it go, Sorrow, or it will eat you up,' Poe said, trying not to smile. The thought of getting under a gorilla's skin did not appeal on so many levels, as the smile upon Poe's face soon turned to a grimace.

'What will eat me up?' Sorrow exclaimed, sucked into the conversation whether she liked it or not.

'Your inner monster, or your inner demons,' said Poe laughingly, unable to help himself teasing his friend. Then an image appeared in Poe's head of a female Dr Jekyll and Miss Hyde and as it did so, Poe immediately stopped laughing, for he did not want to be laughing on the other side of his face, for he knew his inner demons were never far away from escaping from the cage in which they were imprisoned: his skull.

'My inner monster won't eat me up, but it may eat you up if you don't pull your head in!' Sorrow snapped, as her inner monster continued to get the better and the very worst of her. It was often the case that the best of friends could easily become the worst of enemies. Poe did not think that now was the time to play the part of the know-it-all, as gorillas were vegetarians and they may well have been vegans as well for all he knew.

Poe and Sorrow knew they could be their own worst enemies at times, while other times they could be their own best friends. It was time to kiss and make up, as they both knew they needed one another's help if they were ever to get out of this nightmare alive!

Then a giant silver shadow appeared in a clearing, one beating its chest in anger as if to say you do not belong in this world. The truth was, Poe and Sorrow were not sure which world they did belong in. They never felt as if they truly belonged anywhere, like nomads wandering from one place to another, never settling anywhere.

'When in doubt in such a situation as this, I find the best policy is to… RUN!' Poe yelled at the top of his lungs, grabbing Sorrow by the hand as they ran for their lives. By this time, Poe and Sorrow were used to running for their lives.

'I think if I ever get out of this nightmare, I might well make the Russian athletic squad for the next Olympic Games!' Sorrow puffed, bent double as the stitch in her side felt as if someone was stabbing her with a hot knitting needle. Sorrow tried to blank out ghost witches trying to knit her bones together, making it impossible for her to run for her life.

'Either that or the Hunger Games. I could eat a horse. I even think I could eat a unicorn, as long as I had some sweetcorn and brown sauce to make it more palatable!' replied Poe, wheezing like an old man climbing up a very steep hill.

'The Hunger Games, I'll give those games a wide berth if it's all the same to you,' spat Sorrow, screwing up her face so it looked as if she was wearing a death mask.

'Did you notice something strange about that shadow?' asked Poe, bent double, panting heavily.

'You mean that it had two heads?' Sorrow replied, blowing hard as she tried to stand upright.

'I thought I was imagining it,' Poe replied.

'So did I until you mentioned it,' said Sorrow, imagining a gorilla in a cage caught by hunters and then displayed in a zoo, or a travelling freak show, like King Kong.

'There have been many hybrid creatures on earth over the centuries, although some were faked, but I've never seen a two- headed gorilla,' Poe replied, wide-eyed, as his mind took a walk on the wild side.

'It probably wasn't real, just one conjured up by the forest or the forester, the freak whose spirit appears to be running this giant freak show,' Sorrow said with a grimace, looking nervously all about her, as if she felt the forest was listening in on their conversation and taking notes.

'Yes, like the gorillas I thought were ghosts, which almost killed me dead in my tracks. That's the problem. We don't know what is real and what isn't in this forest,' said Poe, speaking his mind but doing so in a hushed tone, in case the forest was eavesdropping in on the conversation. Poe looked over his shoulder; he was sure the trees were all leaning towards where he and Sorrow were standing. It was true that walls had ears, big ears, the size of an African elephant's, or at least Poe imagined the walls of the attic had ears. The fact there was an elephant's head mounted on a wooden plaque on the wall of the downstairs living room may have put this image into Poe's already feverish mind.

'Yes, I agree, no more fighting. Together we stand, divided we fall,' Sorrow said, speaking in a loud voice, as if she wanted to tell the forest it would not break them or divide them.

'Nice speech, do you think that goes for a gorilla with two

heads?' said Poe, raising his voice as he forced himself to laugh out loud, encouraging Sorrow to do likewise, trying to lighten the mood. Poe was showing the forest that they were the sort of people who laughed in the face of death, in other words, idiots!

The forest just smiled. It was playing the long game; it could wait, bide its time. After all, the fun and games in the Forest House of Fun had just begun. Where would the fun be if it killed its prey off now? It would play with its prey first then when the time was right, it would go in for the kill, a slow kill.

Then things got even stranger as a silverback gorilla started to cosy up to Sorrow, as Poe saw the green-eyed monster steam coming out of his ears as the red mist descended. 'The beast, I should give him a damned good old-fashioned horse whipping!'

'I wouldn't if I were you, Poe. He's likely to whip your scrawny ass, pull your lungs out through your throat and feed them to his family!' Sorrow laughed, being just a little too descriptive for Poe's liking. But that was writers all over; they could not help themselves telling it like it wasn't, any more than mischievous elves couldn't help tying children's hair into elf knots while they were asleep. Most stories needed a makeover to make them sound more exciting, even true stories.

Gunfire was then heard and a rustling in the trees of gorillas running scared, as the ardour of the amorous silverback male was quelled as he ran off to defend his family.

'That sounds like the gun of a hunter to me,' Sorrow exclaimed, scowling for all she was worth.

'Come on, the gorillas may need our help,' Poe cried, as he and Sorrow charged into the undergrowth without a thought for their own safety.

26

The Sorrows of Poe Black

'Stop that. You should not be hunting such beautiful creatures, it's wrong,' Sorrow spat, stepping out in front of the hunter, who simply looked at her as if she had lost her mind. The hunter then roughly pushed her to one side so he could get a better shot at the family of gorillas that were all huddled together in fear. That was all apart from the head of the clan, a giant beast that beat his chest furiously and howled in an attempt to scare the hunter off. Birds and animals flew off into the trees, but the hunter stood his ground. What Poe and Sorrow didn't know was that the gorillas were not just protecting their young, they were protecting an old woman, an anthropologist, who often travelled to the Impenetrable Forest, who once upon another time had lived in Poe's house.

But they were in Poe's house, his house of horrors, trapped in the house as surely as gorillas were trapped inside cages in zoos all around the world. Or was that too a lie, a fairy tale? Had they, in fact, slipped into another time and dimension, into another space in another part of the world? Once again, it was hard to know what was real and what was a conjuration of the forest, or the dark mind of the forester.

The anthropologist in the forest in this world had been accepted into the group of gorillas and had taught them sign language. She saw herself as their mother protector, like the anthropologist Jane Goodall, who had studied primates for years, had even given them names, much to the annoyance of her fellow scientists who preferred to give the primates numbers. Unfortunately, the anthropologist in this case had begun to lose her memory, the onset of early dementia, and now it was the gorillas looking after her. The gorillas at times were puzzled by her change in behaviour, every bit as they were by their ever- changing environment, an environment that was changing rapidly as their magical space began to shrink as fast as their species. It was hard to understand man's attitude to its fellow creatures, especially as gorillas and apes were on the same family tree as man.

Whereas before the hunter cut a ghostly figure, one who they imagined was hunting ghost gorillas rather than real ones, now he took on a more menacing appearance. His true form was now revealed, like in a clever conjuring trick, a giant of a man who looked every bit as tall as a redwood tree and every bit as sturdy as an oak. The hunter lifted his gun and with a steely glint in his eye, fired several times, just missing the family of gorillas. The giant silverback gorilla charged towards the hunter in a rage as the red mist descended. If the hunter got his way, the famed mist of the Impenetrable Forest would be a red mist of blood, permanently hanging in the air, like dew in a graveyard in the morning. Sorrow had managed to scramble to her feet, although she was shaky, both of mind and body. But with grim determination, she managed to move quickly enough to trip the hunter up, who was taken unawares.

The hunter looked shocked and fell like a giant tree in a forest as the ground seemed to shake and shudder as he landed. The bigger they come, the harder they fall, was how the old saying went. That was not quite true in this case, as the giant tree man quickly bounced back to his feet. Looking through the eyes of Poe and Sorrow, it appeared as if this was a nature documentary shown in reverse as the tree that had fallen stood straight back up. The hunter regained his composure and his steely glare, his feet firmly planted upon the ground, as if he really were a tree, and an unmovable one, its roots twisted so deep in the earth that nothing would uproot it, not even a twister. The hunter stared right through Sorrow as if she wasn't there. If looks could kill, Sorrow would have died right there and then on the spot, or have been turned to stone, as had happened to the trees in the Petrified Forest.

Then the hunter turned his gun not at the gorillas but at Sorrow, who looked horrified, mirroring the pale, ghostly expression on Poe's face. Poe looked as if he had seen a ghost, the ghost of Sorrow White, as he fast forwarded the film to the end, a bitter end. It seemed the hunter did not mind what he hunted as long as he had a trophy to take back to his home, to hang on the wall next to all the others, both animal and human. No doubt when the hunter passed from this world, he would hunt ghosts, such was his love of hunting.

As the hunter cocked his old blunder-bust shotgun and aimed, a female gorilla appeared out of the mist and charged. In an instant, the gorilla was right in the man's face. The hunter dropped the firearm in shock, his heart in his mouth. Sorrow could see the man had a sidearm, a pistol in a holster slung round his waist like an old gunslinger. The hunter drew the gun with the speed of an old-time gunslinger as Sorrow leapt to the gorilla's aid, just as it was in the process of taking a swipe at the man, but as it did so, the silverback gorilla knocked Sorrow flying. Sorrow collapsed and in doing so, hit her head on a large tree stump and then she lay not moving a muscle. Sorrow never moved again, although a shadow appeared to rise out of her body and fly away.

Poe could not believe it. Sorrow was alive one second, dead the next, and he felt dead too, dead inside.

The hunter was not finished yet. He picked up his gun, reloaded and fired at the gorillas. Poe was so enraged that as the red mist descended, he charged towards the hunter as if he were charging rhino. The hunter seemed to show no compassion, as if he were an assassin trained to kill without remorse, without giving it a second thought, then a shadow appeared out of left field and knocked the hunter to the ground as he fired his gun. It was the tiger Poe imagined had been tracking them the whole time, watching over them. Poe's mind was spinning wildly, first one way then the other, as two of his friends lay on the ground; one human, one animal. Poe wasn't sure who he should run towards so he could comfort them as they lay dying.

Poe stood in the clearing in the forest along with the gorillas at Sorrow's funeral; there wasn't a dry eye in the forest. The gorilla that had accidentally caused Sorrow's untimely death had its head bowed. Poe wasn't sure if the beast was weeping or if it was simply the mist in the forest that hung so low that it was as if the trees in the forest were themselves weeping. Did gorillas cry, did animals cry? Poe imagined that being so close to man, gorillas did cry; they certainly mourned their dead and became attached to human beings who cared for them. Poe walked up to the gorilla and put a consoling arm around him, for he felt its pain. There was a strong connection between man and these beautiful beasts, or at least there should be. It was man who should be protecting them, putting a metaphorical arm around them and the forests they called home.

The funeral was taken by the anthropologist, a good Christian woman named Olivia, who read from her beat-up old black leather-covered Bible. Having dementia herself, her mind, like the forest, was covered in mist, so much so that she was having trouble reading the words on the page. That was until one of the silverback gorillas sat down beside her, pawing at her leg, as if the creature was prompting her.

Poe helped dig Sorrow's grave and did it with a heavy heart, as did the silverback gorillas, with some instructions from the anthropologist. It felt to Poe as if he were digging his own grave. He wished he could swap places with Sorrow, but that was some dark wishful thinking on his part. This was one sorrow Poe Black had to bear on his own, although right at this moment in time, it felt as if he was carrying the weight of the world on his young shoulders. Even more so because Poe knew that he would soon have to leave his newfound friends and be on his way, and do so on his own.

27

The Perfect Forest

Poe trudged on through the forest, his heart heavy. He was alone in paradise, Plato's perfect world, or at least his perfect forest, as Poe found himself in a forest that appeared perfect, without a flaw, not a diseased tree in sight. But without Sorrow it was a hollow experience, a paradise lost rather than found. Poe felt he may just as well have been in a forest full of hollowed-out tree trunks. Poe imagined being trapped in the trunk of a tree, screaming to get out, like the silver birch trees in the twisted forest, as if forced to wear a straitjacket for the rest of his life.

Perfect wasn't all it was cracked up to be. Imperfections were what made us all feel human, separated us from the robots and AI. That's why Poe loved the beauty of the silver birch trees with their willowy appearance and their cracked copper and white rolled gold-like bark.

Poe was imperfect, he knew that, and the same could have been said of his friend Sorrow, for they had been like twins, and twins separated often die quickly afterwards, die of a broken heart. It was as if they were one and could only live as one entity. In Plato's perfect world full of perfect forms, Poe felt out of place. He was waiting for the forest to realise this and expel him from the forest, as the human body does to a foreign body when it enters the bloodstream. Poe would have been happy if one of these perfect trees fell on him; it would be the perfect death. 'Come on, forest, what are you waiting for? Oh no, that's right, you'd rather make me suffer, and suffer alone. Twist the knife in, and do it so slowly as to extend my suffering as long as possible.'

Poe looked up at the sky, or was it the ceiling of the attic? He wondered if Sorrow's spirit was up there, looking down at him, an angel in heaven, or at least a dark angel, her shadow. Plato believed that human beings were living in a shadow world, and that if we pulled back the curtain, we would be greeted by a world of even more wonders than the world we were living in. Poe started to climb one of the trees with a grim look of determination upon his face. Had he lost his mind, did he really think he could climb all the way to heaven? No, he hadn't lost his mind. Poe had had enough of the forest playing with him like a puppet on a string. This puppet was going to finally cut its strings, even if that meant he became a shadow puppet.

Poe had decided this game had gone on long enough. He was the last character left alive in this dark fairy-tale world, but there was no feeling of elation at being the last man standing. He would choose his own ending, a swallow dive from the top of a tall tree. Poe tried not to think of his shattered body lying limp upon the ground; he preferred to think of his shadow flying towards heaven, where he would be met by an angel named Sorrow.

Poe had scaled the mountain and was now standing at the very top of the tree. He didn't have a great head for heights, not that it mattered, for he had made up his mind to join Sorrow in the afterlife. Poe took one last sharp intake of breath, his last, or so he imagined. He wondered who else would breathe in his last breath; probably the forest, the lungs of the planet. Poe hoped that if the forest did suck in his last breath, the forest choked on it, choked to death. If it did, Poe would die laughing. Then Poe stopped himself as he heard a voice. At first, he could not see where it was coming from, then he looked down and saw a large white wolf. The wolf was the wolf that had welcomed him into the attic, welcomed him into the nightmare, more like, the one he had named White Wolf. Could this be the spirit of his mother in the form of a wolf?

'It isn't your time,' cried the white wolf, looking up at Poe as it circled the tree in an agitated fashion.

'It isn't your time. I remember that line from somewhere,' muttered Poe, trying frantically to remember where he had heard that line before. Then it came to him; it was a line from his nightmare, the one where he was trapped in a forest in his pram, surrounded by a pack of grey wolves as a white wolf came to his rescue. But that wasn't the only time he had heard this line. Somewhere hidden in a repressed memory, he heard it again, a distant voice, the voice of White Wolf: *It isn't your time.* The words stuck in his head, repeating like a sharp needle on an old record which then scratched and screeched its way across the vinyl.

'Who says it isn't my time? I'm not a puppet. I can choose my time and it's my time, time to die,' bellowed Poe, picturing Lord Greystoke in a loincloth with a chimpanzee in his arms.

'It is not your time. You must finish the story. The story does not end here, not for you.' The white wolf howled, as if in pain, then turned around and disappeared back into the forest.

'Either that's perfect timing or I'm being played for a fool,' snapped Poe, not sure if White Wolf was real or simply an apparition conjured up by the forest, or the twisted mind of the forester who had built this house of horrors, or perhaps his subconscious had conjured up the wolf? Poe wondered if the forester had built the house knowing full well his intentions were to turn it into a house of horrors. Now that really was a macabre thought, a human zoo, an experiment by a madman who liked hunting people as well as animals. After which, he displayed his kills, the human heads or animals he collected, upon the walls of the house. Poe tried not to imagine his head, or the head of his dearly departed friend Sorrow, on display in the house of horrors. No doubt when he died, the mad woodcutter was hoping his own evil spirit would come back and haunt his house of horrors.

Then Poe heard another voice. This was not the voice of White Wolf but of a friend. It was the voice of an angel, a dark angel, a fallen angel. Sorrow was pleading with him not to give up the ghost. Poe closed his eyes and said a silent prayer for the strength to carry on. He opened his eyes a minute later and thought he saw a shadow pass overhead, but it could just as easily have been a crow or a raven, perhaps one of his shadows that had left him in the Forest of Shadows?

Poe wasn't sure if he was really hearing the voice of his friend from the spirit world or simply hearing the voice in his head. He knew Sorrow would never want him to throw his life away, even if it was a dead romantic thing to do. It was certainly a gesture that a dead romantic poet would have imagined himself doing, although in practice most dead romantic poets, like Lord Byron, were far too in love with themselves to throw their lives away in this manner.

It would undoubtedly leave a bitter taste in his mouth if his last thought on this earth was to give up, lay down and die.

Poe didn't want to be remembered this way. He could see a black marble gravestone with his name on it and his epitaph which read – *Here lies Poe Black, a spineless soul who lived in a world of his own. Good riddance to bad rubbish.* This made Poe smile; it was the kick up the backside he needed. 'You're both right, of course. If I give up now, the forest wins, and it will do so over my dead body,' Poe cried, waving his fist at the forest defiantly. It may well be a futile gesture but it made him feel better and gave him the strength to fight on. The forest remained silent. Poe was half expecting the forest to shake with rage as the tree shook so much that he fell to his death. As he fell in super slow motion, the forest started to laugh uncontrollably. Deep down, Poe imagined the forest would have the last laugh, and those who laughed last laughed longest, so much so that whenever people went into the forest, they would claim they always heard laughter.

Poe climbed gingerly down the tree, fearing he might fall to his death, something he no longer wished for. He would fight the dragon, the forest dragon and any other dragons that appeared before him, real or imaginary. He would fight for himself, his life and for the honour of his friend Sorrow, and anybody else who had lost their life in the twisted forest. If he did lose, at least Poe would go down fighting with his head high, not hung low in defeat.

Poe soon got his wish to fight with a dragon, for a dragon had been laying at his feet the whole time, like Draco the dragon, the star constellation in the night sky sat at the feet of the star giant Orion. The forest dragon was green, brown, black and yellow, and as such was perfectly camouflaged to blend in with any surroundings in the forest. The dragon flew at Poe before he had barely had a chance to get his feet on the ground, smashing him up against the tree trunk he had just climbed down. Poe was winded, down but not out, as he slowly picked himself back up and looked for something to arm himself with. Out of the corner of his left eye, he saw the branch of a silver birch tree. Poe had always imagined this tree to be a magical one. He hoped this was the case, for the dragon was ten times his size.

Then Poe saw something out of the corner of his eye running towards him and the dragon. He couldn't afford to take his eye off the prize, the head of the dragon. At first, Poe thought the figure was a large wolf. Was this White Wolf, another one of his guardian angels, but he was sure it was a large man dressed from head to toe in wolfskin.

'Need a hand, boy?' a man cried, half wolf, half man, or so Poe was imagining, until he realised it was his old friend Wolf the tramp, who had been living with him and had suddenly and mysteriously disappeared.

'I need several. I'm no Beowulf, I'm afraid,' Poe said with a sigh, referring to the epic English poem about a dragon, a destroyer of worlds, and a dragon slayer written in the German folklore style. In the Medieval period, folk really believed in dragons, citing them as the cause of storms and forest fires. These tales were fuelled, no doubt, by the dinosaur bones discovered in the ancient world. The dragon was also seen as the living embodiment of the devil, or so Poe's steam-powered search engine was now telling him. 'Shut up, shut up!' Poe grunted under his breath, as he found himself once again wishing his subconscious further, a parallel world, for instance!

'I'm no Beowulf or a dragon slayer, but I do have wolf blood in me, and wolves are known for their strength and power when it comes to bringing down a larger opponent.' Wolf growled as a hundred other wolves appeared out of the forest, all baring their teeth.

'What happened to you?' Poe exclaimed, unable to believe his senses.

'You mean I look more wolf than man, or why did I disappear from your life without saying a word?' Wolf Man asked, as Poe was now imagining his forest transformation, a wild man of the woods.

'The latter, for I always imagined you as a wolf, not a mad one, a werewolf, although right now I think I could do with a werewolf on my side.' Poe smiled as for a few seconds the dragon disappeared, to be replaced by a giant wolf, or perhaps that was the man giant shadow, large enough to scare and fool anybody in the heat of battle that there standing before them as large as life was a giant wolf.

'Quick version, speed read, I walk in my sleep, had a nightmare like you, although this one was during the day, siesta time for us old folks, found myself in the attic then a short walk from there into this twisted forest,' said Wolf, almost tripping over his tongue as the words came spilling out of his mouth.

The dragon, which had been eyeing the latest warrior on its patch to challenge its authority, once again transformed before his eyes, turning from a dragon fashioned out of a giant tree into a dragon born out of the stars and the universe. Poe and Wolf were now facing the mighty dark star dragon, Draco. How this could be? Poe had no idea, for Draco, he imagined, must be the size of Russia, perhaps even the size of Earth. How was it possible for a dragon so large to fit into such a small space, his old wooden house? It was impossible engineering. Surely the house would go up in flames like a giant tinderbox. The answer to that seemingly impossible question was surprisingly simple. The space was a magical space and thus it could easily contain any number of universes, parallel or otherwise.

Poe was now face to face with the dragon, but at least he was no longer alone, as a wild-eyed wolfman was standing by his side, every bit as fearsome as a Viking warrior. The pack of wolves surrounded the dragon, as if forming a magic circle. Poe did not flinch, and neither did Wolf. Instead, they stared into the giant's blazing red eyes, as if to challenge the dragon to a game of who would blink first. Poe wondered if Draco could read his mind. Did the creature know he was going to try and reach the branch of the tree and use it as a weapon? Perhaps the dark star dragon was so sure of itself that it saw this move as little more than a pawn being used to sacrifice a knight in a game of chess. Poe did not see this as a game of chess, more a twisted game of Dungeons and Dragons, as the dragon in this game was the mighty Draco the dragon.

Poe shifted his eyes to the left and pushed his body forward hesitantly, as if to go that way, but instead, at the last second, he ran the other way, towards the broken branch of the silver birch tree, as if the very devil himself were chasing him. Wolf mirrored Poe's actions and was equally light on his feet for a big man, who now appeared younger than his years. It seemed the old man had been rejuvenated and, like Poe, had found superhuman strength from somewhere. Perhaps they were drawing strength from the magical silver birch trees? The wolves were jumping up and snapping at the dragon, some even biting its tail. Most of the wolves seemed little more than flies to the dragon, to be brushed off without a second thought. However, this distraction, known in magic circles as prestidigitation, at least distracted the dragon so that Poe could make his move.

In one fluid movement, like that of a ninja, Poe rolled head over heels, grabbed hold of the branch and was back on his feet. Wolf did likewise. One more movement and Poe was running up a tree, defying gravity, and from the bottom branch of that tree he leapt onto the head of the dragon. Once again, Wolf Witcher mirrored Poe's every movement, as if they were twins, one old, one young. Now that really was a far-fetched fiction of a fantastical nature.

It was only then that Poe realised the dragon's head was red hot. Poe pictured firewalkers walking across hot coals, not appearing to feel pain. Poe closed his eyes and went into a trance-like state, imagining himself to be one of those firewalkers. It was mind over matter. In this case, it was mind over dark matter, or perhaps even mind over dark energy, for the dragon was pulsing with a fiery energy of a mass that was made up of a trillion stars.

Draco was taken completely by surprise and roared in anger, expelling a jagged jet of flames out of its mouth that Poe imagined was a spiralling galaxy that the dragon had swallowed in the world from which it had just been expelled.

Poe brought three facts to mind, some magical, some not so much. The first was that the Babylonians believed a giant dragon ate the sun and coiled the moon within its tail. This fairy tale was, in fact, an eclipse. The second fact was that dark energy was supposedly leaking from one universe into another, our universe in this case. Poe twisted this fact a little with the help of his kaleidoscopic mind, which enabled Draco the dragon to slip from the Black Sea through a maelstrom in space and into the nightmare world in which Poe was now trapped. The third fact was not really a fact in the true sense of the meaning; it was a quote from G.K. Chesterton: "Fairy tales don't teach us dragons exist; they teach us dragons can be beaten." Poe hoped this beating of imaginary dragons extended to star dragons. If this piece of grandiose wishful thinking wasn't as grand as the universe itself, Poe Black would eat his imaginary mad hat!

Another jet of fire shot out of his mouth, forcing Poe to take cover behind a boulder, expecting Wolf to join him, but he was nowhere to be seen. Poe hoped Draco had not swallowed the sun, for if it had, there would be no light at the end of the tunnel, for him or any other living soul left upon Earth. Poe also hoped the dragon had not swallowed his friend the wolf man. It would be winter all year long, colder than the planet Pluto, the dwarf planet. Poe felt dwarfed by the giant black dragon.

Poe compared this jet to that of a giant fire breather. Perhaps the dragon had swallowed a whole troupe of fire breathers from a travelling freak show, another dark and morbid thought to add to all the others. Poe did not imagine the dragon to be a fire breather in a carnival, for he imagined the flame to be coming out of a flame thrower, one in the hands of a giant.

Poe lifted the branch of the silver birch tree high above his head, as if it were the sword Excalibur and he was King Arthur, or St George about to slay the dragon, or Ethel Red the Viking warrior. Wolf did likewise, as if Poe and Wolf were mirror images of one another. Poe felt he may need the combined superhuman strength of both of these fearsome warriors if he were to defeat this dragon. It is often said that in times of great danger we find superhuman strength we do not know we possess. Poe wondered if this fantastical dragon had been conjured into life by the collective unconsciousness of storytellers from both days of yore and from the days of Poe Black. He may also need to draw on that collective unconsciousness of the same storytellers, of all the great warriors, real or imaginary, if he were to defeat this fearsome and ghastly fire-breathing foe.

'Go back to where you came from, dragon, back to the Realm of Shadows, dark destroyer of worlds. You won't destroy my world, however small and fragile it may appear to you!' roared Poe in defiance, the roar so loud that it was almost as if he had transformed into a dragon himself. In truth, as the words came out of his mouth, he cringed, for Poe knew he sounded like a character out of a thousand and one other fantasy storybooks.

But before Poe and Wolf could deliver what they were both hoping was the fatal blow, their feet gave way beneath them as the dragon tossed its head back and Poe and Wolf found they were being tossed in the air. Poe heard a voice laugh, mocking him. 'Darkling, you and the old wolf man are no match for the firelight of a dragon. Fighting fire with fire in your case is a bit like using a tinderbox to ignite the day star!' Why was Poe not surprised to find yet another dragon talking in riddles? Dragons were not poets or wise men; they were ancient killing machines. This small-minded dragon should stop toying with him, if that was his little game, by ending this game of Dungeons and Dragons.

Whereas before everything happened at lightning breakneck speed, now everything appeared to be happening in movie super-slow motion as Poe and Wolf found themselves falling. And as they fell, Poe and Wolf looked down to see the dragon with its mouth open wide, with a smile on its face as wide as the mouth of the Amazon River. It seemed the dragon agreed with him; no more killing time, it was time to go in for the kill. Poe imagined the mouth and throat of the dragon as a black hole, which meant that if he fell into the mouth of the dragon, Poe would be ripped limb from limb and atom from atom until all that was left of him was stardust.

Poe got the sense that he was mirroring the dragon, or at least mirroring its mind, which made little sense, almost as if the dragon had come out of him. We were all born out of fire, born out of stars, so perhaps this strange thought wasn't so strange after all. Could the dragon be a shadow, one of his own shadows, "darklings" as Poe had thought of his lost shadows, as hadn't the dragon referred to him as a "darkling"? A Shadow

Dragon, or a giant shadow puppet being manipulated by a giant shadow puppeteer? Once again, Poe's mind was racing with possibilities and imaginings, wild imaginings at that.

Poe had the distinct feeling that the Sword of Damocles was hanging over him, as he imagined the dragon with the sword in its hand, about to wield it with impunity. Poe could clearly see an image of a castle full of dragon men, all pointing gleefully at a head on the wall of the castle, and it was his head they were pointing at!

Poe could not see the light at the end of this tunnel, a dark tunnel, if he were to end up in the mouth of the dragon, or its belly, which Poe was already imagining to be full of acid. Bathing in a bath of acid or a bloodbath was not Poe's ideal of a rejuvenating experience. He would stick to the forest bathing if it was all right with the dragon. The dragon was already bathing in its own glory, or so Poe imagined, as the giant iron clamp-like jaws of the dragon started to close around him.

28

Monsters of the Mind

Then something big and strong came tearing out of the forest and slammed into the side of the dragon, knocking it off its feet. The something big turned out to be a giant wooden spike.

The dragon howled out in pain. The roar was so loud that the whole forest appeared to shake, causing leaves to fall like giant snowflakes. Another flaming jet of fire was expelled from the dragon's mouth, but this time it was not aimed at Poe, who was now spreadeagled upon the ground, his wooden sword still in his hand, but at a giant. Except that this giant was not a giant of a man but a tree giant, one that appeared to have uprooted itself from its stationary position so it could join the fight. Too often, the giant trees of the forest had to stand idly by, watching their own kind be cut to ribbons. Now it was time for one tree, a tree giant, to rise up from the earth, stand up and be counted. Poe had already re-imagined this giant tree as the Tree of Life. Poe wished with all his might that the tree giant would save his life; perhaps, for once, wishful thinking would actually work.

The tree giant dragged its raggedy-looking roots across the forest floor, leaving a trail of large clumps of mud and stone behind it. To Poe's mind, the roots of the tree looked not unlike the tentacles of a giant jellyfish. The tree drew back one of its giant arms, which were attached with long, sharp, spiky branch-like fingers, and thrust it into the side of the dragon. Once again, the dragon howled out in pain as the forest was shaken to its very roots. Poe imagined that if the battle raged on much longer, all that would be left of the forest as far as the eye could see would be a long line of ghostly-looking trees as the Twisted Forest became the Ghost Forest.

Poe and Wolf, of one mind, mirror minds, reflecting the other's exact thoughts, saw their chance, although they only had a split second to react, for it hadn't taken the dragon long to free its body from the branch upon which it had been impaled. The dragon then engineered its long, bulky, scaly frame into a position whereby it could attack the tree giant head-on. The dragon roared and flew at Poe and Wolf. Poe lost his balance and fell. The dragon was now standing over him, breathing fire. Wolf reacted first, appearing to fly through the air, causing the dragon for a split second to take his fiery red eyes off Poe and direct them at Wolf. Poe scrambled to his feet and ran for cover. For Wolf, there was no cover, as the dragon bent down and stared wild-eyed into Wolf's face. Wolf did not blink; he simply turned his head towards Poe, winked and then turned his head back towards the dragon and spat in his face. The dragon snapped the old man up as if he were little more than an insect and then Wolf was gone. Poe could not believe his eyes. One minute his friend was standing by his side, the next moment he was gone. Poe knew Wolf had sacrificed his life to save his. Poe saw a large shadow appear from the nostril of the dragon and imagined it was the spirit of his friend, which floated into the air and disappeared. Of course, it could just as easily have been black smoke expelled out of the nostrils of the fire-breathing dragon. Poe preferred to believe the spirit lived on, imagining Wolf as a cloud, like a Native Indian spirit walker, one who was now walking across the clouds as if they were stepping stones in the air.

The dragon once again transformed itself, this time from a star dragon into a mechanical dragon, with black armour plating and two flame throws coming directly out of its mighty nostrils. The wings of the black dragon were massive, like two giant metal shields bolted together with rivets. The dragon's tail had sharp metal pointed stars, medieval-like, which snaked back and forward like the tail of a giant scorpion.

The whole body of the black dragon seemed to be on fire, as if it were still being forged in a furnace of hot molten metal, forged in the fires of the universe. Poe imagined the dragon was being reborn, growing stronger and more powerful with every beat of its black heart. Great jets of hot steam were now pouring out of the dragon's mouth so it looked like an old steam engine. Perhaps it would combust; wishful thinking, Poe imagined on a grand scale. The dragon flew at the tree giant, setting it alight, then it clamped its metal jaws on to the trunk of the giant tree, bit down hard then spat a large piece of the trunk out, roaring as it did so.

The dragon clawed at the air with its giant metal feet in such a rage that Poe thought this mechanical dragon would tear him, the forest and his house down around his ears. Poe imagined the dragon must have been forged in the fires of hell by the devil himself.

The dragon drew itself up to its full height, which was so great that it appeared to touch the stars, as if it truly believed it came from the stars and, like Draco the dragon, belonged there and not on Earth. Poe felt the whole forest shake with fear, or was that the house being blown down, like in the story of the three little pigs as the dragon huffed and puffed and blew their house down? Perhaps he should let it blow this house of horrors down. Why stop it? It might be the best thing for all concerned. As the dragon slowly turned its lumbering metal frame 180 degrees, it knocked half of the trees in the forest down with its massive tail. Trees flew all about, as if they were little more than leaves, dead leaves at that.

The fire-breathing monster then mysteriously stopped dead in its tracks, as if it had run out of steam, remaining silent, its great metal eyes shut. Poe nervously walked forward. Why he was walking towards this mighty metal creature when every brittle bone in his body wanted him to be walking away, for the life of him he did not know. It was almost as if he felt compelled to confront the dragon, or perhaps comfort it, as he imagined it was dying. Poe could see black blood pouring out of the gaping wound caused by the tree giant, who also lay motionless on the forest floor, until, bending down, he sniffed the patch of ground and to his surprise he realised that it was oil, not blood, seeping from the dragon's wounds.

There was an overhanging tree close to where the dragon stood, so he climbed it and jumped off onto the dragon's head. Unlike last time, the dragon's head wasn't as hot as burning coals. This made Poe think the dragon was dead. More wishful thinking from the mind of Poe Black, for no sooner had this thought entered his head than the dragon opened its eyes. The dragon roared and expelled another jet of fire, shot from out of its giant jagged jaws. Then, much to Poe's horror, the black dragon started to flap its giant metal wings, which creaked and groaned and, before he knew it, Poe was flying. As a child, Poe had wanted to be a dragon rider, a standard dream, and one a lot of children had, but this wasn't the sort of flying that could be said to be dream-like, more like a nightmare. The dragon lumbered over the trees like an old Lancaster bomber on its way back from a bombing mission, leaving a trail of oil behind it. Poe imagined it would only take one spark and the whole forest would go up like a tinderbox.

The dragon then began to splutter as it began to run out of steam. Poe could see the dragon was about to enter a death spiral, and one that not even an experienced dragon rider would be able to pull out of.

Poe closed his eyes, sure that this was the nightmare ending to his short but eventful life story, one last nightmare for old times' sake and one where he crashed and burned. Still, at least he was going down in a blaze of glory.

The dragon skimmed the trees then it started to roll, and as it did so, its right wing clipped the canopy, causing it to burst into flames then cartwheel across the top of the trees like a giant Catherine wheel, setting over a hundred trees alight. Poe felt himself falling but unlike the other times, he did not fall in slow motion as he crashed through the canopy of the trees, hitting every branch on the way down, snapping them in two. Poe felt every one of those snapped branches, not that he was feeling the tree's pain, more his own. He was sure he had broken every bone in his body. He looked up and saw stars, not sure if it was because his head was in a spin or if it was the spiral galaxy above his head spinning wildly out of control, if his head, the world and the universe were all spinning wildly.

The next thing Poe knew, a wildcat was standing over him. Why was he not surprised? From one nightmare into another one. What was he complaining about? He'd had a break, he'd been dreaming, he had flown a dragon, even if he had crashed it, and now he was going to be eaten alive. Talk about out of the frying pan into the fire, and there was a fire spreading through the forest, between a nightmare and a bad dream. Poe wasn't sure which nightmare would get him first, being eaten alive by a wildcat or being burnt to death. Pick a nightmare, any nightmare. Then Poe realised that he recognised the wildcat; it was the white tiger. Poe was too weak to get up so he reached out his hand to stroke the tiger, but his hand went straight through its body; it was a ghost. No, it wasn't a ghost; ghosts didn't exist outside Victorian storybooks and the movies. It was a spirit, the soul of the creature. The white tiger raised its left paw as if beckoning Poe. Eventually, after several failed attempts, he managed to lift his weary body off the ground. It seemed that seeing a friendly face, even if it was only its spirit, had lifted his spirits.

Poe was on his feet, but his troubles were far from over, quite the opposite, in fact, as the fire spread like wildfire. Poe stumbled behind the tiger who he presumed was leading him to safety. The spirit of the animal stopped, but they were nowhere near out of the forest. The tiger appeared to smile then it turned its head and walked away, disappearing into the flames. Poe wondered if the spirit of the tiger had gone bad, turned from a benign spirit into an evil one, leaving him to his fate. As the tiger and Sorrow were buried side by side in the forest, Poe wondered if Sorrow's spirit was close by. He thought he saw a shadow out of the corner of his eye. The shadow was ablaze. How many more nightmares did he have to endure. Perhaps this was the last?

'Don't give up the ghost, Poe Black, or at least not yet,' said Poe, grimacing, trying to get himself going. Once again, Poe's black humour had come to his rescue, although there seemed little hope of being rescued. Poe could see the forest as a giant graveyard, the trees little more than giant twisted charcoal sparklers, and his twisted and charred skeleton in the middle of that cemetery. His mind turned to the Tunguska event in Russia in 1907 and then to the present day, where he had seen many pictures of forests burnt to cinders. Poe feared there was no fairy- tale ending for the forests of the world, and it seemed like the Fairy King Ludwig II, also known as the dream king, no fairy- tale ending for Poe Black.

Poe could see giant pillars of twisted flames all around as giant black phantoms appeared in front of him, ones conjured up by the black smoke. This was rare phenomena in forest fires, occurring when a swirling wind created a twister of fire, although not one Poe much cared for. Except that the fire twister came with a twist. There was always a twist when it came to the Twisted Forest, as inside these giant pillars of fire the trees were encased. Poe thought he saw faces in the trunks of the trees, ones that were twisted in agony. It was as if the whole forest was screaming. He tried not to picture all the poor souls over the centuries that had been burnt to death at the stake. As the trees looked like giants to Poe's mind, and had souls, as was believed in ancient times, was it any wonder he had to avert his eyes?

Poe realised he was in a small circle, one that had been cleared of all twigs, branches and leaves. He recalled a programme about forest fires in which a firefighter was explaining what you should do when trapped in a fire: clear a small patch of ground from all foliage and lay down in the middle of it. Poe was now imagining he was in a magic circle. Only time would tell if this wasn't yet more wishful thinking.

29

The Living End

As he lay prostrate upon the ground, Poe thought he heard the trees screaming, or perhaps that was the ghosts of the forest shrieking. Shadows suddenly appeared above him. Perhaps they were angels, angel of darkness and angels of the light, moths and butterflies all fighting over his soul. Poe saw a giant copy of the Old Testament open up. In his mind's eye and out of the pages flew pestilence, floods, locusts and the fires of damnation. Black silhouettes cut from paper that turned to black ashes, or burnt black butterflies' and moths' wings gently falling to the ground like snow. Then he saw an old rowing boat hanging from the ceiling of a church, a custom in Finland, no doubt, in case the snow turned to ice water, as the Arctic Circle continued to melt at an alarming rate. Poe was now surrounded by a circle of fire as the flames licked at the trees, as if a giant fire eater was enjoying his last meal on earth. This was no magic circle, unless this was black magic, as the circle was shrinking fast and he was at the centre of it.

To Poe's feverish mind, there seemed no way out. This was to be his bitter end. The forest had won. Poe was waiting for that last laugh to come as he closed his eyes for what he imagined was the last time. The dream was over, time to step into a never-ending nightmare. Poe clasped his hands over his chest as if on his death bed, his hand on his heart, one he imagined would soon be as black as charcoal. This was not quite the full story, for Poe was holding on to his yang symbol and the silver chain as tightly as if holding on to life, for he felt that if he let that slip from his grasp, he really would be lost to this world. But which world would Poe Black be lost to? The spirit world, earth, a parallel world, another time and dimension? Poe was holding on so tightly to his yang pendant that it dug into his skin, causing his palms to bleed. Poe was sure that if they found him, he would have the pendant imprinted upon his palm, like a tattoo.

Poe heard a rasping voice cry out in the dark. 'Come with me, climb on my back.'

At first, Poe imagined he must be dreaming, although as he was trapped in a nightmare, this could not be the case. Poe saw the outline of a creature covered in fur and wondered if this was the bear man, Rasputin once again, back from the dead. It seemed you couldn't keep a good man down, or a bad one for that matter. Good or bad, Poe did not care if this dark character saved his life. Poe forced his weary body up off the ground, opened his eyes and saw that it was not the mad monk Rasputin, the man of magic, it was White Wolf, who had come to his aid.

Poe staggered wearily to his feet. Standing by the side of the wolf, he steadied himself by holding on to the body of the wolf then after drawing another breath, he sat astride the wolf. Poe was now a wolf rider; he had earned his spurs and perhaps if he was lucky this wolf could fly. This was not the case, but the wolf seemed to have superhuman strength as it fought its way through the smoke and fire as trees and branches fell all about them.

'I want to tell you a story,' said White Wolf, not moving his lips as he made his way through the burning forest with Poe clinging to his back, digging his long fingernails into the wolf's body. The wolf did not appear to feel pain; it really was as if it were a being from another realm, the Realm of Dreams, or so Poe imagined.

'This seems a strange time to be telling me fairy tales,' replied Poe, wondering if this tale included them getting out of the forest alive. His wondering led to a further wondering: what if this white wolf had a darker side as he turned into the Big Bad Wolf in the fairy tale and ate him alive? The wolf would find him tough to chew, what with him being burnt to a cinder, like a burnt piece of steak on a barbecue, leaving out burning Cinders, Cinderella, to cinders on a barbecue.

The word "fairy tale" could be found in a thesaurus under the heading of a fabrication, a lie. Perhaps White Wolf was not immortal after all. Perhaps the wolf imagined that this was the last story he would get to tell. And for Poe, the last story he would get to listen to before the grim reaper, aka Dr "Deadly" Nightshade, tucked him into his bed, his deathbed. And as he turned out the light for the last time, he uttered the line, 'Sweet dreams. Fat chance! A sweet dream in the midst of a nightmare, dream on!'

'I suppose it does seem a strange time to be telling you a fairy tale, but then again we are living in strange times. In fact, I've never known stranger,' White Wolf replied, raising his bushy eyebrows so it made him look like a snowy white owl. The wolf's shadow had changed many times while it had been shadowing Poe and Sorrow through the forest. It was his camouflage, for the white wolf was a chameleon-like creature.

'So, what is this fairy tale about?' Poe asked, holding on to the coat of the wolf for grim death, hoping his death would not be a grim one as he burnt to death.

'You. It's about your dark fairy-tale life, or should I say the beginning of it,' the white wolf said, sounding mysterious.

'I suppose I should hang on tight then.' Poe smiled as he held on tight for a rough ride through his childhood, or so he imagined, one as rough as the ride he was being given now and as rough as the one in the Forest of Nightmares. Poe was now imagining he was being chased by the nightmare catcher, who was close to catching up with him, or perhaps that was his past, or past lives.

White Wolf told Poe a most extraordinary tale of his mother giving birth to him in the old house in the attic, and that he had a twin who was found by another woman who took her in. The woman had not chosen to ignore or turn her back on Poe, as if she imagined he was the evil twin; it was just that she did not realise Poe was still in the attic, having crawled in there through the door, the one that led to the Twisted Forest. The wolf had rescued Poe as a pack of grey wolves came in for the kill, telling him it was not his time. White Wolf then took him back into the attic, carrying him in between his teeth, which is where the wolf left him, returning to the forest, or at least the one in the attic.

'So, Sorrow is my twin sister?' Poe exclaimed, trying hard not to choke on the black smoke now spiralling up towards the sky, or the ceiling of the attic, for now the ceiling of the attic was clearly visible. But so was the sky as the house of horrors began to burn and crumble all about them. Ashes fell like snow, black snow, some falling on top of Poe and the wolf, who seemed not to feel the ashes as its fur began to smoulder. It was as if the white wolf was in a trance, like a firewalker who walked upon hot coals. If the wolf ever got out of the forest, its coat would no longer be white but coal black.

'She is,' White Wolf replied, sounding as wise as Buddha, although it seemed to Poe that he was wise after the event. Wouldn't it have been better to tell him this dark fairy tale at the point he had welcomed him back into the forest? Poe Black had reached the darkest hour, or the darkling hour, as he had always imagined the darkest hour. But as the old saying went, "It's always darkest before the dawn." It dawned on Poe that perhaps it was written that he was not to die, or at least not yet.

'And she is dead, and I never got to know my sister for who she really was,' sniffed Poe, whimpering like a wounded animal, a tear not far away.

'Does anything really die?,' White Wolf said once again, sounding like a wise man who knew more than he was letting on.

Poe could see a giant shadow going up in flames out of the corner of his eye as ashes rained down upon him and the wolf, a twisted column of black smoke winding its way up to the ceiling of the wooden shack. Poe wondered if the giant shadow was the spirit of the forester burning. Poe was sure he heard a terrible cry of a tormented beast in agony. Or perhaps it was just a giant tree going up in flames. After all, according to Nordic tradition, trees had souls. It wouldn't be the first, and Poe was sure that as deforestation continued, it wouldn't be the last; another forest that, if it could speak, may utter the line, *Just as well I am leaving, for my soul is unwell.* Perhaps the forests of the world would be saved, yes, saved in a parallel earth, or at least their forms would be saved, if you believed in Plato's perfect world.

The next thing Poe knew was they were out of the darkness, into the light. Poe looked round and the wolf was gone, and he was left looking back at the forest as it burnt. Poe saw a black door and ran towards it. The door opened without him having to turn the door handle, which was fortunate, for he imagined the door handle would be red hot.

Poe was free from the nightmare, standing in the snow in his bare feet, looking back at the burning house. But how could he be happy, for he knew Sorrow was inside the house. She was being cremated. Poe wanted to rush back into the burning house to find her body and give her the burial she deserved. But it was too late, for the house was a burning inferno. Nobody could survive in that firestorm, not even a forest, so magical that every spring, come rain or shine, it sprang back into life from the jaws of death, winter.

Poe hoped that the evil spirit that haunted the house had also gone up in smoke. Perhaps this was more wishful thinking on his part, but the thought that evil was still about in the place that he loved sent a chill down his spine.

30

Event Horizons

Poe walked further out into the snow, taking big gulps of cold air into his lungs. It hurt, made him choke, but it felt good. Pain was a good thing, for it meant he was still alive and it felt good to be alive, so good that he wanted to shout, *I'm alive, I'm alive*. Poe may not have been shouting on the outside, it wasn't his way, but he sure was shouting on the inside.

Another dark thought crossed his event horizon as he found himself wondering if he had just breathed in one of Sorrow's last breaths. Poe had seen so many event horizons come and go, inside and outside the Twisted Forest, that he was beginning to feel as if he was going around in ever-decreasing circles, dark magic circles.

After this near-death experience, Poe felt sure his death wish would disappear, like the falling snow in summer. He certainly hoped this was the case. If he could not learn from this nightmare, his dream of a better life, a happier life, would all go up in smoke. The dark humour that had helped him through his darkest hour, the darkling hour as he liked to call his darkest times, made him smile, at least one more smile for old times' sake. Poe had reached the state of happiness, leaving the state of unhappiness far behind him, or so he hoped.

Poe looked around and thought he saw three shadows appear out of the door of the house. He imagined the shadows to be Rasputin, for one of the shadows was a giant, followed by two smaller shadows. The smaller shadow he imagined to be Anastasia and Ivan, not the Terrible but Ivan VI, the prince who had spent his whole life in a prison.

Was this side of the black curtain really so bad? Were we all so disenchanted with our world that we all wanted to escape into some sort of perfect enchanted forest, a model of perfection? Surely it was the imperfections that made us humans unique, special. And despite the darkness of our world and for all its faults, it was a beautiful and wonderful world, full of light and hope.

The more likely fairy tale was that the shadows he had seen coming out of the fire were all in his mind, Poe's romantic, poetical side conjuring up these images for him. He stood transfixed to the house as thick black smoke poured into the cold morning air, curling and spiralling upwards to form clouds, or dark angels, as Poe saw it, through the eyes of an imaginer and poet.

Poe had lost a part of himself, his twin sister, and it hurt like hell, and as the realisation struck him like a hammer, he fell to his knees and wept uncontrollably. As the tears flowed like a river, he knew the tears were both ones of sheer relief at being alive and mourning for his twin. Sorrow was the better half of him. He wondered how he would cope without her, even though for all the time he had known her in life, he had not known she was his twin. Poe felt a twinge of guilt, for he had been attracted to Sorrow, felt she may be his soulmate, another dark thought to twist its way into his head.

Poe suddenly felt a presence as he thought he saw a shadow move out of the corner of his eye. Perhaps it was Sorrow's soul, her spirit, his dark angel now, his guardian angel watching over him. This wasn't the first time he'd had this thought. Perhaps it would be a recurring thought throughout the rest of his life, as every time he saw a lone magpie, he would imagine it to be his long-lost friend. Then Poe heard a ghostly voice but quickly realised this was no ghost as he got up off his knees and was amazed to see a girl staring back at him. It was like looking in a mirror, a dark mirror, slightly bowed, like in a crazy funfair mirror maze.

'Cheer up, poe-face, it may never happen,' Sorrow called out, cheerily smiling for the first time in her life.

'B-b-but you are dead, or at least you were?' stammered Poe, almost afraid to believe his eyes. Poe feared Sorrow was a ghost, either that or the spirit of the forester was conjuring up another nightmare for him as he twisted the knife in one last time. A further thought then occurred. Was this the real Yarra, Sorrow, or had she been sucked into this world with the dark energy from yet another parallel universe? Here, Poe was picturing Sorrow being both alive and dead at the same time, as in Erwin Schrödinger's cat in a box theory, except Sorrow wasn't a cat, unless she had been reincarnated from an Egyptian cat that once upon a time belonged to Cleopatra.

'My death was greatly exaggerated, mostly by you, I hasten to add. I can't say I cared much for my obituary, so I rewrote the ending of my life. I was buried alive, you see, not as dead as we both imagined. When I awoke, I found myself in a dark place. Thankfully, I'm used to dark places and spaces, buried seven foot under. A large white wolf dug me up out of my shallow grave. I thought I was going to be eaten alive. I saw the wolf's fangs and imagined I was Red Riding Hood on her last legs. One nightmare after another, the never-ending nightmare, the nightmare that keeps giving, and one I'd gladly have given back. But instead of the white wolf eating me alive, it simply turned tail and disappeared back into the forest.' Sorrow gasped, almost running out of breath in her excitement as she retold her not-so-sad-and-sorry tale.

'You're my sister, my twin sister,' Poe exclaimed, not being able to keep this secret any longer, as if it was burning a hole in his soul. Poe could not help feeling that he had been trapped in a nightmare within a nightmare, perhaps within a nightmare as if a giant Russian doll had been a casket.

Here, Poe brought to mind Edgar Allen Poe's quote, "Life is like a dream within a dream." Then Poe brought to mind Edgar Allen Poe's dark tale *The Fall of the House of Usher* and the story told by the main character. You see, the man buried his own twin sister alive in a tomb in the basement of the house, not realising he had done so. And within that book, a story inside a story, as one of the characters read a passage from a book during a wild storm involving King George, the most fearsome dragon slayer of them all. Both the storm and the slaying of a dragon had happened in the Twisted Forest, Poe starring in both incidents. It felt to Poe that he had been trapped within the book itself, *The Fall of the House of Usher*, trapped within his house of horrors, the House of Poe trapped within his own mind or the mind of the forester, the spirit, the entity that had created this whole dark mindscape.

'And I thought coming back from the dead would steal the show, but I think you may have trumped that and stolen my thunder and the show, all at the same time,' Sorrow said, her mouth agape, her eyes every bit as wide as the Big Bad Wolf's on spying his next meal, Little Red Riding Hood.

'I know. Everything is perfect in this world, Plato's world, as I will now call it, but a perfect world is imperfect in my book on philosophy, the one I one day hope to write and publish. I don't want to live in a world where everything and everyone is perfect. I wouldn't match up. In fact, I'm surprised we haven't been expelled from the forest already. Who wants to live forever? Everything must die. It is the natural order of things, as is disorder. Every story must have an end. Immortality is a living death, to my mind. I would go mad if I thought I would live forever, so, Plato, thanks but no thanks, I'm going back to my imperfect world, that's if I can get back to it, that is,' Poe said, feeling all the trees were gods, immortal gods who were all now looking down their noses at him. Poe realised something else was perfect: Sorrow's English. In truth, it had been perfect for quite some time, ever since she and Poe had stepped into the Twisted Forest. Perhaps, as time went by, Sorrow would go back to speaking broken English, or perhaps not. Poe did not want to break the spell of this perfect reunion by mentioning such a trifling little thing. If Sorrow had now been residing in the spirit world then Poe may need a necromancer to be his voice in that ethereal realm.

'Yes, I agree, Poe, there is something beautiful in the imperfect, a beautiful imbalance,' Sorrow said, sounding as po-faced as Poe and Edgar Allen Poe. 'The beautiful image I had of my mother in my head, God rest her soul, will most certainly be imperfect from now on.'

'You must not think too unkindly of her. She was just a poor woman who no longer wanted to be alone,' Poe said.

'Of course, you're right, but it's still a shock to think of how many secrets my adopted mother kept from me,' Sorrow said, sighing with a heavy heart.

'I've got something to show you,' said Poe, as if he were a magician.

'As have I,' said Sorrow, as if she too were a magician and not the beautiful assistant. Sorrow and Poe were both now holding the exact same thing in their hands; it was a pendant of the yin and yang symbol, with a twist. The twist was that Poe was holding the yang symbol, the symbol of maleness, and Sorrow the yin symbol, the symbol of femaleness.

'I have always felt there was something missing, as if I had a twin, and it turns out I do,' Poe said, trying not to well up.

'Snap,' Sorrow replied through misty eyes, for she was so overcome that that was all she could say. Poe stepped forward and put his arms around his sister in a warm embrace. Sorrow felt as cold as an ice sculpture and, for a split second, Poe wondered if his sister was a vampire. Vampires had been done to death, Poe thought, and thought no more about it, for he felt warm inside, for he was no longer alone. And while he had a sister, his twin, Poe would never be alone again, not even in death, for this extraordinary adventure had shown him that there really was a spirit world, another plain of existence after death.

31

The Twisted Forest – The Final Twist

'I think finally I can say without fear of contradiction that we are finally out of the woods. You see, I said we make a great team, the dream orienteering team, able to find our way out of any forest in the world, having been dumped there for a reality TV show.' Poe laughed in relief at having finally come out of the nightmare forest into the light. Poe was hoping nobody was going to contradict him, like a giant of the forest, or a giant wolf in sheep's clothing.

Poe wanted to kiss and hug Sorrow as if they were characters out of a scientific romance, and then remembered that their closeness and synergy was that of twins, not lovers. One day, they would make a good scientific team, like Marie Curie and her husband, who would not accept the Noble Prize for Physics from the committee who ran the awards unless his wife, Marie, was recognised for her contribution. And Marie Curie's contribution was a big one. Poe and Sorrow were both mightily relieved they had not become any more than close friends. Thankfully, they were both green horns in the old love and romance department.

'We're not out of the woods yet,' Sorrow replied, her face mirroring the figure in the painting *The Scream* for, unlike Poe, she did not want to tempt fate, 'although we may well be out of the Twisted Forest, out of reach of its grasping, clawing hands.' And as Sorrow finished the sentence, a sort of smile broke out across her face, although with the facial disfigurement she had had since childhood, it was hard to tell if Sorrow was smiling or frowning. This was something that had got her into trouble more times than she could recall, which is why, like Poe, she was drawn to the solitude of nature.

'I hope while we've been in the woods, we're out of the woods, I mean, regarding the coronavirus,' Poe said, trying to explain the unexplainable. 'Look up ahead in the distance. People. And I think they are waving at us,' Poe exclaimed, his voice raising an octave as the light at the end of the tunnel finally appeared to be coming into sight.

'I'm not sure these people are friendly,' Sorrow replied, sounding suspicious, as she was of most strangers, as was Poe himself.

'Let me take a closer look through the spyglass,' Poe said, peering through the old brass spyglass into the distance, one he had had in his pocket from the very beginning of the nightmare. Who on earth sleeps with a spyglass in their pyjama pocket? Poe Black, that's who. After all, it's important to be able to see into a dream just to make sure it's not a nightmare in disguise. If this was the curious case then it appeared he was not now holding a brass spyglass but a kaleidoscope! 'I-I-I don't, I don't believe this!' Poe stuttered, hardly able to believe his eyes, for he was sure what he was seeing was Nazi soldiers with SS symbols sewn into their grey uniforms.

'What?' exclaimed Sorrow, wanting to be put in the picture, although by the sound of Poe's voice, perhaps it would have been better not to be put in the picture but taken out of the picture. Like a figure in a painting that looked uncomfortable and out of place. In truth, Sorrow was imagining the worst, that Poe had seen Bigfoot or an army of Bigfoots, all marching towards them with sharpened trees in their hands. She imagined the trees whistling through the air like giant arrows, at first missing them by a whisker until one tore a great big hole in Poe's body as he was poleaxed. She turned to run as trees whistled over her head then her worst fears were realised as a tree thrust its way through her body, like a knife through butter, and she felt blood spilling out of her mouth, like water out of a fountain.

'Forget what I said about being out of the woods. I think we are back in the woods, and they are darker than ever. Nazi soldiers, I think we've gone back in time to World War Two, and they've spotted us. They are running towards us and they've got guns. Run!'

'The Nazis, they are monsters, an army of monsters led by a monster of a man named Adolf Hitler,' spat Poe, shaking his head, trying not to think of what these monsters had inflicted on men, women and children.

'Hold on a minute. No, look, the uniforms aren't grey, they are blue, and that isn't an SS symbol, it's the Rescue Services and the Red Cross,' Sorrow cried, finally getting a clearer picture of reality from the blurred images of another reality. At times in life, it really was hard to see the wood for the trees.

'Hey, you over there, can we help you? We are digging out survivors of the avalanche that happened last night,' cried a man, now fifty yards from where Poe and Sorrow were standing frozen to the spot in fear, or like ice sculptures slowly melting in the sun.

'No, but thank you, we're all right. It's my house, there was a fire. I must have knocked over a storm lantern during the night,' Poe replied.

'I can get some men to try and put out the fire,' the man bellowed.

'Don't worry. You've got more important things to do. It's an old house anyway. I can always rebuild it. It'll give me something to do in the holidays,' Poe called back cheerfully, coolly lying through his teeth. He wanted to add to the lie, fairy tale, and call back, *Yes, don't worry. We are the sort of people who just love to set things alight, just to watch them burn. We are part of the Pyromaniacs Society. We even had an old fire engine that shoots pink champagne into the air. We chase fires then set up tables for a fire party. Of course, as it's almost New Year, we can make this fire a part of the traditional Nordic bonfire parties, as an offering to the gods of fire and ice.*

It seemed that despite being trapped in a dark world of many nightmares, the fire inside Poe Black was still burning as brightly as ever. It would take a lot to extinguish that fire and snuff out that dark, twisted sense of humour of his, which paradoxically was exactly what got him through the dark times.

'I didn't realise you were such an accomplished liar?' Sorrow said through a fixed smile, which made her look like a politician on a walkabout during a campaign trail through the Twisted Forest.

'Storyteller, I'd much rather like to think I'm an accomplished storyteller, or teller of fairy tales than a liar,' Poe replied, as he waved the man off as he turned and trudged back through the thick snow to join the rescue service.

Something cold struck Poe on the back of the neck. His first thought was a mad axeman who was attempting to decapitate him with a rusty axe. Poe whirled around like a whirling dervish to see Sorrow with a snowball in her hand with the biggest, brightest neon smile on her face that he had ever seen, one that made the Northern Lights and the luminescent light of Venice pale in comparison.

'Got you!' Sorrow beamed. It took a few seconds for Poe to process what was happening, reality blurring the lines as it had done throughout all of Poe's life, before he mirrored Sorrow's smile as he too beamed from ear to ear before speaking his mind.

'I will never get most of the female of the species, but I get you, Sorrow Black,' Poe said, trying hard not to blush as he replaced the surname White with the surname Black. Sometimes life was black and white and, in truth, sometimes life was better shot in black and white, as old movies were sometimes better than ones shot in Technicolor.

'What you said, replacing female of species with male of the species,' Sorrow said, mirroring Poe's expression, 'is that line as corny as I imagine it to be?', hoping to break the awkward moment with humour.

'I hope so. We're both a couple of old romantics ahead of our time!' Poe said, trying to think of a funny line, and while not exactly succeeding and bringing the house down in the outdoor theatre, the line didn't die on its feet either.

'I imagined forest fire started in gingerbread house as witch left oven on while baking a man with ginger hair and cake with fairy on top of it. It looks like old witch baked herself at the same time, cooked her own goose, so to speak,' Sorrow replied, as she pictured a similar tale of woe, the Great Fire of London, which started in Pudding Lane in a bakery.

'I imagine the fire started in Pandora's house or the house that belonged to Pandora, as I have re-imagined the house and the fire. The door of her house was left ajar, designed like a giant box, and all the fires of hell came out, setting the forest on fire. Alternatively, the nightmare catcher, being a pyromaniac, set the Twisted House alight because he finally realised how ugly it looked.

'Or perhaps a fireball came out of an alternate reality, a parallel world, as I imagine happened in 1907 in the forest in Tunguska, Russia. This left the forest and the trees looking like giant charcoal matchsticks leaning to one side.'

'Right, enough of alternate realities. I think we have both had enough of those to last several lifetimes. Time to get back to reality, whatever that is,' gabbled Sorrow, sounding both sorrowful and joyful all at the same time, as clearly, like Poe, she too was a crazy mixed-up kid. But what was wrong with a little craziness as long as the craziness was kept under control?

'Both time and reality are an illusion, but you're right, time to get back to the present, and as long as that present isn't a fake future where we are all hooked up to a machine, the futurists' dream world, a waking nightmare to my mind, I can live with that,' Poe replied, feeling that as he was the one directing this dream-cum-nightmare, he should have the final line.

Sorrow was happy to let her friend take the limelight, for she knew it would be the last time, as they both stepped back into the shadows, where they felt most comfortable. Plato's perfect world, however amazing it was, was not for them. These Siamese dreamers preferred the imperfect world, with all its many imperfections.

Paradoxically, Plato had called our world, the one we were living in, a mirror or a shadow world, and perhaps he was right and perhaps he was wrong. Or perhaps, just perhaps, he was both right and wrong, if you believe in the many worlds theory of physicist and maverick genius Hugh Everett III.

Sorrow reached out her hand and Poe gladly took it, and after all, there was warmth in human contact, and it was a cold day despite the warm weather, that and now night had almost fallen and the only moon out was the black moon, as it was called in the Orient, the new moon. Then Poe and Sorrow walked off into the night as if at the end of a silent movie shot in black and white, as the image they were framed in, shaped like an oval mirror, shrank until they had both disappeared from the shot.

As they were walking out of shot, Poe had one more last thought, one that was like trying to recall a dream when you awoke as it started to quickly fade like snow on a sunny day, an imprint on his mind, a film negative. That was funny. Before Poe entered the forest his mind was full of the names of storytellers who seemed to be every bit as colourful as the characters they had created. And like their characters, they back stories were weird and wonderful, with as many twists and turns, ups and downs. It seemed these storytellers, like Poe, had a mirror mind, and their thoughts, traits, hopes, fears and sorrows were reflected in those characters.

While Poe was in the Twisted Forest, there was no mention of the creators, the authors, just their characters; no Hans Christian Andersen, Mary Shelley, Bram Stoker, not even his hero, Edgar Allen Poe. A world without Edgar Allen Poe seemed unthinkable to Poe Black's mind. There was no writer or poet better at reflecting how Poe felt than his hero; they were both of the same dark mind, mirror mind, both on the same page. Yet as soon as Poe was back in the real world, their names sprang to mind as if out of a children's pop-up book. It was as if once upon another time in the forest, the characters had cut their strings and left their storytellers behind in the other world. In the forest, the puppet masters could not control or manipulate them. Poe was going to say the real world, but he was no longer sure what the real world was supposed to look like. Both worlds at times appeared to feel unworldly, the one he was now in and the one he had just left.

It was often said by storytellers that after they had created the character, it was as if they had taken on a life of their own, leaving them to run wild. The characters did as they pleased, leaving the storyteller desperately trying to rein them in like a naughty child or a mischievous elf.

32

The Day After the Fire – Part 3

'All that's left of my dream house is charcoal and charred broken wood,' Poe said, kicking the smoking wooden timbers out of the way as he walked through what was left of the house he once lived in and the house he was born in.

'All that is left of your nightmare,' said Sorrow, giving Poe one of her I-think-you-are-looking-at-this-all-wrong looks.

'Perhaps you are right. Perhaps now the nightmares will

disappear for good,' Poe replied, trying to look on the bright side of the nightmare. The bright side of the nightmare was always the dream, or as Sorrow once put it, there is always a dream waiting for you at the end of the nightmare.

'I for one am glad I opened the Pandora's box in my head,' Sorrow said reflectively.

'So am I,' Poe replied, mirroring the expression on Sorrow's face, then added, 'However, now I've shut the lid and locked it, I won't be reopening it anytime soon.'

'You're probably reopening it now in some parallel universe,' Sorrow said laughingly.

'Then I pity that me,' Poe replied, managing a half-smile to match the half-smile on the face of his twin sister.

Sorrow reached out her hand and eventually, after picking his way carefully through the embers and broken bones of his old house as if he imagined he was walking upon hot coals, Poe stepped into the dark space where Sorrow was standing, taking her outstretched hand in his and said, 'Better go home, I suppose.'

'Where do you suppose this supposed new home of yours is?' Sorrow enquired thoughtfully.

'Any place, anytime, anywhere,' Poe replied, all smiles as he and Sorrow walked down the mountainside towards the nearest town.

'That sounds like old slogan for travel company to me.'

'Nothing's new. It's all been done before.' Poe laughed, finally seeing the funny side of a horror story. 'Hey, I've just noticed, Sorrow, while I've got my memory back, you've lost yours, or should I say your lexicon has shrunk.'

'Woe is me. I am full of sorrows. At least I have not shrunk, like Thumbelina or Alice, so I live with speaking poor English, no drama,' replied Sorrow, first painting a scowl on her face with her finger then a few seconds later, painting a smile upon her face with her finger. 'You say it's all been done before, even our journey into unknown, even snowflake, and what about dreams and nightmares? Poe, surely they have not all been done before,' Sorrow added, running ahead, bending down, making a snowball and playfully throwing it at Poe.

'You'd make good scriptwriter. We should do film together,' said Sorrow, with a deadpan look upon her face.

'Do you think that's a good idea? I imagine the whole project would be a nightmare from beginning to end, beset with disasters, like the publicity hype for an old horror movie,' Poe replied, throwing three snowballs Sorrow's way in rapid fire. Sorrow ducked in true movie slow motion, or as if she were a ninja.

Then Poe took something out of his pocket, one more twist in the fairy tale as Sorrow instinctively caught it in her hand and was amazed to see it was an egg. But this was no ordinary egg; this was a quite extraordinary egg. 'It's a Fabergé egg. Where on earth did you get it?'

'I twisted Rasputin's arm, the old Chinese burn, and he gave it to me, cried like a baby. It was embarrassing really,' Poe said, as his nose began to grow like Pinocchio's, or so Sorrow was imagining, for she was sure he was telling her a fairy tale, in other words, a bare-faced lie.

'But how did you really come by egg? Surely you did not pick Rasputin's pocket?' Sorrow asked, determined to get to the bottom of this latest twist in the dark fairy tale.

'That's exactly what I did, picked the pocket of a brown bear. My grandfather, or should I say our grandfather, was a magician back in the day, although I suppose you could say our day now. He taught me some sleight of hand card tricks and how to pick a pocket or three, three being the magic number,' Poe said, beaming from ear to ear. 'Of course, I'll return it to the royal collection. I wouldn't dream of selling it for profit.'

'That was Rasputin's nest egg, and Anastasia's too. I hope they not starve to death,' Sorrow said, looking a little disappointed in her twin.

'Rasputin, the old rascal, he can take care of himself wherever he may be in time and space, probably still in this space, hiding in the forest. Nothing would surprise me, not anymore. And as for Anastasia, well, we saw her as an old lady, Anna, remember, in the Black Forest.'

'I'm hardly going to forget that, that's if she was the real Anastasia and not fake, and I take it the Fabergé egg is real and not fake?' Sorrow said, raising her thinly plucked eyebrows.

'It's real, all right,' Poe replied, taking out a jeweller's optical eyepiece from his pocket and examining it in the cold light of day.

'You're full of surprises, Poe Black, a regular magic man, like Harry Houdini or Blackstone the Master Magician,' Sorrow replied, bending down and painting a giant smile in the snow with her finger. 'But you're not only one who can astound and amaze with feats of extraordinary magic. Perhaps you recall seeing shadow in perfect forest. You may think is this not a little unusual, what with Plato's theory of our world being the shadow mirror world, and there being another world, perfect world with one perfect form for everything? Is such thing as perfect shadow, for all shadows have rough edges, like wings of moth, raggedy around edges?'

'It had occurred to me, yes, but at the time I wasn't thinking straight. I was, as usual, thinking around corners, left-field thinking, while thinking outside the box, belonging to both Plato and Pandora,' Poe replied stiffly, and more than a little po-faced.

'Well, before you saw the shadow, you had your eyes closed. I presume you were saying silent prayer, which gave a certain magpie mind a chance to slip golden egg in your pocket. A nice twist, I thought, as it is mind of magpie to take shiny objects, not put them back. That and I not know if I get out of forest in form of magpie,' Sorrow said, painting a double smile, parallel to the one she had drawn earlier in the snow, with a stick, a sort of mirror image.

'Well, you could knock me down with a black feather from a giant raven,' Poe exclaimed, recalling how his shadow had transformed into a giant raven. In truth, he felt as if a giant wing of a raven had been hanging over him for the longest of times, but now it felt as if that shadow had been lifted.

'I hope I haven't stolen your thunder or ruffled your feathers,' Sorrow said, smiling on the inside and the outside.

'The god and goddess team of Thor and Nike stole both our thunders if I recall, while we were in their worlds, and as for ruffling my feathers,' Poe said, pretending to flap his arms like a bird, 'I think my raven shadow has flown the coop. Still, I imagine I have quite a few other shadows I can cast in any number of different species of both bird and animal,' Poe added, mirroring Sorrow's smile.

'I don't think this last twist in life story of Poe Black,' Sorrow smiled on the inside, 'although I would like to think you won't twist that kaleidoscopic mind of yours for a little while at least.'

'I, Poe Black of sound mind, promise I will not push my existential Viking boat out any further than I have already pushed it out. Furthermore, I will stick with the twisted world we now see before us, even though it may well be an illusion, cross my black heart and hope to die,' said Poe, smiling on the outside.

'And if you believe that, A, you must be out of your brilliant mind, and B, you'll believe anything, including fairy tales and quantum wonder tales,' replied Sorrow, raising her eyebrows as the song *Brilliant Mind* by the band Furniture started playing on the cracked jukebox in her and Poe's heads, in this and every other time and dimension imaginable. And in doing so, this proved without a shadow of a doubt that Hugh Everett III's many worlds theory was correct one million per cent. In the reality Poe and Sorrow Black were living in, however, there was still a huge shadow hanging over Plato's shadow\mirror reality. Perhaps one day physicists would be able to prove Plato's weird and wonderful theory one way or the other, in theory at least?

'Do you know what the first thing I want us to watch on the television as twins is?' Poe said, looking smug.

'*Twin Peaks?*' Sorrow replied, looking equally smug.

'Close, but no, exploding cigar, the Big Bang, the little black and white dots the background radiation,' said Poe, raising a half-smile.

'Good choice, it's like watching miniature snowflakes fluttering down from the heavens,' Sorrow replied.

'It's nice to know we are both on the same page of the old black and white television guide,' Sorrow and Poe said as one, as they both disappeared into a world of their own making, one world, a world in which they both took the starring role.

As Sorrow and Poe departed the scene, little more than ghostly negatives on an old roll of film, they did not see the imaginary camera pan back at the house, slowly trawling through the burnt wreckage, until it stopped dead. The image was of a model of a forest, the *Twisted Forest* Poe had made as a child. It was the classic horror movie trope. Could this be the end to the Life and Times of Poe Black, a bitter end? Like a doll in a glass case in a basement in the dark, as the eyes opened and shone like the beams of a torch, as the credits rolled on the silver screen. The silver screen in this case was the silver birch forest. Or would Poe's end be a bittersweet one, for he had found his sister but lost his first love, imaginary love in this case.

The pandemic, like climate change, was a stark warning for mankind that it needed to learn lessons from such disasters.

Poe and Sorrow, being twins, both feared the same thing, that this change of attitude of mankind towards nature and its fellow men and women would not last very long before everything went back to normal. The new normal being replaced by the old normal; it was human nature.

Nature may need to hide, take refuge inside Pandora's giant box as it became a sanctuary, nature, which included the forests and creatures that lived in the forests of the world, if it was ever to survive man's monstrous ways.

Poe and Sorrow decided their normal, abnormal to most people's minds, also needed a makeover, a change, and, after all, how many times had they seen their own shadows change from man to beast and back again? Mankind really needed to learn from the shadows he cast.

Poe and Sorrow were casting their net wider than they had ever cast it, no longer content to live in a world of their own, for in dark times the world needed bright, brilliant and beautiful minds to illuminate it. Even if those minds were flawed, or saw the world through kaleidoscope eyes.

It felt to them both as if they had let the blackbirds in the attic of their minds go to fly free; ravens, crows, and the like, and as such Poe and Sorrow felt as light as a feather, as if they could fly to the dark side of the moon and back.

The world most certainly needed people who could think both inside and outside the box belonging to Pandora, those with kaleidoscopic minds. For it was those inventive minds that changed the world for the better, worlds for the better, the Kaleidoscopic Worlds of Poe and Sorrow Black.